SHOAL WATER

ADVANCE READER COPY

SHOAL WATER

KIP ROBINSON GREENTHAL

Homebound Publications

Ensuring that the mainstream isn't the only stream.

HOMEBOUND PUBLICATIONS

WWW.HOMEBOUNDPUBLICATIONS.COM

HOMEBOUND PUBLICATIONS IS A REGISTERED TRADEMARK OF HOMEBOUND PUBLICATIONS

Look for our titles in paperback, ebook, and audiobook wherever books are sold. Wholesale offerings for retailers available through Ingram. Homebound Publications and its divisions are distributed by Publisher's Group West.

All Rights Reserved
Published in 2021 by Homebound Publications
Cover Design and Interior Design by Leslie M. Browning
Cover Image © Robin L. Lindsey
ISBN: 978-1953340269
First Edition Trade Paperback

10 9 8 7 6 5 4 3 2 1

Homebound Publications, is committed to ecological stewardship. We greatly value the natural environment and invest in environmental conservation. For each book purchased in our online store we plant one tree.

FOR STANLEY

—═╪═—

WHO PLAYED MUSIC
THROUGH ALL THE YEARS
I WROTE THIS STORY

PART I

1

THE DARK, forbidding clouds closed in, the wind, its high-pitched universe.

Basil Tannard turned and saw the rogue, its steely wall of water topped by foam just before it pitched him from his Cape Island boat. Hurled into the Nova Scotia sea, he reeled, his body churning through cold swells, his eyes wide open in the briny bubbles.

After some minutes, the angry sea coughed him up from its depths like a derelict buoy.

He floated on his back watching the sky and fought off the panic swallowing him. Seawater sloshed in the hollow of his ears.

Yet he could feel something towing him through the black, heaving ocean.

Half his body was numb from cold, while the other half grew warmer from something slick moving alongside him.

This must be dying, he thought.

He hadn't been a very good Christian. He drank too much, but he'd worked hard all his life and never was unfaithful to Ellen.

Pain ripped down his back and he realized he couldn't be dead. Wasn't pain kept for the living? Strong, fin-like arms worked their way under him, dragging him over razor-edged slate. A fleeting image of a woman's face.

Basil woke up wedged in a small salty space of black rock. A circle of light lay at his feet and he heard the hiss of the incoming sea. His cheek was slashed against the stone but he could not lift a hand to soothe it. Seaweed tangled beneath him and his lips tasted of blood. I'm alive, he thought. A sensation of warmth radiated from his back as if a large heavy blanket was rolled up beside him, hard and breathing. But he was too stiff to look around. Saltwater dripped in cold pinpricks on his skin, and Basil drifted in and out of sleep while the sound of waves heaved through the still air of the cave.

He woke again to a cold hollow on his left side. The blanket that breathed had moved away and he longed for its return. Suddenly a piece of raw fish was shoved into his mouth and Basil swallowed, choking on the mix of grit and bones. He glanced up to see black eyes and thick whiskers in the sea light. He knew then that he was in the care of a seal.

Basil recoiled. Seals raised havoc in his nets, attacking fish, and he often had to shoot them. Some said if you shot a seal, it would bring you bad luck. He was not a superstitious man.

The creature turned and shook the folds of its half-dried coat. For a long time, it moved around him, tending to his bed of eelgrass and cleaning the mackerel.

Basil grew stronger day by day. Once, when his fingers fell on the silver fur of the seal's neck, it seemed to peel back from its head and shoulders. Startled, Basil watched the seal leave the cave and move out onto the reef. Sun blazed through the sea air, and the seal groomed itself on the rocks. Waves foamed over, and the seal stretched and arched its tail.

The seal seemed to know that Basil was watching. Prying its fur coat from its head and shoulders, the seal unsheathed the breasts and hips of a woman. Her nipples were firm and deep red. The wind lifted long black strands of matted hair so that Basil could see the features of her face, the watercolor wash in her skin. And then he heard her sing. She sang through the push of the tide that swirled around her, long low notes that rang through the cave.

Basil clasped his hands over his ears, and the rock spun around him.

Later when he woke, the seal was beside him, black eyes heavy with light and sorrow. He smelled the cool salt in her fur. He remembered the woman who sang. She might have kissed him. He might have touched her nipples with his fingertips.

Basil had heard the stories about fishermen finding selkies in their nets or on the beach, but he'd never believed them. He'd heard about their long strands of hair and brilliant blue eyes and exquisite beauty, and how a human spirit could enter the skin of this creature capable of existing in the deep regions of the sea, human above the waist, and seal below, their sea dresses allowing them to travel from one world to another.

When he touched her, her skin was smooth.

Suddenly he found himself lifted up and shoved outside the cave. Daylight blinded him. The seal rolled him over the reef, pushed him with her nose across the slate and into the icy water. With her fin, she clasped him to her. Moving at a supernatural speed, just under the waves, the seal took Basil to the opposite shore.

When he opened his eyes, he recognized the cliffs of Skerry Point. The rocks were hard beneath him, and he sat. The sun was behind the bank, the shore in shadow. Stunned, he stared into the ocean's vacancy. When he stood up, he was surprised to find that his strength had returned, his clothes were dry, and his body showed no injury.

He looked again toward the reef, where the sea shimmered.

There was no sign of the seal.

Would his wife Ellen ever believe him?

2

FOG DROWNED THE NOVA SCOTIA COASTLINE. **Kate** sat beside Andy Farrell in a yellow 1957 Chevrolet truck, straining to see the thin gray road unwind ahead of her. She felt as if she were traveling in water and not on land, even though she knew the Atlantic was on her right side. The smell of salt caught in the back of her throat like a gulp of the sea.

It hadn't helped that the battery went dead in Yarmouth. Andy had to find someone in the campground with cables to jump start it, and they got to a service station to replace it. That was when Kate Black was first unsettled by the fog, its massive cloak surrounding her while they waited. "I'm sorry our trip started off this way," Andy said to her.

"Oh, it's okay," she said, knowing she wasn't telling him the truth, that she was already ill at ease here.

With each turn the old truck bounced, springs creaking, while Kate tried to balance herself on the sticky black vinyl seat. She watched Andy, his black hair swept back from his pale forehead, his crystal gray eyes, as he drove through the blinding white air with confidence. He'd been coming to this place since he was twelve years old and she tried to take some comfort in this.

"This is the landscape I love," he said.

Weathered fish stores floated past her like apparitions. Houses painted tangerine or eggshell blue seemed to drift along the rocks as though caught in a flood.

This was not the Nova Scotia Kate had imagined. Her Nova Scotia had been the clear one, the place of her mother's happy stories as a girl visiting Baddeck. In fact, Kate grew up sleeping beneath an old lithograph her mother had hung over her bed in their New York City apartment. For as long as she could remember, her eyes had traced the scrolled and faded capital letters at the bottom, N O V A S C O T I A S C E N E R Y. A blue bay with schooners, small glacial hills, a channel leading into the Atlantic. A house stood above the bay, with a fence and a gate where a woman held her daughter. Kate liked to pretend this woman, in a long brown dress, was her mother. And that she was the little girl in the mother's arms, looking up into her tranquil face and admiring the wide-brimmed hat that she wore. There was a black dog barking by the gate in the lithograph and this became her dog, named Smokey. And the spruce and oak trees braced in the landscape under a copper stained sky held the same wind in them she could hear then outside the window while she dreamed.

She could still hear Andy inviting her—*Kate, come with me to Nova Scotia*—and how she'd barely thought, just said *yes!*

But now, she was traveling on the south shore of Nova Scotia. Looking at the map, she realized the province was in the shape of a large whale projected out into the Atlantic and the south shore they were driving on cut along its belly. Cape Breton was its tail, farther east. Seven hours away.

Right after they'd graduated from college, Andy had paid

three hundred dollars for the Chevrolet. He'd spent days building the wood-shingled covering for the truck bed where they now stored their Coleman stove, sleeping bags, and tent. Some clothing, paper, journals, and pens; a few books of poetry—T. S. Eliot among them—lay in the bottom of the cab at their feet.

Kate remembered her last night before joining Andy, how she'd sat on her childhood bed in New York City toward the open window, the June air swarming with the smell of fresh leaves. A small lamp caught her reflection in the glass covering the lithograph, its light touching her high cheekbones, her brown eyes and long black hair, as she looked down toward the flat of her stomach, her breasts full and small with dark, pointed nipples beneath her nightgown. She was a woman now at twenty-one, she told herself. She'd had a boyfriend before she'd met Andy; Michael had dropped out of college and been sent to Vietnam; a shock, it all happened so quickly. He'd returned after a year of service, and visited her at Sarah Lawrence, but didn't want to talk about being "over there." He did tell her in a short breath that half of his platoon got lost; that he changed out of his uniform at the airport and stuffed it in his bag because he was afraid of being ridiculed for being a soldier. She felt guilty because their last time together didn't go very well. He had to go back, and she was going to protest. In fact, she'd met Andy at an antiwar rally and she knew she wanted to be with someone who was against the war, not fighting in it. But Michael haunted her, the way he'd lost hope in everything he had wanted to do.

Now she was leaving her old bed with the carved floral

posts, the lithograph beside it, and the thick embroidered curtains her mother had chosen.

What on earth are you going to do in Nova Scotia? her father had asked her.

She had to leave New York, the apartment her mother died in. Even though she hadn't known Andy for very long, she was ready to jump into his truck and sleep in the small tent he had bought at Sears; she was ready to cook on the Coleman stove with their cast iron pan; she was ready for exploring a wild place.

But now in the truck, days later, Andy watched her. "Are you okay?" he asked.

Closing her eyes, she wished she could recover her initial excitement. "This fog makes me seasick," she admitted, not quite knowing what'd possessed her to come here.

"Do you want to stop? There's a great beach here."

"Sure."

He turned off the main highway, drove down a dirt road to a beach. There were no houses or wharves here. The sudden quiet inside the cab let in the ocean's dull roar.

Even in her sneakers, she stumbled over the heaps of granite as they aimed for the surf. The water hissed in close with a seething of small stones. Fog thinned to a gauze over the waves, and the air was warm and humid.

"The ocean!" he cried, and picked her up and swung her over the waves. She clung to him, relieved by his laughter, even though the fog veiled over them again and hid them with the sea.

"No one can see us," he whispered, as his hand slipped

beneath her T-shirt, cupping her naked breast in his palm.

In haste they peeled off their clothes, cotton khakis already damp, and stood back to gaze at one another while the fog slid like silk between them. Kate stepped up and Andy lifted her, surprising her with his strength, and leaned in to kiss her, clasping her damp thighs around his waist. They braced, barely moving, locked with the liquid heat inside their mouths and bodies.

There was nothing now but their own desire. Andy collapsed on his knees and held Kate tight against him in the sand. The sky and the fog exploded in Kate's eyes as she fell back, the wet earth sucking beneath her as Andy arched, piercing inside her with the ocean roar, her mouth filling with the smell of waves. The sea swam up through their legs and hips, flooding her with memories of all the times they had made love, as if each time was related to that first night in Andy's small dormitory bed where they lay naked with their shoulders tight beneath the sheet so they wouldn't shiver. They'd talked about their good fortune in meeting each other, and how *the Vietnam war* had consumed their college years, the wrongness of it, and the people they knew getting drafted and sent overseas. Then of the *coincidence*, first of Nova Scotia, and then of death, losing a parent—yes, each one of them, losing a parent—a finality that had linked them, and the way they'd shared the details of their parents' deaths with the intimacy of exploring each other's bodies, raw and all too soon, Kate's mother and Andy's father, both deaths too painful to fathom. So their conversations stayed mainly with Nova Scotia and how they wanted to *go there*. And Andy told Kate how he wanted to work *with his hands* and build boats; how they could be *self-sufficient*, raise a garden, have chickens, a few pigs, and maybe a milk cow. Kate could still hear those words now on the beach with Andy's weight on top of her, his scrambled hair blocking the sky.

The fog pulled away and startled them, naked on the shoulder of the sea. Quickly Andy got up and pulled Kate with him towards the surf. "Let's swim," he said, laughing, and Kate looked around to see if anyone was on the beach. The waves crashed in and pulled back, whipping spume on her skin while the gulls dove about, and in spite of the cold, Kate lunged in after Andy. The sea roiled up to her waist and lifted her, until she floated like a flower on the water.

იი

Back on the road, the afternoon darkened and Kate fell asleep as Andy drove.

His voice woke her.

"We're coming into Slate Harbour."

Kate sat up. The road narrowed over a windswept field and wove through masses of rock knotted with scrubby juniper and blueberry bushes. In minutes the fog receded, and an arm of land jutted out like a puzzle piece into the Atlantic. A surprise blaze of sunlight brightened a blue cove full of Cape Island boats and dories. Fish stores lined the water's edge, and farther back on the rocks, the houses of Slate Harbour.

The road ended abruptly in the middle of the village as if they had just pulled up into someone's backyard. Andy stopped the truck, and in the quiet, a foghorn cast a low-pitched cry out at sea.

They slid out of the truck then, Kate's skin sticky on the

vinyl, and they stood in the cool air. Curious faces appeared in the windows of the nearest houses, and she shivered, hearing the surf she still couldn't see. Andy nodded somewhere beyond the houses.

"Look out there at the end of the point."

Those letters Andy had written her after they'd met, with photographs of the Tannard house. *This is my family's house at the end of Skerry Point. I've spent my summers there since I was twelve. Nova Scotia and these people have given meaning to my life.*

Kate had put the picture of the house with two men standing in front of it on the wall over her desk at Sarah Lawrence. A young man around Andy's age, Ivan, with a serious expression aimed straight for the camera, and another beside him, Karl, older, in overalls, grinning so she could see his blackened teeth. The house stood on barren rocks behind them, and Kate thought of Sartre, whom she'd just been reading, and the search for meaning in "the bare existence of things."

The house looked isolated, suspended on the edge of the world.

This is the story of a place on the coast where life's only purpose is survival, a place where people fish for several months and then exist for the rest, Andy had written. He sent an article with photographs of white box-shaped houses on a scoured rock coast, Cape Island boats anchored in a cove. Andy used the word "survival" twice, underlined it with the thick point of his pen. *These people live in harmony with the land and sea,* he wrote. *It is a tragedy that the inshore fisherman is being sacrificed to the greed of modern technology. I want you to meet Karl and Ivan, and Ivan's parents Lena and Will. These are people who are made happy by simple things.*

ख

A figure emerged from the fog. "It's Will," Andy whispered.

Kate had heard something about an accident, but nothing prepared her for the shock of the old man's face: his crushed eyelids and blazing, gray eyes. His stitched skin zigzagged from his cheekbones down to his neck, each patch a gray or pink color as if a stocking had been pulled over his head.

"We're so sorry about your father," Will murmured to Andy, walking right up, embracing him, and Kate wondered how much he knew about the circumstances surrounding his father's death. During their days traveling here, Andy had been having nightmares about his father. This worried her, and she felt this again while observing the closeness she saw now between Andy and Will, their long history as they stood close together on the rocks, and she stepped back, ashamed by her reaction to Will.

"Is this Kate?" he asked, looking over.

The day seemed cruel now to withdraw the fog and reveal more completely the specter of his face. Kate swallowed hard, holding out her hand to shake his. At the same time—in the flood of sunlight—a voice rose up not far offshore. The three of them turned, and out in the cove beyond the rocks, a woman sang as she rowed a yellow dory. Gray hair pulled back into a bun, the woman wore a white cotton shirt and an apron as if she might have just come from the kitchen. She seemed playful, her face turned up toward the sky, and the dory moved over the purplish water while she pulled the long oars as hard as she could, blades hitting the surface of the sea with a clap, and pull; clap, and pull.

Transfixed, Kate listened to her sing, her voice ricocheting from the rocks to the water with long *aahhhs* that rang out like a bellow from the cove itself.

She saw them and waved.

Andy smiled and waved back. He said, "And that's Lena."

3

WILL TOOK ANDY OFF TO THE WHARF, and Lena invited Kate up to the house for tea. Walking close behind her, Kate watched the drops of mist rest in Lena's gray hair. The foghorn called somewhere close, and everywhere was a blurriness, of small houses with gardens smelling of rockweed. Clotheslines on spruce poles swayed back and forth in the offshore breeze.

Lena ushered Kate through the door of a lime-colored house. A fresh smell of wax filled the kitchen and everything gleamed: the linoleum floor, the nickel stove, the plants on the windowsills. Stacks of knitting lay piled on the dining room table, and clothes draped over a sewing machine.

"Let's choose our cups," Lena said, and led her across the room to a glass cabinet filled with porcelain cups in different patterns. "Which would you like?" Lena's voice was soft and rhythmic, with almost an Irish lilt.

Kate breathed more easily now, relieved to be inside and away from the fog. "That one," she said, pointing to a cup with coral roses on a sapphire background.

Lena picked up the teacup, light as a shell, and handed it to Kate. Choosing one with yellow roses on a maroon background, she said, "Now let's you and I have our tea."

Kate watched Lena set the kettle on the stove. Something about Lena reminded her of Margaret, the Irish nanny her father had hired, whose calm in the dark storm after her mother's death had soothed her. Now Lena was soothing her, her expression tranquil, though the lines in her face betrayed resignation or even sadness. Kate, on the hard wooden chair, felt her muscles unwind, her damp skin still salty from the ocean.

Lena put the teabags into an enamel pot and when steam began to rise, she filled it and covered it with a crocheted cozy. Kate knew she was watching someone who had practiced this ritual most of her life. She thought of Will and wondered about their relationship and the accident that had scarred him. She wondered if Lena's hair was prematurely gray because of such hardships. Now she watched Lena's care as she poured condensed milk into a small pitcher and set it beside the crystal sugar bowl. At last she sat and filled their cups. "Such fog," she sighed, looking out the window, short wisps of hair escaping her bun. "It's been a long trip for you, I imagine."

"Yes, three days." Kate stirred in milk and sugar. "Have you lived here all your life, Lena?"

"Yes, all my life. Though I did entertain other thoughts when I was younger, mind you." She held Kate in the gaze of her large blue eyes. "I had wanted to be a schoolteacher."

"Really?"

"It didn't work out, though. I was born to a life of fishing, see." Lena swirled her fingertips around the gold rim of her teacup. Then she looked back up at Kate. "See, when you live beside the sea as we do, it's our livelihood. But now I'm spared it, mind you! Will got out of fishing. Those scars you saw, they're the mark of a hard lesson, I can tell you that. We run the store here in Slate Harbour now, have for a number of years."

Lena paused then, brushed the small strands of loose hair behind her ears.

"Ivan," she continued, "our son, works at the tire plant. Got his training as an electrician, he did. He almost went fishing by choice, mind you!" She laughed and sipped her tea. "All those years Will and I worked so hard at the store, and Ivan, all he wanted to do was go fishing with his uncle Karl. He came to his senses, though, after a while." Lena paused, and then asked, "You're staying at the house then, with Andy?"

"Yes," Kate said, suddenly aware of what people might think. Her father had trouble with their not being married, and Nova Scotia was surely farther behind the times. Kate could never admit that to Lena that she had come here on impulse, the way she had *just done it*, driven north with the belief they could choose a simple life despite her father's questions—"What will you *do* in Nova Scotia? You're driving there in a *truck?*" From inside the cab Kate had watched Andy's face move past the Atlantic sky and the fog and the blurry grasses along the coast, and the movement felt like running; Kate, the fastest runner in her class as a girl, felt the world was benevolent as long as she could run.

Lena put her cup down. "I'm sorry about Mr. Farrell," she said. "He was a fine man. I'm glad you're here with Andy. Mrs. Farrell did tell me he was murdered. . ."

"Yes. . ." she said, hesitating, remembering the night in the college room when Andy had told her: "*In the kitchen*," he'd said. "*Stabbed.*"

"Must be so hard, not. Why, I watched Andy grow up. He used to stay with us a lot when Mr. Farrell went away. Same age as my son, Ivan."

"Went away?"

"He was often called away," Lena said. "Worked for the government, that was all we knew."

Andy had told Kate he never knew where his father went when he left on business. She'd known he worked for the government, but she didn't know what kind of job he had. Andy said he believed he'd escaped the draft because of "the strange circumstances" surrounding his father's murder. She knew that it bothered him, that he didn't get drafted while some of his friends had to go to Vietnam.

"And his mother? Do you know her well?"

Andy's mother didn't want to come back to Slate Harbour after his father's death. "It gets too lonely out there," she'd said, easily agreeing to let them stay in the house this summer. Kate had met Andy's mother once before they left. Frail, with high cheekbones, and her graying hair clipped back from her face, she'd seemed despondent. Andy apologized for her, saying she was obsessed with trying to find his father's murderer.

Lena cleared her throat. "I'm not sure she liked being here. She was a hard person to get to know, you know what I mean. I could never sit and talk with her, well, the way I'm sitting here talking with you."

Kate blushed. She thought to herself, maybe I can try to live here as long as Lena lives here too.

တတ

Following Lena down the path, Kate still had no sense of direction. She couldn't even recall where they had parked their truck. Lena guided her through the houses, past red tulips rising from small gardens, the ground beneath her feet dry, even though the fog still swamped them.

"We need rain," Lena muttered, but then she stopped: "Oh, I must check in on Flossie! I always help her out this time of day. Would you believe, she's ninety-three. Excuse me, Kate, for just one moment. I'll be right back."

Lena vanished into the nearest house around the corner, and Kate stood there alone, the sunlight fooling her while it flashed on and off the rooftops of surrounding buildings, and again Kate thought of how Lena reminded her of Margaret.

რა

Margaret, her soft white hair woven back from her face, her skin smelling of rosewater. A gold cross hung from a chain just below the neckline of her blouse. As a child, Kate had been fascinated by how the sun caught its golden light. When she'd asked, Margaret told her that God was her protector.

"What does God protect you from?"

"From feelings that are too big to bear on my own. Like sadness, or loneliness." The Irish lilt in her voice gave these words a mysterious ring.

Kate said, "I wish I had a brother or sister. I wish I had someone who knew Mommy as well as I did."

"Maybe you can pray about it," Margaret said, her voice very low. "God can help you with your loneliness."

Her father wasn't religious, so one Sunday Kate asked if she could go to church with Margaret. And there in the vestibule, she saw a bigger shape of Margaret's cross. She knelt in the pew and prayed towards it. "I wish, dear God, I had a brother or sister."

She knew this didn't make sense now that her mother had died, but it didn't matter. Her loneliness had made up its own rules. At home, she made an altar. She tuned her radio until she found music she'd heard in the church. Then she drew a cross with bright colored crayons, hung it with Scotch tape in the center of the soundbox. It looked too bare, so she spread a cotton scarf with pink roses over the desk at the radio's base.

A week later, she found a watercolor leaning against the radio. An older woman with gray hair, dressed in a white uniform, was holding hands with a young girl. They were standing in a smooth green meadow backed by a cobalt sky and small childlike beings with wings were flying over their heads. She ran to find Margaret.

"Margaret, did you paint this? It's so beautiful!"

Margaret blushed, rubbing a soft cloth against the spout of a silver teapot. "Yes."

"Who are these?" Kate pointed to the flying figures. Their eyes, shadow-lidded and serene, were looking down at her. Wings sprouted from their small shoulders in fine quilled feathers.

Margaret peered. "Angels, my child. God's angels will always take care of you, and help you not feel so lonely in the world."

From that time on, Kate could only think about angels. At night she prayed until she felt the pinch in her forehead, the dark closed around her like water. The streetlamp outside cast a phosphorous glow on the shade over her window. She rose and pulled up the shade. Light burst into her room and cast a shock of brilliance against the opposite wall. When she turned, her shadow leaned, a dark, velvet presence crisp against the brightened wall. She lifted her arm, beckoning, and smiled at her silent replica. Soon their fingers invented shapes, and Kate began to laugh and dance with her shadow, in perfect, synchronized motion. The wind was on their cheeks and the stage lights came on in blue and red and the loudspeaker introduced them. They spun on ice and waxed wood floors, and the crowds stood cheering while the partners embraced each other in a shower of roses.

For nights she did this. She created costumes with her shadow, and they danced, and in the mornings, she would get up alone and exhausted and go to school.

Then one night, when Kate began to dance, light swamped the room. Margaret and her father stood in the door. "My dear Kate, what are you doing?" Margaret's voice was worried.

Kate stood, half losing her balance in the invasion. The wall where her shadow had danced was flat and lifeless. Tears filled her eyes, and she could barely ask: "Did you see the angel?"

"Yes," Margaret answered, almost whispering. "I did see the angel."

స్త

Now Kate stood beside the house Lena'd entered, feeling shy about the immediacy of her feelings towards Lena. She guessed this memory might be giving her a clue of Lena's importance as she began her first days in Slate Harbour. Those years ago she'd been too young to understand the importance of creating a companion to protect her after her mother's death. But some part of her knew that she had this magic, to believe in the solace of something otherworldly. And maybe Lena had that too.

The fog seemed to smother all sound and there was no wind. Curious, she stepped off the dirt path and walked a short distance over the rocks and past another building until she could see the cove. Water spread out like polished silver at her feet. The tide was low and rockweed lay in golden heaps. A few dories sat veiled offshore.

"My God, there's a young woman now," came a voice with a screech in the back of it. "What brings you here? Ah ha ha ha . . ."

Startled, Kate turned. On her left, maybe eight feet away, sat an old woman on a bench against the shingles.

"Hello," said Kate, nodding towards her.

"Hello, my God, what a thing to say now! What in the name of God brings such a young woman as you to these parts? Ah ha ha ha . . ."

Showery air diffused the old woman's laugh, and Kate tried to bring her face into focus—her swollen pink gums, a few scattered teeth.

"I'm here, visiting with Andy Farrell," Kate stammered, trying to make out the red scarf around the woman's head, her black rubber boots.

"Ah, you been to the house, not?" The woman's eyes seemed skewed and Kate wondered how well she could see.

"Not yet," Kate said, turning to look over the cove. Nothing made any visual sense anymore: the water, laws of gravity, and light. The black rocks bordering the cove seemed to float in the air. "We just got here."

"That'll be Basil Tannard's house, you know that, you! Hah! It'll always be Basil Tannard's house." The old woman rocked as she ranted, her hands clamped to the bench.

Basil Tannard. Andy had told her the story about Basil being lost at sea and then saved by a seal but no one believed him. Not even his wife, Ellen.

"The future ain't good, no."

"Why do you say that?"

"The young fellows want to be up in Greenport, that's where they go. No use fishing no more because there ain't no fish in the sea." The old woman chanted and rocked, and Kate began to feel as though she were suffocating.

Suddenly the woman turned a piercing look on her. "Mr. Farrell's dead, isn't he, now? Dead now?" she called out.

Everyone in the village must know about Andy's family, Kate thought. She tried to concentrate. "I'm sorry, but I have to go," she said, stepping farther up the rocks.

"It'll always be Basil's house! They say he haunts it . . ."

"Kate!" Lena shouted from the road.

Relieved, Kate waved good-bye and stepped gingerly up the path towards Lena. Yet the old woman's voice trailed her. "It'll always be Basil Tannard's house, you!"

4

"THAT'S JUST CRAZY OLD SADIE. Pay her no mind," Lena said.

"Do you think a seal saved Basil Tannard?"

"Yes, I can believe it, but no one else did. Except for Sadie." Lena's voice grew quiet. "Sadie had a hard life, see. Her two boys froze to death hauling lobster traps during a bad winter storm. Ever since, she sits out there on the wharf saying whatever comes into her mind."

"How old were her boys?"

"About eleven and thirteen. See, if boys didn't like school those times back, they went fishing." Lena paused and looked at Kate. "When Sadie's boys were found, they were caked in ice. The ice just grew around their bodies during the storm."

Kate supposed such a loss could make anyone crazy, and she wondered if other things Sadie said might be true.

The tide was out, and the wharf, now high on its pilings, stretched into the cove. A Cape Island boat sat at least seven feet beneath the dock. Their steps clapped through the inlet, and Lena looked back. "Be careful, now, the planks aren't nailed down to avoid a storm's damage, not."

Trying not to skid, Kate breathed in the gull droppings and fish scales pasted to the boards. A hum of voices rose through the sodden air. When they reached the end of the wharf, Kate peered down into the hull of the boat, awed by a world she knew nothing about but had dreamed of; a well of nets, coiled rope, fish boxes, and pails, packed inside the vessel for the single task of fishing.

Andy, black boots on, his shirt sleeves rolled up, sat beside Will and a man she guessed to be Karl. "Kate!" Andy greeted her, a reckless look of pleasure on his face.

For a moment, Kate panicked. He looked so at home on the Cape Islander's curved railing. Her ignorance about fishing and boats and the men who navigated them made her embarrassed, even a little ashamed. Here was the *real work* on the sea; she could smell the labor of it, and see the strength of it in Karl's forearm as he lifted his hand in greeting. "Hello, Kate. Climb aboard, you."

She saw the ladder nailed to the piling, and put her foot on the top rung, concentrating on her descent. Salty steam hissed in the low tide and her head pounded from the marine pressure. The boat rocked when her feet hit the deck, and Andy grabbed her hand. She smelled alcohol on his breath when he kissed her on the forehead, and the smell mixed with the gasoline from the engine box.

"Welcome to the *Lena!*"

"The *Lena?*"

Karl said, "Yep, we named our boat after the best woman in Slate Harbour!"

Kate saw the look of pleasure pass over Lena, who still stood on the wharf looking down at them. Laughing, she called out, "Come again for tea soon, Kate. I best be going now."

"Here's to you, now, Kate," Karl said, toasting her with a green bottle. Kate wondered if Will might look like Karl if he hadn't gotten so scarred up—gray curly hair, bright hazel eyes, a deep russet skin.

Andy leaned in. "Have a sip of sherry."

She fought off feeling hurt that Andy was drinking in the middle of their first day arriving in Slate Harbour. She took the bottle and smelled the lip, gaseous and sweet. Everything was so different from what she'd imagined. She sipped the runny darkness that at least purged the taste of seaweed and dry fish in her mouth; and then she took another sip, the liquid buzz down her throat. Karl and Andy laughed, and Kate passed the bottle back.

"I don't touch the stuff," Will said.

Kate looked at Will now, not so disturbed by scars netting his face. She saw the look of intelligence in his eyes.

A shadow fell over the well of the boat. Kate looked up and squinted. A man stood silhouetted with his hands on his hips. He wore khaki pants, a plaid wool shirt, and leather boots. His hair was thick and disheveled around his face.

"Hey." His voice was deep and slightly hoarse; his lips curved into a smile.

"Ivan!" Andy shouted. He grabbed the rungs of the ladder, managed to climb up the side of the wharf. The two men embraced, laughing and pounding each other's backs. Kate watched from below, feeling the joy in their greeting, seeing Ivan's strong, hardworking arms circling Andy, and Andy's, longer, slimmer, around Ivan.

Something unexpected overcame her—as if in their embrace she saw Andy freshly: his body, slighter than Ivan's, though more refined, his chamois shirt, his loose khaki pants. Ivan was rugged, and *from* this place, a Nova Scotian from a world so different from hers, and she realized how much she and Andy were trying to change their lives by leaving their past and college educations and troubled protests against the war. Andy had encouraged his roommate Tim to burn his draft card and come to Canada, but Tim had registered instead and now months later, Andy still hadn't heard from him. So now here they were in Canada, greeting Ivan, who was not at all a part of their life in the States, yet who'd spent those summers with Andy when they were boys in Slate Harbour, part of the reason Andy wanted to move here. And in their embrace on the wharf, Kate knew this.

ཀྵ

Finally, they left the *Lena* and headed for the house. Arms of fog burned off in the late afternoon and they drove the truck as far into the field as they could, then walked the path with their bags towards Skerry Point. A wash of blue soaked through the air, and Kate could hear a roll of thunder ahead, the great North Atlantic. Perhaps it was the sherry that gave her a vague sense of peril as the wind came over the cliff.

When they entered a clearing of windswept grass, the sun flared. The Tannard house almost blinded her as it rose on the field's edge. With no trees around it, it was much larger than the saltboxes inside the village of Slate Harbour. A second-story dormer window reflected a brilliance that forced Kate to shield her eyes, yet she adjusted her fingers so she could gaze upon this house pouring inside her and taking shape like a dark shingled castle on the horizon.

ଔ

Their feet grew wet in the grass as they crossed the field to the front entry. The gray weathered shingles glistened in the lowering sunlight and a cool ocean breeze whipped around the house, its roof cutting a steep angle through the sky. Andy put down his bags, unlocked the red ochre door. "Welcome," he said, and kissed her. His mouth was warm and Kate tasted the sherry, still disappointed he'd drunk so much on their first day here.

They stepped through the entry and stood in a room filled with old pine furniture and hooked rugs covering the wood floors. The stagnant air mixed with the smell of cotton, wood smoke, and dust. Two family portraits hung over a fireplace, and the mantel was cluttered with tole painted trays, copper plates, and kettles. Andy put their bags down by the fireplace, then opened windows.

"It's beautiful," Kate said. Small paned windows of rippled glass faced Northeast. She was mesmerized by the closeness of the sea.

Andy circled his arms around her waist. "It's good to be here with only you."

"Yes, it was a busy welcome."

"Everyone wanted to meet you."

"I even met old Sadie on the way to the wharf."

He laughed. "She's sat on that wharf as long as I can remember."

"She said Basil Tannard haunts this house."

"Yes, it will always be his house. For years no one lived here. All the windows were broken out. I remember coming up and looking in through that window and seeing a kid, sitting right here on a crate, smoking a cigarette," he said, pointing to the floor on which he stood. "The kid got up and yelled at me. *Get out of here!* That was the first time I saw Ivan."

1958

VAN JABBED THE EARTH WITH HIS FORK. Twelve years old this August, he was late bringing in the potatoes for Lena. The Atlantic air blew up from the cove and he shivered thinking about the first frost that would come any day now and leave the ice in the fields. Yet he didn't know if it was that or the thought of Will getting home soon from the hospital that made him shiver.

He kicked at the earth with his rubber boot. Hilled rows of potatoes stretched out in front of him, the plants dry and withered. He worked the prongs of the garden fork. New potatoes unraveled like a nest of eggs from the dirt, and Ivan reached down, broke a potato from the roots and turned it in his palm. Small, darkened pocks erupted on all sides of the tuber's coarse skin.

"Shit, scabs." He tossed the potato and it landed with a dull thud in the wheelbarrow, a sour smell of roots erupting in the air. Ivan knew the crop should have been planted where the soil wasn't so sweet. They'd done a bad job this season after Will got burned up. Lena had stayed with him in the hospital and had asked Ivan to plant the potatoes, but he hadn't been sure where to put them. That old frustration welled inside him, he couldn't do anything right.

He wiped his nose with his sleeve. Across the cove, the old Tannard house stood clearly in view at the end of the point, its gray shingles lit by the lowering sun. For a moment, everything was gold: the tips of dried summer grass, the moss on the rocks, the abandoned house beckoning like a shelter.

He shoved his fork into the earth. Maybe he had time for a quick smoke before Lena came home. Digging his hand into the pocket of his jeans, he pulled out an old pack of Exports he'd found. Three cigarettes.

He set off across the field, down the path that rounded the cove. His socks slipped down as he ran, knotted under his arches. He came off the path through the tall wild timothy towards the Tannard house, remembering how he'd run away here on that terrible night, still feeling the strength of his father's muscles and fists, and smelling the rum, and only wanting to get away to smoke.

The broken window by the front entry was his mark. He placed his hands on the sill, and with one jump, swung through. Making his way across the rotted floor, he grabbed the tin of matches he'd left there, and went to sit by the large window looking southeast over the Atlantic. Balancing himself on an old crate, he swept the wooden match against his jeans.

A neat flame exploded in a crisp smell of phosphorous. Ivan brought it to his cigarette and tried to picture again what might have happened that night; had Will dropped a match on his clothes, or a cigarette? He watched the tobacco catch fire as he inhaled, the miniature lit coils tight in the paper skin. Was it the wind from the cove that had turned the small embers into flames up Will's body?

Now Ivan inhaled the smoke and released it slowly in drifting rings, growing dizzy, floating as if he were in tune with himself, the house's only inhabitant. He'd grown accustomed to the whir of bats and the occasional slam of a door. Basil Tannard's ghost, of course, he'd laugh to himself. He loved the peace he felt as the sun lowered and drained the light from the inside walls of the house.

A silhouette flashed from the window out of the corner of his eye. He turned, his breath in his mouth. A figure stood against the glass on the opposite side of the room looking right in at him.

Ivan leaped to his feet. "Who are *you?*" he yelled.

The image of a boy about his age took shape through the glass. Ivan could see his startled eyes and flushed cheeks; a straight line of hair cutting across his forehead. Their faces were not eight feet apart. The boy's mouth was open, but he did not speak.

Ivan slapped at the air. "Hey, what do you want? Get out of here!"

He saw the boy's eyes open wider with surprise. A gray shirt buttoned up to his chin. Ivan took another step, and the boy turned, vanished. Ivan ran to the glass, seeing his figure disappear through the grass back towards the village. Jabbing his cigarette out, he ran from the house, chasing the boy through the field.

"Don't...come back! *Get out of here!*"

༚༚

"You got to take risks sometimes, Ivan," Karl said the next

day. Sitting on the wharf mending the nets, Ivan worried about that boy he'd seen through the window and how he was going to tell Lena about the scabby potatoes.

"The old place is just waiting to fall to the ground. Standing empty all these years. Those people from New York offered me a good price, you. They'll fix it up. They've got a boy about your age."

"Yeah, I've seen him," Ivan said, pushing the wooden needle through the net.

He'd spent most of the summer with his uncle Karl. He'd always known Karl was smarter than Will, he never drank the way Will did, but now he was upset Karl hadn't told him about selling the house. He'd seen that strange car driving down to his house.

"Besides, there's something queer about the place," Karl went on. "Ever since Basil died and Ellen deserted it, almost thirty years ago, not."

"What will you do with the money?" Ivan got the courage to ask. He briefly fantasized about Karl getting a new engine for his boat and taking him out on more fishing trips.

"Well, with your father in the hospital and all…"

"Ivan!" Lena's voice startled them. The sound of her feet echoed on the loose boards of the wharf, and Ivan guessed she had discovered the scabby potatoes. He lowered the netting on his lap, raised his hands to shield his eyes from the light. She came to a stop in front of him, wisps of her long hair circling her face. "We're going to open a store!"

"Store?"

Briefly, she looked over at Karl, who was smiling.

"Has Karl told you he just sold the old house yesterday? He's giving us money to start a store right here in Slate

Harbour." Lena bent closer, still catching her breath, and put her hand on Ivan's shoulder. "Will's coming home soon, Ivan, and everything's going to be different, you wait and see."

But Ivan only stiffened.

Lena stared down at him, her eyes wide open. "Karl is going to give us the money so we can have another chance, you."

"Another chance at what?"

Lena walked to the edge of the wharf then, and leaned against the railing. Ivan knew what would come next, the anger he knew inside his mother. He heard the sea churn against the pilings, and then he heard her voice.

Ivan, can't you see what the problem was? It was the fishing. The men all turn to drunks out here in Slate Harbour, Ivan, you better believe it. Now we have another chance. Listen to me, Ivan. No way will you fish, Ivan, hear me? Over my dead body will you be making a living on the sea!

ཉ

He went back to the potato field with still enough light to dig up a few rows. The fork and wheelbarrow were where he'd left them.

Karl had always told him that to fish well you had to learn to use the senses in your head. Staring out at the old house, he saw it standing there like the old men of the village who would sit out at the end of the wharf and watch the fishermen. They would lean back, have a smoke with each other. Karl said that seeing an old man at the end of the wharf before you went out meant that the sea would spare you. He said that a man who lived past seventy should go out of this world with dignity as a reward for his hard life of fishing, so why couldn't the Tannard house die the same way?

Ivan reached for his fork and began to dig. A cloud of mosquitoes hovered at his face and the fury seized him. He threw away the fork and began to dig with his bare hands until his fingers burned and chunks of dirt got clogged under his nails, and all he could see was the house as it had been, before Will's burning and his secret climbs through the broken window for a smoke and the view of the blue moving ocean. He knelt in the soil and wept, hands pressed into the deep and decaying smell of it. Finally, then, he felt the rage that blinded him from helping Will that night.

For a long time, he sat in a quiet field.

"Ivan?"

The voice startled him. He looked up. Lena peered at the potatoes. "Digging the potatoes so late?"

"They're full of scabs," he said, wiping his cheeks with his sleeve.

"I've seen scabs on potatoes before."

"I planted them in the wrong part of the garden."

Lena looked closely at Ivan. "It's not your fault, Ivan. I should have helped you more. I've been so distracted this summer . . ." Lena's voice was sad. She picked up a potato, twisted it in her palm, threw it in the barrow. "Tomorrow just dig them up and put them in the shed. It's late now." Lena looked at him. "I'm sorry, Ivan, it's been so hard…"

She turned and walked quickly down the hill then, and Ivan watched the wind blow her dress away from the walking shape of her body.

1971

THERE WAS NO MOON on their first night in the old Tannard house, only kerosene lanterns brightened the room as Kate and Andy sat talking after dinner. Andy lit the woodstove and Kate had cooked the haddock Karl had given them. Andy uncorked a bottle of white wine and poured it in two glasses. The sherry from the afternoon had worn off, and the wine tasted fresh as they listened to the surf wash through the window.

"Ivan wants to take us out in the dory tomorrow," Andy said quietly.

"Great," Kate said, looking out the window, and a cold draft moved through the rooms.

"Kate, you're cold, let me get your sweater," Andy said, rising.

She folded her arms, wondering about those who'd lived here, looking at the old stone fireplace and hanging iron cook pots, imagining Basil and his wife, Ellen, and wanting to see their faces.

Andy returned, wrapping her sweater around her. "Let's go outside for a moment," he said. "The fog still hasn't come in and I want you to see the point."

They walked in darkness through the grass towards the end of Skerry Point. The house, its lit windows loomed behind. The sea surged near. Adjusting to the dark, Kate began to distinguish a steep bluff and she breathed in the salt air. Large boulders lay scattered through the water along the shore and strange caws and popping sounds came from them.

"Seals," Andy said. "They lie out on the reef and talk to one another at night."

Of course, seals, Kate thought. They must be all around here.

When they turned to go back inside, Kate saw a dark shadow lit by the kerosene lantern pass through the house. Startled, she said, "Someone must be inside."

"Oh, that's just the flame flickering," Andy said.

∽

The house was warm after the chill outside. They cleaned up, Kate carefully drying the blue porcelain plates and crystal glasses. She felt the good fortune of being in the midst of such beautiful things and thought about Andy's mother not wanting to come here, how sad it was after all the care she must have taken to choose the Le Creuset pots and flat silver, the framed seascapes, and maroon patterned curtains.

Then Andy led her up the stairs to his room on the second floor and she thought about the two of them being here by themselves. She began to feel like an adult, beginning the first part of her dream. They got sheets for the bed, and before spreading them, she turned to kiss him, slipping his hands under her shirt and pressing them into her skin. She closed her eyes and leaned back, unzipping her jeans, overcome by the mystery of this place and their finding each other, desire deep in her body and Andy whispering, "We're really here."

Afterward, he slept, and she moved from under his arms and lay on her side, staring at the unfamiliar walls and ceiling, the dark windows.

An unmistakable knocking sound came down the hall, perhaps someone walking. Kate sat up.

"What is it?" Andy asked, waking.

"There's a strange noise," she said, remembering the shadow she'd seen earlier.

They listened for a moment, yet the house was silent.

"Perhaps the seals."

"Maybe," she said. Though this sound was different.

"Or bats, sometimes there are bats. Don't worry. There're always strange noises in this house."

She slipped down further under the covers, close beside Andy, telling herself she wasn't afraid.

The foghorn called, and already Andy had fallen back to sleep. Slowly she breathed. For how many years, she wondered, had the fog hidden this house on the point and the lives of people inside it, and the room grew dark as if it were rocking her out at sea.

And if that noise had been Basil Tannard, he'd quieted.

7

THE NEXT MORNING. Ivan waited at the end of the wharf. Kate and Andy descended the cove, a low tide scattering golden rockweed in a circle at its base.

"Good morning to you, now," he greeted them, wearing baggy khaki pants and a plaid cotton shirt, his gray eyes brightening.

Such a distance Andy had come with Ivan after all these summers. It was his father who had been so persistent about the two of them getting along. "Don't show Ivan you're afraid of him," his father would say, leaving him those times as a boy to stay with Will and Lena.

"Let's get the dory now," Ivan said, putting his hand on Andy's shoulder, Andy glad for its weight as the three of them walked along the shore. The sea seeped in through the heaps of rockweed and made the crackling sound of a rising tide.

Ivan leaned in to draw the rope, guiding the dory in. The bow slid onto a patch of gravel and the stern swung around, beaming its bright yellow planks on the water.

Ivan looked down at Kate's sneakers. "Hmmm. Don't want to spoil those shoes getting in, now."

She looked down at her feet.

"I'll give her my boots," Andy said, taking his off and handing them to her.

Ivan held on to the bow while Kate struggled with her balance as she took off her shoes and pulled on the boots. Even in her awkwardness, Andy was reminded of Kate's beauty; her thick black hair as it fell over her shoulder, her long, thin legs. Her cheeks flushed as she concentrated.

"So when you're ready, climb aboard and sit there," Ivan said to Kate, pointing toward the bow. "Andy, you go aft now."

Kate waded in. Supporting herself with one hand on the gunwale, she put one foot in the bottom of the dory and hoisted herself in.

"Well done," Ivan said, nodding.

It was inevitable, Andy guessed, that Ivan would think Kate beautiful, and a wave of worry swept through him as he climbed into the stern. Ivan chuckled as he pushed the dory out from shore. "This should be some fun, you," he said as he jumped aboard, and Andy could see Kate watch Ivan's every move as he slipped the oars through the tholepins.

Here were the two people Andy loved most in the world. He wanted to believe the good fortune in this, as Ivan rowed out through the rocks towards the ocean, his strokes strong and rhythmic. Andy looked past Ivan at Kate, who sat facing Ivan's back, her eyes ablaze with the newness of what surrounded her. The village receded, while the Tannard house stood alone at the end of Skerry Point, small squares of light flashing from its windows. Andy still remembered those first nights he had stayed with Lena and Will and Ivan, and how he would wake up frightened in the middle of the night and watch the house from Ivan's window. He remembered traipsing through the wet grass to go out there, it must have been near morning. He would look inside the front window, wanting to believe it was his home, yet he always wondered who lived in this house while no one was there. Even still, Andy could feel like a trespasser.

"How is it now, Andy, being in the house?" Ivan called out. "Without your father and all . . ."

Even though Ivan's expression was thoughtful, the question for Andy was a hard one. He felt his body being out of sync with the pulse of Ivan's rowing. "It helps that Kate's here," he said quietly.

Andy's and Ivan's eyes met then as if they both knew the influence a woman could have in their lives. Then Andy gazed over the sea's horizon looking for a visible sign for what had changed. The light was different, as if his father's murder had the power to change the color of the day.

"How long do you and Kate intend to be here now?" Ivan asked, breathing harder between strokes.

"Hopefully for a year. That is, if we can get jobs."

"Really, a year! Now that's a good thing, you. What will you do for work?"

Andy hesitated, an American trying to get employment in Canada. But he forged ahead. "I'm hoping to try apprenticing at the dory shop in Greenport. With Sherman, if he'll have me."

"Oh, yes, I always knew you liked those dories. You spent enough time hanging out with Sherman, that's for sure."

"We're thinking about applying for our landed immigrant status."

"Now that's good!" Ivan grinned. "Verlene will love to have you both as neighbors."

"How's your work going, Ivan?"

"Pays the bills is all."

Andy heard the flat tone in his voice. Ivan had married Verlene last summer and since that time, had worked at the tire plant outside Greenport. Andy couldn't picture Ivan at a tire plant, even if it was electrical work he was doing. He knew Ivan wanted to fish. Now he was embarrassed he'd mentioned working at the dory shop, his own life's dream, while Ivan didn't, or couldn't, pursue his.

"Do you ever consider anything else?"

"Fishing? Ha, over Verlene's dead body!"

Ivan rowed harder, and Andy, annoyed with himself, changed the subject. "The dory's in good shape. Did you help Karl paint it this spring?"

"Yep. I like that outside work, not. Oh, and I volunteer for the fire department. We practice every Tuesday night and I like that well enough."

"That's great, Ivan," Andy said. "I'm sure that's not an easy job."

"You're right. In fact, there have been some strange burnings around here."

Ivan turned to look as they approached the reef. It surfaced like a small mountain range from the waves; the same reef visible from the Tannard house. About fifty feet away, shining, dark seals camouflaged on the ragged rock broke up the blue horizon. As they got closer, a few seals turned their heads to watch them, but they did not seem afraid.

"There, Kate, have you seen seals before?" Ivan asked, a quiet enthusiasm in his voice.

From long ago, Andy knew of Ivan's love for seals. He remembered that time when they were boys, out fishing with Karl and Ivan on the *Lena*, when something had interrupted their work, attacking the fish in their nets.

"Damn seal!" Karl had called out, grabbing a spiked pole and racing to the stern. Cursing, he'd taken aim. Small whirlpools whipped up by the float line, and Karl jabbed at them with the pole.

"What is it?" Andy had asked, surprised.

"They eat fish," Ivan said.

A shining black head rose in the water, looked right at Karl. The seal's whiskers flickered in the sun, its black eyes watery like a dog's. Andy had never seen one so close before, something looking so benevolent rising from the sea. Karl aimed his pole right between its eyes.

"Karl, don't!" Ivan screamed.

The seal disappeared.

"Why the hell, not, you!"

"Don't kill it." Ivan's voice was steady.

Everything grew silent then, even the movement of the sea as Andy stood with his feet rooted to the deck, relieved by Ivan's outburst.

Karl dropped the pole by his side. "What's gotten into you, Ivan?"

"It's bad luck," Ivan said, looking out over the water, and Andy looked out too, fearing he might see the creature's body floating with its warm blood on the ocean. But there was no sign of him.

"Since when is it bad luck?" Karl spat into the water, wiping his mouth.

"It's just a feeling," Ivan said, looking away. Andy pictured the seal underwater somewhere, down close to the sea floor maybe twenty-five feet beneath the *Lena*. He imagined it escaping over the reef, darting for a deeper current.

ରୟ

Now, in the dory, Kate said, "I've never seen a seal this close," and she bent forward in her seat. "I heard them last night." The sun beat down on the resting mammals, warming their bodies. She laughed like a child when one lifted its tail to dry.

"They're not very shy," she said.

Ivan turned to see her. "We'll let them sleep, you."

She said, "They're watching us . . . I can hear them breathing."

Their eyes met then. Kate swept her hair behind her ear, giving Ivan a half-curved smile. A flare between them out here on the sea. In Andy's imagination, a gold flame on the water.

Even as a boy, Andy knew, in the smallest moments, anything could change. Was it so simple that both Kate and Ivan being enchanted by the seals could throw Andy off course now? As if, in this one act of their looking at each other, the air around them could quicken a dark and secret light of attraction. Now Andy did not want Ivan to think Kate was beautiful. Breathing in heavily, he imagined losing everything.

He forced himself to sit straight up in the dory, and he watched Kate's body sway in the bow.

Ivan, oblivious, rowed thirty or forty feet from the reef and nodded towards Andy. "Look under your seat, there, you'll see the hand lines. We can jig off the shoals, you!"

Ivan's voice brought Andy back. Yes, now *they could jig off the shoals*, a phrase of words that resonated with the place where they became friends. The sea slapped against the dory, and Andy could see his own beginning with Ivan: their tough first days, Ivan's strong, sinewy arms pulling them through the water, little bits of light rising and slipping from the oars, yellow or white or just blazing from the sun.

Andy grabbed the hand lines from under the thwart. Ivan drew up the oars, and the dory rocked in the trough of the ocean while they put chunks of salt cod on their hooks for bait. Andy glanced at Kate, who smiled at him from the bow, still lost in the expanse of water and sky and her search for the seals.

They cast their lines over the side, unfurled them from the jig. Andy thought about what his father had told him, learning survival from these people in Slate Harbour. How these people had *real values* making their living from the land and the sea. "Unlike urban people who have lost touch with what's real," his father used to say. Though Andy wondered what his father had *really* been looking for in Slate Harbour, for it seemed he'd never escaped the danger of his own job away from this place.

The sun pounded his back and stuck his shirt to his skin, his eyes smarting from the glare on the water.

Then, Andy's line jerked. "Jesus! That's fast!" he yelled, his jig line zigzagging back and forth in the water.

"Christ, Andy, hold on tight!" Ivan hollered, almost standing up in the dory.

Andy grasped the jig with both hands, his teeth clenching in the strain.

"Come on, Andy, bring her in!"

Slowly, with all his strength, Andy wound the line around the jig and started to pull the fish in. "God damn," Andy cursed under his breath.

"Ha!" Ivan laughed. "It's a good thing to hear you curse, now, Andy! You got yourself a big one!"

Andy struggled with the fish and worked out a rhythm for bringing it in—moving into the slack of the line when the fish jagged off to the side, then wrapping that slack quickly around the jig. He knew his hands were no match for Ivan's, but this was his fish.

He managed to haul the fish up to the dory's side. It flapped wildly in the water, a small leviathan, and with one gigantic pull, Andy flung it over and into the bottom of the boat.

"It's a goddamned haddock, now, Andy!" Ivan yelled in triumph, slapping Andy on the back.

Andy caught his breath. The large, silver fish panted in the bottom of the dory.

The fish was suffocating. Andy couldn't make himself do anything.

In a fury, the fish flipped wildly, then lay still again, pulsing its gills. Its soft white underbelly glared against the dull yellow planks of the dory.

Ivan grabbed a small wooden club from under his seat, whacked the fish twice on the head. "This will put him out of his misery," he said, under his breath.

Now the fish lay lifeless in the bottom of the boat, blood's bright stream flowing across its gill. Its eye, a glass bead, was wide open.

Andy's stomach twisted.

"You've got dinner, Andy!" Ivan yelled.

Andy sat rigid on the thwart, forcing his eyes out to sea. The swells in the ocean rocked him, spewing out pictures of his father's murder like a torrent from his stomach, up through his lungs, and into his throat. It was the blood that made him sick.

෨෨

He never liked what he saw in his mind. Always there was a feeling of not being prepared; as if there were something he should or could do to prepare for obliterating the terrible pictures coming over him, a giant wave hurling him through the troughs of blood. He heard his mother's voice: *Don't talk to anyone about your father's murder.* Why had she done that— force that same hateful secrecy on him that he'd had all his life? Except for the few things he'd told Kate.

He closed his eyes.

When he closed them, he saw the packed snow and wind filling the March New York morning.

He saw the police cars out in the street, their red lights turning like flames over the white shining metal.

He saw the security men guarding the front door to his building.

"It's his kid. Let him through," someone said.

A man with fleshy lips took Andy by the arm, up the elevator, and down the hall towards the large oak door he had known all his life. A cold chill slipped through Andy's body knowing this man in a dark suit was from the Secret Service and was leading him to his own home. The man's thick hand opened the door, and a few unfamiliar people stood around inside speaking in low voices. The apartment had the smell of wool soaked in warm water, and Andy found it hard to breathe.

The man nervously looked around. "Where's his mother?" he asked.

A different man nodded towards the kitchen. "Don't let him go in there," he said. "I'll see what I can do."

A rush of adrenaline shot through Andy. He broke away, running through the kitchen door that swung open and hissed shut behind him. A sea of awful red flooded the black-and-white checkered floor around his mother, who was the only person he wanted to see, his mother, who sat at the table holding her head in her hands with her black hair hanging limply down her shoulders. The room was strangely raw with a smell of fresh-baked rolls, and when his mother looked up, her blue eyes were blacker than Andy had ever seen them. When she opened her mouth, no sound came from her.

"For Christ's sake, get the boy out of here," someone said.

The walls and cabinets came into focus then. Blood—sprayed over the white paint—lay in thick pools on the floor, reflecting the bright light overhead. Someone touched Andy then. But Andy wanted to walk over to his mother. Her head had fallen back on the table, her hands pressed up against her ears. When he walked over to put his arms around her, he knew he was walking through his father's blood. His shoes almost slipped before he leaned down, putting his face against his mother's so hard he could feel the tears on her skin.

Andy lifted his eyes from his mother and focused on the tins of golden rolls cooling on the white tile counter. Their fragrance mixed with the scent of blood and Andy knew that if the air smelled sweet, it was because of them. A simple thought came to him—when did the cook take the rolls out of the oven? Then his eyes traveled along the counter, and he saw his father's pipe lying on its side.

ແນ

Waves knocked the dory.

"Andy, are you okay?" Kate called from the bow.

Andy barely heard her voice, his head swirling.

"You're seasick," Ivan said, his voice a million miles away. "Let's get back."

Ivan set the oars, brought the dory around. "Won't take long now, we're going back with the incoming tide, you."

When Ivan began to row, Andy watched the horizon with the *clap and row* sounds from the water, and he tried to wash away *that sight* in his mind, that physical strain of death and blood beating inside his temples as if in rhythm with Ivan's rowing.

They approached the cove, and Andy's eyes found Kate's.

He opened his mouth, but he couldn't get any words to come out. He put his head in his hands.

"Andy, we're almost back," Kate called out.

The sea swelled around them with a slight breeze on its edge. "I'm okay," he lied, feeling the power of Ivan and Kate's presence, the deep relief of the two of them facing him in the dory.

Ivan kept rowing, breathing hard now. "I'll get us back."

Ivan rowed with that sound—*clap and pull, clap and pull*—as they approached the cove, and Andy felt his sickness replaced by a deep exhaustion, even though he was still wondering if the act of accepting death was a higher skill, one that had to be developed like a muscle. For example, the way Ivan had killed the haddock. It was their dinner tonight. He looked up and watched Ivan's hands cup the wooden handles as he rowed. Down, lift, and up. The sea in small blue streams from the oar's blade. He tried to regain his senses, for there was a different order of the universe out here in the dory. Death was necessary here in order to live. But Andy's father's death wasn't necessary. It was evil.

ოი

They brought the dory in and tied her to the buoy. Sunlight moved lower in the sky. Andy sat on the rocks and Kate put her arm around him and watched the tide while Ivan carried the haddock back to the fish house. He returned with a bottle of rum and handed it to Andy.

"Here, drink some of this," he said, sitting down beside him.

Andy took the bottle with his free hand and sipped a long drink and wiped his mouth. Now on the shore, he'd begun to feel his equilibrium return. He said, "Something happened out there on the water."

"Yep," Ivan said. "It's different out there. The sea has its own rules with us."

He took another swig of rum. The wind was quiet then, and the sea.

He said, "I saw my father. I think it was the blood."

Ivan nodded.

Andy said, "In high school I figured out my father worked for the CIA. I'm sure that's why I didn't get drafted to go to

Vietnam. I was against the war and *they* didn't want any trouble from me. I felt bad watching my friends go. Especially Tim."

He took another swig of rum.

"Remember, Ivan, how my father used to wait for Karl to come in on the *Lena*? And then, when he was away on one of those business trips, I'd do just what he did and run to watch Karl unload the fish?"

"Sure, I remember," Ivan said.

"Karl would ask me, 'Where's your dad?' and I'd say, 'On business,' and he'd say, 'I thought he was on vacation when he comes down here,' and I'd say, 'He's never really on vacation,' and he'd say, 'Well, I got a big halibut for you, now!'"

"I remember."

They sat a while longer, the three of them.

Finally Ivan got up. He said, "Well, let's go dress out that haddock, you."

= 8 =

HROUGHOUT THE WEEK, Kate grew more familiar with the Tannard house; its drafts and changing views through the windows; how the anchored boats in the harbor turned with the prevailing wind while the northeast side of the house pressed its back to the moods of the sea. When the party line rang, Kate recognized its signal: *Long short long.*

Lena telephoned to invite Kate to come meet some of her lady friends. Kate felt shy, unsure how the women of Slate Harbour might feel about Andy and she living together without being married.

She went upstairs to change her clothes. The southwesterly plowed up the sea, and the old house rattled and sighed as if it had sails. The high ceiling and large old windows created an inside space for fog light, and her skin chilled as she went into their bedroom. Her suitcase was still lying on the floor. A flower print blouse and her favorite green wool cardigan, she decided. She changed and stood under the light, studying her features in the mirror, sensing how different she might look from the women she'd meet. Her eyes were dark and tired, she thought. Nervously she straightened her hair, still worried about how Andy had been in the dory that time, his restless sleep.

She turned from the mirror and walked to the window facing the sea. The fog thinned for a moment, revealing the gray unsettled surf of the Atlantic slanting towards Slate Harbour.

მდ

Lena waited for Kate in the fog. She wore a light brown scarf around her head, a cotton skirt, and a red checkered blouse. Kate followed her past the church to a bright blue house and into a kitchen where a group of women sat chattering around a quilting frame. They looked up, and silenced.

"Ladies," Lena announced, "This is Kate. She's come with Andy Farrell to live here."

Kate blushed feeling their stare, and her eyes fell over to the quilt. A pattern of small red triangles unscrolled on a large white sheet, looking like red wheels over a field; needles, thimbles, small scissors glinting; the smell of fresh cotton dried in the North Atlantic air.

"Oh, Kate, I'm so glad to meet you," blurted out a plumpish woman with short, yellow curls, younger than the rest. Her brown eyes narrowed as she searched the features of Kate's face. "I'm Verlene, Ivan's wife."

"Verlene," Kate said, surprised. She had imagined Ivan to be with someone prettier. Verlene's nose had a strange upturn; or maybe it was her body, the way her white arms bulged from the short sleeves of her blouse. But she managed to say, "I'm so glad to meet you."

There was Irma Morash, Mary Eisnor, Judy Heckman.

"This quilt pattern is called *Fisherman's Reel*," Verlene spoke out.

"Lovely," Kate said, mesmerized by the illusion, feeling now, as she had felt looking down into the Cape Island boat, her complete lack of knowledge or confidence. The only thing she knew about sewing was how to replace buttons.

"Here, come sit by me," Verlene said, pulling over a chair. "I'll show you what to do."

She sat and watched Verlene thread a needle for her. She wondered what Ivan might have told her about their dory trip, still seeing Ivan while he rowed, the sparkle of sun on the water.

"You want to do the running stitch—like this, see." Verlene's swift fingers pushed the needle up and down like a little silver fish. Lena smiled at her from across the table while a beginning rain scraped the windows.

Trying to imitate Verlene, Kate took the needle and plunged it through, hoping

not to tangle the thread.

"Go nice and slow," Verlene advised. "No need to rush."

She was just like Ivan, Kate thought. That voice she'd heard in the dory, calm and in control. She stole another look at Verlene, and Kate could see her more clearly under the lamplight. She thought of those Rubens paintings she'd studied in college, of plump, smiling, languorous women. She could almost taste Verlene's hairspray and wondered if she liked books, or if that really mattered; maybe she could learn other things from these women who were so different from her. She began to think of the friends she'd left behind. Lizzie, her childhood friend, who would be surprised if she saw her sitting at this table quilting. Lizzie certainly never wanted to sew; she was too busy applying to law school.

They worked over the frame while the rain ticked.

"Kate, how long will you be here in Slate Harbour with Andy?"

"Well, we thought we'd try living here for a year."

"Ah, and what will you *do?*"

Kate sensed some suspicion in the ladies' gaze upon her. Coming from so far away, how could she tell them what she was hoping for, that she and Andy would like to start from the beginning—as if they were starting their lives all over again— and be self-sufficient here in Slate Harbour. Get jobs, plant a garden, and raise their own food. Grind wheat berries for making their bread. Yet that might sound odd to these women who've probably worked hard on the land their whole lives and might love to get clear of it.

So she said, "Well, Andy would like to get a job with Sherman at the dory shop."

"Oh, the dory shop," the women chanted in staggered whispers.

"And I will be looking for a job too," she said hastily.

"Well, a fine young lady such as yourself, with such a good education and all, mind you! What kind of work would you like?" one woman asked, her voice sounding a bit nasty.

"I'm really not sure . . ." Kate looked down, trying to resume the running stitch.

"Remember to go behind the thread," Verlene whispered.

"You know, a lot of people take issue with Harbour House. But I know they are looking for nurse's aides," another woman offered.

"Perhaps I can look into it, then," Kate said, still nervous.

"Oh, and dear, we do need to say how very sorry we are about Andy's father's death. *A murder*, no less, such a terrible thing," someone burst out.

Kate looked over at Lena, wanting some help in responding to these women.

Verlene said, "Kate, I'll drive you if you like to Harbour House. Maybe tomorrow? I know people who work there."

= 9 =

ANDY WALKED DOWN THE ROAD TOWARD the dory shop built alongside the Greenport wharf. Everywhere was fog and the smell of fish. Even the large buildings along the shore looked waterlogged.

Sherman had been building dories now for thirty-three years. As a boy, Andy had done odd jobs for him: carrying boards, hammering nails. Once Sherman brought in a model dory for him to see.

"You could build one of these, now, Andy," he'd said, his eyes shining towards a hull no more than a foot long.

Straightaway Andy had wanted to build a miniature dory. Shaped to the larger boat, its oars and thole pins and thwarts were light as matchsticks when he lifted them. Sherman'd given him pine scrap and reassured Andy that he could learn to build these little boats he hoped to sell to tourists. In one summer Andy did learn to build them as Sherman taught him. Andy's father had set up a workbench in one of their spare rooms of the Tannard house, and Andy would cut and sand and glue the small pine pieces to make these replicas.

Now, years later, he wondered about the next step— learning to build the larger boats—though doubts nagged him, as he thought of his own inexperience in the presence of this master builder.

The shop was small on the edge of the harbor; it stood on thin pilings between the shore and the tidewaters. Now in the damp, its boards were dark as charcoal. Two yellow dories lay overturned on the ramp, and Andy climbed past them and pulled open the door.

The interior was dim but for the light from six high windows. In the center of the room, a half-built dory rested like a skeleton of fresh bent wood inside the molds. In its growing sheer, anyone could tell it was headed for the sea.

Andy stepped inside, pulled the door closed. Daylight glowed in bronze dust from the windows. Sherman, dressed in overalls, was bent over the dory's stern, and when he heard Andy, he looked up, his eyes brightening beneath his framed thick glasses.

"Andy," he said, grinning, and put down his saw.

"Sherman. I don't mean to interrupt you."

Sherman tipped back his cap. His large brown eyes lost their customary shyness while the two men shook hands. "Here for a while?" Sherman asked.

"I hope so."

Sherman, now in his fifties, was a humble man who walked as if he were permanently bent over a dory. When he spoke, his voice was gentle, and his hands were thick with the muscles it took to build these boats. Wood molds and saws hung from the ceiling, and shelves were jammed with paint cans and brushes, tins of galvanized nails, planes, and chisels. Power tools rested on the bench or on top of stacked lumber, and clamps hung by size along the wall.

The only place absent of clutter was in the center of the room where Sherman worked, all the light in the room seeming to move towards him.

For Andy, there was no use waiting. "I've come here today to ask you, Sherman, if you'd take me on as an apprentice."

Sherman scratched his head beneath his cap. "I don't have a lot of work right now, Andy." Then his face shadowed. "Andy, I'm real sorry about your father. I should have said so straightaway." He bent his head toward the dory, then looked back up at Andy. "A terrible thing, you."

The skeletal dory grew bright in the window light.

Sherman took a deep breath. "Well, what's the next step for this dory, now?"

"I see you have the stem and stern on, planks along the garboard," Andy said, knowing Sherman was quizzing him. "Well, the next step is to fit the knees in, right?"

"You bet. Come over here, now."

Andy followed Sherman to the other side of the shop where some lumber was piled.

"Now before we do anything, I want you to understand that the dory is built from the Nova Scotia forest, see. You know the sides are planked with white pine because pine bends nice."

Andy nodded, breathed in a forest smell.

"The oars, spar, and gaff, they're made of spruce. That hardy grower you see around here, not. They grow tall and straight, see."

Dreams. What are dreams when they finally begin to come true? Sherman's voice seemed to float beside him, on his right side with a slight humming sound. The sensation of joy overcame him, as if the simple logic of building a dory was giving him the chance to re-arrange the synapses in his head. He breathed in deeply, trying to concentrate, remembering his father, years ago, when he carefully lay lines of glue between the boards to set the bench in his childhood workroom, and for the first time since his death, Andy could see his father's face clearly and undisturbed.

Sherman scrutinized the spruce boards with the palm of his hands, bending them to test their spring. Andy knew this would take time to learn.

"Now the stern and stem are made of oak, which comes from the valley," Sherman went on, putting the boards down, looking around. "I don't have a lot of it here in the shop right now. But I do have some hackmatack. That wood makes good knees for the dory because their roots are tough and bent."

Andy remembered the lacy fernlike tree that stood out among the spruce. "What kind of tree is that?" he'd asked his father years ago. "Hackmatack," his father answered. "Conifers that lose their needles in winter and grow them back in spring. That's why they have such a bright emerald color." Ever since, Andy loved these trees because he could hear his father's voice in them.

Sherman took a long clear board over to the workbench. Choosing a medium-sized plane from his collection, he bore down his weight over the board and pushed the plane forward, bringing it back up through the air to push the blade down again with the strength of a rower. Shavings spilled from both sides with a pungent smell of resin. Then he handed the tool over to Andy, who leaned over, trying to balance his body the same way Sherman had, pushing the plane along the rough pine surface. Shavings curled and fell in stiff ribbons to the floor, and the more he pushed, the easier the motion became, the sweet scent of trees filling him with the memories of walking through the forest floor with his father.

"Okay, then, Andy," Sherman said. "I've got some orders, not that many though, but let's give it try."

When Andy left the dory shop, the fog had lifted. In fact, the sun now lit up the drenched boards of the buildings so brightly that when he looked up and saw the blue sky, he could barely contain the elation heading him towards a possibility he could not name.

— 10 —

KATE WANTED NEW CLOTHES for her interview at the Harbour House. She'd heard Rudolph's clothing store in Greenport was the best place to look. Maybe she could feel more at ease if she could blend in better with the women of Slate Harbour. Most of her own clothes were out of place—long patterned skirts, Mexican blouses, bell-bottomed jeans, T-shirts.

In the store's musky air, she began her search, inhaling polyester as she browsed the rack of skirts. A fluorescent light hummed over her head as she looked for size six or eight, and went hanger by hanger, through the blue, khaki, or plaid skirts, all in pleats, looking as if they were made in the fifties. She pulled out a couple, then searched for some tops on a table, where blouses and shirts were mixed up like a salad. Kate dug her hands through—perhaps a long-sleeved cotton shirt, she thought—but none of the colors were right, they were all pastel and she knew she couldn't wear yellow. Finally she settled on a white jersey blouse with small buttons, size six. She looked at the price tags and saw that they were reasonable—in fact, far less than in the States.

The woman managing the store watched Kate. "Can I help you?" she called out.

"Thank you, I'm still looking." The moment she spoke, Kate knew she was seen as an outsider. A voice with a funny accent. She pushed herself on to find a jacket. She had always loved jackets, ones that were a little different to add some flare to her appearance. But she saw only blazers in beige, red, or navy blue, or car coats. Forcing herself to pull one out, she took her piles of clothes up to the counter.

"I'd like to try these on," she said, and the pale woman, hair pulled back in a tight dark bun, nodded and led her to the back of the store.

Behind an old curtain, a bare bulb glared over a long mirror on the wall. The unsmiling woman nodded towards it, and Kate thanked her and went behind the curtain to try on the clothes. She removed her jeans and T-shirt. Her breasts and thighs looked too soft to her in this light. She tried on the things she'd brought in and regarded herself. She knew she didn't look right. She rubbed her cheeks, hoping for more color in her face. The cut of the skirt was old-fashioned and hemmed at her knees. The blouse was too loose, the jacket too boxy. Wondering what to do, Kate just stood there, pushing back her long black hair, pursing her lips, trying to convince herself to buy these clothes. She envied Andy that all he had to get were overalls and plaid flannel shirts. She stood up straighter and looked at herself in the mirror, tilting her head to what she thought was her most flattering angle. After all, these were the clothes women buy here, so if she did too, she'd fit right in. If only Lizzie, with whom she used to shop, could see her now. She wondered if she was beginning to miss New York, browsing in the small shops in Greenwich Village and the Lower East Side.

༄༅།

Verlene waited for Kate by the church. Her 1971 blue Dodge sedan was parked off the dirt road. Verlene wore a pink skirt and a white pressed blouse, with a pale green sweater cast over her shoulders.

"Okay, let's go to Harbour House in our new car!" she said, smiling, and Kate climbed in, smelling the new vinyl and admiring the clean, polished dashboard. Verlene glanced at Kate with a victorious half-smile and said, "Ivan's so proud to have bought it." Kate thought of the irony of their having a 1951 Chevrolet truck.

They wound around the rocks through the fields on the way to Greenport. The day was clear and the sky very blue against the sea. Verlene wore bright red lipstick and dark mascara, and her tight blond curls were deeply sprayed. Kate pulled her new khaki skirt down over her knees, and her boxy jacket felt like cardboard over her blouse. She guessed Verlene might think she looked plain with no make-up, but she would never change that. They drove talking of small things, their favorite foods to cook.

"And your job, Verlene?"

"I cut hair in Greenport."

They crested a large hill overlooking Greenport Harbour. There at the top was a new gray building with large picture windows. Inside, the air smelled of disinfectant. She announced herself to the young woman at the reception desk and a tall smiling woman with black hair came out to greet her. Her body was strong and thin beneath her white uniform, her eyes gray.

"Thank you, Verlene, for bringing Kate to us. My name is Ann Whynacht. I'd love to show you around."

Verlene winked at Kate to go ahead. "I'll wait here."

Kate followed the head nurse down the hall, gleaming with a freshly waxed floor. In small white rooms overlooking the harbor, elderly people lay on beds or sat hunched in chairs, casting their eyes in various directions.

"Have you had any experience working with the elderly?"

"No, not really. But I'm eager to learn."

"We're very proud of our new facility. But it does take the people from here a while to get used to the idea, you know. I'll get you set for a training and you can see for yourself..." Now she scrutinized Kate closely again, her skin with a slight accent of make-up beneath her crisp white nurse's cap. "All the way from the States, are you? Your husband must be a draft dodger?"

"No, actually not," she said, surprised that Ann assumed she was married.

"Good, then. I'll show you the recreation room."

≡ 11 ≡

THEY WERE STANDING BY THE LARGE window in the Tannard house looking toward the great width of the sea, when Andy said, "Marry me, Kate, please marry me." His voice was strong, and Kate's heart stopped. A lifetime commitment. They'd gone to get their immigrant status, and discovered it would be advantageous to be married.

"I want to spend my life with you."

Suddenly the space seemed small as Kate tried to imagine what a lifetime meant. She took a deep breath and wanted to believe that Andy was the right man for her. She heard her father's voice before she left for Nova Scotia: *You're not even married.*

"I will marry you," she said hastily, while a breeze came in through the room and she knew that she had no idea what she wanted. *Yes, maybe that is what I should do.*

They walked to Tannard's General Store. Will and Lena were usually there on Saturday afternoons, the busiest day, when the fishermen came in and talked to Will and got those things they needed: fish hooks, line, tobacco, rain gear. Even those fresh apple pies Mary Dauphinee always baked.

Kate wanted someone to talk to and was relieved to find Lena up on the ladder re-organizing the yellow oil clothes.

"Such a mess, Will," she called down, and then she saw them, and smiled.

"We got jobs!" Andy announced proudly. "Sherman's taking me on at the dory shop, and Kate will work at the Harbour House in town."

"Now that's some cause for celebration! Let's make some tea, not. It's almost closing time," Lena said, throwing a stack of oil clothes to the floor with a loud thump. A pungent smell of rubber exploded in the air.

"I'll help you fold them, Lena," Kate offered, feeling shy with all their news.

Lena hummed as she climbed down the ladder. She picked up the clothes and motioned for Kate to follow her to the back. Andy and Will shook hands, then fell into conversation with a few fishermen standing around.

Lena's small gestures showed her pride in being in the store: the way she pulled up a chair for Kate and began the ritual of preparing tea, putting the kettle on, and getting out cups. Kate watched Will still out in front. A few fishermen crowded around him, leaning against the counter, smoking their cigarettes, and talking about their catch as if he were one of *them*, a fisherman. Kate wondered if Will would always be *out there*, in that watery line between land and sea no matter what had happened to him those years ago. Somehow his scars were diminished in the bright store light, as if watching him at a distance helped Kate imagine the features Will once had.

Lena began to fold the jackets, and Kate moved to help her.

"That's good, now, you have a job, Kate. A nice beginning for you both. You must love Andy very much to come all this way to live with him."

Love. Kate wondered, from the tone in Lena's voice, if Lena was seeing herself as a young woman again. Was she remembering the first time Will lifted her skirt, perhaps down by the fish store? Now Kate remembered Andy's first kiss, his warm lips on hers while a quarter moon shone through their college room window. "Yes," she said, "Yes, that's true," and as she said these words, she wanted to believe them.

"I hope it won't take you too long to feel at home in Slate Harbour," Lena continued, with a faint sigh, getting up to fetch the boiling water. She put two tea bags into a teapot and poured the water in. Coming back to sit, they listened to the rain, a veil of water streaming down.

"To work here, Lena, we need to get our landed immigrant status," Kate blurted out. "And it helps to get married..."

"Married! Oh, Kate. That's wonderful. I hope... Well, I mean, I imagine that's what you want?"

"Yes... I think so. It feels inevitable... To get married."

She saw herself running the way she'd watched the grasses flow through the truck window coming to Nova Scotia with Andy. And now she was getting married, a thought with a strange whistling sound inside her head.

Lena smiled over at Kate. "I married Will when I was sixteen. Imagine that!"

"When did you meet?"

"Before I can even remember. He lived three houses away from me, you. We're mostly Tannards, see, and we all know too much about each other, that's for sure!"

"But, you fell in love with him...?"

"Oh, yes. When I was a girl, I believed Will Tannard was different from most men in Slate Harbour. He didn't drink down on the rocks with the others. He was considerate and waited for me to walk to school. I was able to tell him things, like how I thought this place was the end of the world."

She fell quiet and picked up her teacup then, swirling her long fingers around its rim, as though she wanted to say more, but didn't.

Lena couldn't tell Kate how, when she was a child, she would lie in her bed in the dark and sing a little tune to the white painted wall of her room. Far better than listening to the drunk, chair-smashing racket of her father downstairs. And how her singing took her to the far-off places, the moving Atlantic sky, past the rooftops, and the steeple of the church standing against the ocean. She'd have her father's nautical maps hidden under her pillow, and she'd let the tips of her fingers rest on a choice of cities: *Boston. Vancouver. San Francisco.* In a chocolate wool suit and an ivory silk blouse, Lena was going to be a schoolteacher and walk down aisles lined with wooden desks for her students in a place far away from Slate Harbour.

"Did Will want to leave too?" Kate asked.

"Oh, yes," Lena said. "Even though Will fished with his father, Angus, he told me he might start a general store someday, and move to Halifax… But that never happened."

Kate waited again, looking at Lena. Their eyes met, and Kate blinked, feeling the intensity of whether or not she would marry Andy. She wanted to know more about Lena and Will's marriage, as if that might help her, even though she knew she had no right to ask those personal things. Kate couldn't help herself but imagine when Lena and Will were young, maybe fourteen, and perhaps they met down in the fish store, and Will had told her, "You're so beautiful, Lena;" and how he might have gently turned her and lifted himself on top of her. Kate wondered if Lena came alive then, with her breath and heated skin all mixed up with Will's, and if she might have mixed up this aliveness with her dreams, and then mixed up her dreams with Will.

"I became a fisherman's wife," Lena admitted to Kate, slowly. "Just like my mother. Though that wasn't what I wanted."

"So you never did leave?"

"No." Lena looked at Kate and sighed. "I became pregnant with Ivan, see. So Will had to keep fishing…"

"For how many years?"

"Until Ivan was twelve, mind you. I was a fisherman's wife…"

A fisherman's wife. The woman who watched from the kitchen window for her husband to return from the wharf, who worried about his life on the treacherous sea. Who worried about his mouth around the lip of a sherry bottle, his unquenchable thirst. Suppertime was always the hardest time of day. Potatoes to wash and peel for the cod chowder, the plunge of hands into a bowl of water to scrub the skins down. Looking out the window, she might hope her fisherman was walking up the path, but usually he wasn't. Usually the path stared back at her with its usual emptiness. And he would be *down there* with the other fishermen in the abyss of their own exhaustion and light, their sacred place this time of day with the hard work done, all of them in a pact protecting one another in their unburdening and the drink in them, poisoning themselves.

Lena leaned over and patted Kate's hand. "Things got hard,

mind you, but Will's a good man. We got ourselves out of a big mess."

Kate knew Lena was not prepared to tell her the most difficult part of the story. She could feel it in Lena's eyes. It would be much later when Lena told her how on some nights, she used to stay up waiting for Will, when he'd shove his body through the kitchen door and she'd beg him to stop fishing like he'd promised. "You can start a store!" she'd cry. "Remember our dreams?"

"Fishing is all I know, Lena," he'd cry back, then weep, his lips like loose rubber on his face. And Lena would coil on the floor when he came at her, his fists a frustrated shadow beneath the kitchen's bare bulb. She didn't know what to do then. She didn't know how to hide from Will or herself or the pain of what they'd become.

"Remember our dreams?" she'd cry.

And she knew their son Ivan was watching them from his bedroom door.

∽

Now, a decade later, Lena told Kate: "The Farrells came and bought the old Tannard house, see. I remember watching them come to Slate Harbour while Will was in the hospital, their large gray Buick winding its way down the road. The Farrells, mind you, would have picnics on the rocks overlooking the ocean, right in front of my house. A tall man, a woman who always wore a hat, and a boy. I guessed that boy was the same age as Ivan."

And then Lena described how they'd pull out a camera and

take pictures while they posed against the Cape Islanders and dories anchored in the cove, and that was the first time she'd noticed that the rockweed on her shore was the same gold color painted on the dories.

Lena paused for a moment, then looked intently at Kate. "I wondered what brought these people to such an isolated place I'd always dreamed of leaving. But they bought the Tannard house, mind you, and that saved us. Your Andy is a part of that."

Your Andy. Kate took a deep breath, sensing the importance of the Farrells in Will and Lena's life. And she realized, at that moment, that her destiny was linked with Andy's.

"I'm glad you told me all this, Lena," she said quietly.

Just then, Andy and Will came through the door and pulled up chairs beside them.

Lena's face flushed and she turned and said, "Let me get you some tea."

"Thank you," Andy said, smiling. "Did Kate tell you that we're planning to get married?"

Will sat back, took in a deep breath. He looked with his disfigured eyes at Kate and Andy. "Well, now, I wish you both well! That's a big step, you."

Lena returned with more cups and filled them. "My congratulations to you both."

They sat with a soft rain wrapping around the silence of the store. Andy leaned to take her hand. "Kate is the best thing that has ever happened to me." His eyes were bright. His words seemed to make it true; and for the first time, she *knew* she was going to marry him. As if this dream about Nova Scotia had started a long time ago and any questions seemed to vanish beyond her control. Perhaps, no matter what happened, life itself could guide her.

Yet there was an uncomfortable sensation of pressure as if her blood rushed inside her and blocked out the sound of her own voice. She wished, suddenly, her mother was alive and she could talk to her. Why did she feel like she was sacrificing herself because Andy loved her? And did he really love her, or did he just want to marry her to get their immigrant status, and she knew these two things were not the same.

"We've talked about getting married at the courthouse, and asking Ivan and Verlene to be our witnesses," Andy told them.

"Now, that's a fine thing!" Lena said. "Not too long ago they got married."

Will said, "Well, being a husband and all, I'm glad you've got a good job, Andy." Then he paused a moment. "Somehow you make me think of Ivan, you. It's selfish of me, I know. I just wish my son Ivan could like his job the way you might enjoy yours. I just wish he didn't want to fish, you."

"You really mean that, Will?" Lena asked cautiously.

"Yes," he said, lowering his eyes. "I know there's no future in it. The men come in here, talk about those draggers out there destroying the sea bottom. We know those draggers are killing what feeds the lobsters and fish, not. There's nothing left for us."

Since coming here, Kate'd seen these proud men up before daybreak, longlining from their Cape Island boats. Built with a high bow and low stern, the Cape Islander was their home on the water, its wide beam giving a good open workspace. She knew the daily schedule: how these men unloaded their fish into tubs on the wharf, stood over the trestle table, and cleaned the fish. How the seagulls flew in a crazy turmoil over their heads and spun shadows over the fish stores like black specks in a kaleidoscope. After a hard day's work, they left their boats, sleeping birds on the cove's still waters.

"The tire plant's not such a bad job, Will," Lena said softly, looking over at Will.

Will rubbed his cheeks now, the scarred patches perhaps softer over the years, and looked at Lena. Kate could see they still loved each other. Though she guessed they had many things to work through; *hard* things. She longed for a love that could last, and she thought about her mother again, who had died too young. She longed for the freshness of seeking a new world. And that, she told herself, was what she would do with Andy Farrell.

"ANDY'S GOTTEN A JOB AT THE DORY SHOP." Kate told her father over the phone, lifting her voice so he could hear her pleasure. "And I've got a job at the old people's home." She couldn't quite tell him they were going to get married.

"Really," her father said. His tone was so flat, Kate's hand grew sweaty holding the receiver.

"We're going to try living in Nova Scotia for a year."

"How far is Cape Breton from where you live?"

Cape Breton. She knew he thought her coming to Nova Scotia was about her mother, in the same way she knew he had never remarried because of her mother. They both knew they were linked with how suddenly her mother had died. Now they were both left to know this pain when they found it hard to speak.

"I've heard it might take four or five hours to drive there," Kate said, words gathered like wool in her mouth.

"You might go there sometime? Look up your mother's relatives?"

"I might."

"Perhaps I can find the phone number for your mother's cousin, Emily."

She got that empty feeling again trying to imagine her mother's relatives whom she'd never met. "Oh…" she said.

"Perhaps I could even come with you…"

"Come with me?" she asked.

"To Cape Breton."

"Dad, I'm just not sure about going there anytime soon…"

Her father's silence breathed over the wire. "Okay," he finally said with the disappointed voice Kate recognized. They both did this. Neither of them to blame, the search still on for her beautiful, mysterious mother.

Kate lifted her voice to a higher tone. "Dad, I *do* hope you come to visit us sometime soon," and she knew as she said those words that she was cutting him off.

"Yes," he said. "We'll work that out."

Their conversation lingered in the room after she hung up the phone. The ocean gleamed like a brilliant blue dream through the window. Could it be so simple, she wondered, that she wanted to live here in order to find *that place* where her mother had been happy? She could drive to Cape Breton. She preferred to go on her own, though, to see the small brown house where her mother had slept viewing the bay, the same house in the lithograph. From the road she could watch, like a stranger.

She crossed to the southwest window. The sun cast its golden light above the ragged spruce. She wished she could feel that pure desire to live here; not plagued with ambivalence since the first foggy day, and now, planning to marry Andy.

Looking through the window, she puzzled over an old fence in the distance bordering clumps of field grass. Lupines swayed on its edge, a wild rose climbed up a post. A garden gone to seed? she wondered. Top on her list was starting a garden, growing their own food. She went outside and walked through the grass. Sea air swept the field and she arrived to find posts and rails running along a rectangular space probably cultivated a long time ago.

A ridge divided the field from the plowed land, and some soft green leaves climbed through the grass at her feet. She picked a sprig and rubbed it under her nose. A clean, green fragrance filled her; no itching, no burning, only the effect of purification. Mint!

She knelt on the warm earth. Ivan had offered to plow up some ground for their garden, and perhaps Andy could call him right away, get a start. She'd like that. Grass twisted under her and pricked her jeans.

She thought again of her mother, how she used to say: *"After my father died, those summers in Cape Breton were the happiest in my life."*

∞

It had been the constant worry, what would make her mother happy. For as a child, it had seemed to Kate that the source of her mother's unhappiness revolved around the words: *"My father died when I was eight."*

She remembered mornings before going to school when she would check up on her mother just to hear her breathing. She would peek through the bedroom door and see her mother's eyes closed, her lids sunk so deep inside her skull that they looked like large unopened seeds. Her long black hair, rolled back on the pillow, was a reminder of night. Kate would pause then. What if she were to run into the room and kiss her mother on the lips. Would she wake up? Ashamed to imagine this, she knew there was a dark spell around her sleeping mother. No one, including her father and Margaret, had told her that her mother had leukemia. Even after the doctor had come, her father would only say, "Your mother is very sick. But we all believe she'll get better." She remembered the shots, the frequent visits to the hospital. She remembered the feeling of her mother vanishing in front of her eyes.

In the late afternoon when Kate returned from school, after walking the long city blocks, she often climbed the carpeted stairs in her apartment hoping her mother would be up. On good days, her mother would be standing in front of the mirror in her dressing room getting ready for the day, and she would sit on a stool then, mesmerized as her mother bent and brushed out her long black hair, lifting it into a black halo around her head. Her brush crackled. *This is a good day,* she'd think.

Her mother, too thin, Kate knew, would scrutinize herself in the three-way mirror.

Kate would lean in closer. "Will you tell me more stories about when you were a girl and went to Nova Scotia?" she'd ask.

"Yes," she'd say, moving in an inch from the glass, working her hair with bobby pins and hair spray to make a perfect "S" wave along her temples.

"*My father died when I was eight...*" she'd start, searching for the wave's perfection in the glass. "After that, my uncle, who was my father's twin, invited me to Nova Scotia."

A hissing shower of hair spray would suddenly drown her.

Kate would wave the spray and ask, "What kinds of things did you do in Nova Scotia?"

"We flew kites. And sailed in the bay. There was a garden where we picked sweet peas." Her voice was momentarily happy.

Did your uncle look like your father?"

"Yes…" she'd say, shifting her eyes.

"Because he was *identical?*" Kate loved to slow that word down.

"Yes."

"Did you pretend he was your father?"

"Yes…"

"I like to make things up, too," she would tell her mother, hopefully, but her mother would only sigh and say, "I only went to Nova Scotia two times. Those summers in Cape Breton were the happiest in my life."

"You only went twice?" Kate said, startled.

"Yes. After those visits, my mother forbid me to go again."

"Why?"

"Because my mother married another man and didn't consider herself part of *that* family."

Her mother's eyes turned away from the mirror then, and Kate would always wonder if that was when her mother's illness began as if stress could be the cause of it.

☙❧

Now in the raw field, looking over the old garden, Kate felt calm. Maybe it was good she was here and not in Cape Breton.

Light from the setting sun fired her imagination. Was it too late to start a garden? she wondered. She could get a start on planting and learn how to do it. Her father could visit and she could make soup with her own fresh vegetables, and she could begin freezing and putting things up for the winter.

For a brief moment in the field's hum, she dreamed of peas and lettuce, and strawberries and beans that she would soon be picking for dinner. She couldn't wait to tell Andy.

 roa

Days later, Ivan came on his John Deere tractor to plow the old garden. Kate watched him steer back and forth over the earth, its great rear tires churning. Soil lifted like dark brown waves in the sunlight and she breathed in the dank sweetness exploding in front of her—*her first garden!*—watching Ivan, as if he were also part of the dirt and the light and the sea.

Now and then, he glanced towards her. She hoped he would come closer when he was done, but instead, he turned the tractor back on the road and raised his arm out to wave good-bye. "Got to get home for dinner!" he called over the engine noise.

Kate cupped her hands around her mouth. "Thank you… Ivan!" and her words rang out over the soil.

The next week Ivan came to disk the plowed garden. Again when Kate heard the engine, she ran outside and watched Ivan swing the tractor back and forth over the turned ground, this time the blades leaving a grid of long dirt hills. Joy filled her. She couldn't wait to learn about gardening. She scooped the soil in her palm and squeezed her fingers into a fist. The dirt smelled sour and sweet and she knew she would soon be planting.

"You'll need some rockweed and manure to work in," Ivan called out when he pulled the tractor up along the road by the house. This time he did not leave right away but turned off the engine. The sudden silence stirred in the air around them. He jumped off the tractor with the same coordination she'd seen while he navigated the field, then leaned against the rear tire, and cupped his elbows in his large hands. A sudden shyness overcame her as she thanked him.

"You're very welcome," he said, tipping his cap. "Andy home soon?"

"I'm sure he will be," she answered, peering down the driveway, confused by her own awkwardness. She swept back her hair and asked, "Would you like some water, Ivan? It's hot today."

"Yes, thanks," he said, his gaze still on her, and waited while she ran to the house and filled a glass for him.

A disarming breeze blew up over the cliff as she walked back and handed him the glass. She saw his disheveled hair and bright gray eyes as he leaned back to take a long drink. "Very much appreciated," he said, wiping his lips.

Kate tucked her hair behind her ears, looking down the driveway for Andy.

"Usually we plow in the fall, disk in the spring," he said. "But at least this summer you can get a start on it." He chuckled, looking right at her.

A strange light possessed the hill now. A mixture of fisherman and farmer, embodied the earth and the sea, she thought. Her opposite, perhaps. Maybe that was why she felt so uneasy. His eyes, now resting on her, made her think it would take her years to learn the things he did naturally. Kate tried to picture him working at the tire plant, but she couldn't imagine him inside.

"I've never gardened before," she admitted.

Ivan smiled. "Well, it's good to get a start on it this summer, then you'll be learning, you. Lena can help you."

"Yes, she's given me some lettuce seeds already. And she says she has tomato starts."

"That's good, now."

"I found some old gardening tools in the woodshed beside the house," she went on, talking too quickly. "They're a little rusty but I think I can use them. And I've been reading *Rodale's Complete Guide to Gardening* and the *Vesey's Seed Company Catalogue*." The words poured out while Ivan stood steady against the tractor.

"Never heard of…what was it? Rodale's?" he asked as he leaned towards her to give back the glass.

Their eyes met then. So simple, here by the field. She told herself she was being initiated into one of man's oldest arts of husbandry. What was this attraction she felt as they gathered themselves for one moment in the blustery air? Every pore in her body was flooded with heat she was not prepared for, and she blushed and turned away, too late for him not to notice.

Then Andy was driving up the road, gravel spitting beneath his tires. She waved at him, relieved. He parked and got out of the car and she met him on the drive.

"Sorry I'm home late today! Thanks for bringing the tractor, Ivan," Andy said. "How much do I owe you now, Ivan, for all this good work?"

"You don't owe me a thing," Ivan said. "Let's just consider it a trade, the way we've always done."

"That's generous. I'll remember that," Andy said, and the three of them walked over to admire the fresh-turned land.

"It's fertile enough for this year's planting," Ivan said.

Kate watched the two together and wished suddenly her eyes had not met Ivan's the way they had minutes earlier. She took a deep breath, telling herself she couldn't be feeling *real* desire for Ivan since she had never felt attracted to anyone else since she had been with Andy. She folded her arms. Whatever this was, she didn't want it to spoil things. She just hadn't met anyone like him before. And by the guarded way Ivan smiled at her when he turned to say good-bye, she guessed that he was thinking the same.

13

T STARTLED ANDY TO SEE KATE AND IVAN standing there. Something about the angle of their heads, as they stood alongside the tractor in the sunlit field. It shot through him as he got out of the truck. Such a simple sight.

Of course, he'd been the one to ask Ivan if he could help out. He couldn't be jealous. Still, he felt black needles in his chest as he walked over to them.

How much do I owe you now, Ivan?

A feeling straight from his gut told him he could lose everything in a moment.

You don't owe me a thing, Ivan said.

Later, at dinner, Andy admitted, "You looked so happy standing beside that tractor with Ivan. I got a little jealous."

Once Andy had looked up the word *jealousy* in the dictionary. Derived from the Latin root *zelosus*, it was related to the word *zeal.* He liked that the emotion connected to zeal and ardent passion.

She only smiled and said, "I was happy about the garden!"

That night in bed, he felt soothed by the nearness of her body. He rolled on top of her, finding her awake and responsive, and his desire filled him up like the sound of the sea outside. He rocked her then, tasting salt on her skin as he spread her thighs with his knee. And when he came inside her, an electric shock exploded through his body, squeezing his eyes closed.

You will be my wife, he thought, breathing hard, and he tried to let his fear course away, even though behind his eyes he still saw Ivan.

14

IVAN HAD ALWAYS SEEMED a little dangerous to Andy. When they'd come that first summer in 1959, his parents had left him with Will and Lena for four days. They paid them, of course, like they paid Karl to look after the Tannard house during the winter when they weren't around.

For the first two days, Ivan had avoided him. Then suddenly one morning, he brought out a burlap bag from under his bed. Taking a glittering piece of rock from inside it, he asked Andy, "What do you think this is?"

"I'm not sure," Andy said, faltering, surprised Ivan was talking to him.

"It's *pure* gold," Ivan said with a slightly menacing tone.

"Really?"

"It's from the sea cave. I read the tide table, and you can go in at ebb tide. Want to try?"

The challenge was clear. "Sure," Andy said.

As he followed Ivan along the path over the rocks, he tried to fight off feeling flattered that Ivan was paying attention to him. The wind soared around them as the sun rose over Skerry Point, and the ocean lay white-capped beneath them. Ivan carried a small hatchet fastened to his belt, for chipping gold, he said. They climbed down the bluff, sliding on the steep rock.

"People come from all over looking for gold," Ivan shouted back at him. "But so far, I'm the only one who knows where it is! We're pirates, you!"

"Wow!"

Ocean spray-coated them as they landed at the cliff's base, and Ivan pointed towards a dark mouth at the edge of the sea.

"The tide's out now," Ivan said. "We can go inside."

Andy followed him move for move over the wet rocks and into the dark interior of the cave, wanting to prove to Ivan that he was brave, and could do this. The deeper in they went, the more muffled the sea became, outside. Andy inched his way along an exposed ridge, and the dark stone drew around him. The slippery seaweed smelled like urine. Yawning to relieve the pressure in his ears, Andy felt the rock close and suffocating. He fought off dizziness while water dripped onto his head.

Ivan stopped. Removing the hatchet from his belt, he began to chip at the wet rock's glowing metallic streaks in the water light. A few chunks fell to his feet on the ledge, and Ivan handed a piece to Andy.

"Is this real gold?" Andy asked, incredulous, looking at the rock shining like crushed sunlight.

Ivan laughed. But then he smiled at Andy for a moment. "Fool's gold," he said.

"Fool's gold?"

"Pyrite. It's pretend gold, see. I brought some to school and that's what my teacher told me. Now just you and me know the truth, you!"

Andy stood in the cold, dripping cavern. All of a sudden, he wished his parents had never bought the Tannard house, that his parents hadn't left him, and that Ivan didn't hate him, but the feeling was too big, and Ivan was smiling, and Andy had to do something, so he smiled too. "Pyrite!" he yelled, and Ivan turned back to chip at the wall and hand the chips to Andy.

They lost track of time. The tide began to flow in, covering the rocks and soaking their feet. Andy assumed Ivan knew what he was doing, even when the triangle of the cave's opening began to shrink. But then Ivan's face changed, and he put his hatchet back into his belt.

"The tide's moving in too fast," he said to Andy. "Follow me now."

"What about our gold?"

"Leave it!"

Ivan slipped past Andy along the ledge, and Andy followed him. He knew if he lost his balance he would fall into the crevice filling up with the incoming sea. The water surged over his boots, drowning them and the rock he walked on, and fear rose in his throat as he floundered behind.

Through the bit of light left at the cave's opening, a seal appeared. Its dark black eyes looked straight into the cave at them. A calm sensation overcame Andy before the seal disappeared.

"Did you see the seal?" Andy asked.

"Yes," Ivan said, reaching back to grab Andy's hand. He pulled Andy through the water now circling their thighs and the great cold weight of the sea tried to knock them over. But they stuck together, Ivan maneuvering them over underwater rocks. Andy, half swimming now, felt Ivan pull him towards the spot where the seal had surfaced, and they found better footing there and climbed out onto higher ground out of reach of the sea.

Ivan let go of Andy's hand then, and lay back, panting. Andy tried to catch his breath. The sea churned inside the cave, and the sight of it chilled Andy, and he wondered if Ivan had saved him from drowning and if the seal had shown Ivan the way. He knew Ivan hadn't meant to hurt him, but he also knew he hadn't kept his eye on the tide.

= 15 =

THEY MEASURED THEIR FINGERS AT A JEWELRY store in Greenport, and chose 18 karat gold. Kate flexed her ring finger, thinking a lifetime. An ease had come to their days while Andy worked at the dory shop and Kate at the nursing home. The garden was growing on the point, lettuce and peas were the first to be eaten, and she was learning to preserve strawberries and pickled beets. Dirt crusted beneath her fingernails from digging and washing potatoes and carrots, and soon she'd have tomatoes and squashes from the vine. Pouring over recipes, she surprised Andy with ratatouille or stuffed zucchini and borscht for dinner when he arrived home.

Even their lovemaking was easy and a bit reckless when they stood in the kitchen, Kate bent over holding on to the counter, feeling Andy's desire for her in every pore of her body. She gave her entire self to him, as if that day with Ivan tightened her resolve to not let her thoughts be impure or wrong or mistaken, and she'd breathe in the warm act of sex as if it cleansed her skin and muscles and heart beneath Andy's searching hands.

At night they would lie together and share passages of poems or novels they were reading before they turned out the lights. Then they'd stretch back, their naked bodies cupped together as they listened to the sea murmur outside their window. And Kate let the ocean flood her. *Yes, I can live here,* she almost sang to herself, and she kept thinking, with a determination or stubbornness, she couldn't tell which, she was in a practice saying *Yes.*

On a bright afternoon, they found their way to the courthouse, a stately brick building surrounded by huge deciduous trees. Kate wore her floral cotton skirt with a white blouse and cardigan; and Andy was dressed in his best khaki pants, blue chamois shirt, and pullover sweater. Ivan and Verlene stood beside Kate and Andy in front of the judge in the big wooden room. The front door was left open and fresh air with a scent of salt drifted in. Kate signed her name on the marriage certificate and said out loud: "*I do* commit myself to you, Andy Farrell."

Verlene wore a bright blue cotton dress, and her eyelashes were thick with tears and mascara. She said, "You are just going to be *so* happy."

Ivan came up to Kate with his hands in his pockets then, his thoughtful gaze toward her. He wore a navy cotton shirt and brown khaki pants with suspenders. Kate had rarely let herself meet Ivan's eyes since that day in the garden, even though now they were playing bridge together in the evenings. It was possible to control these things, she told herself, while she watched Verlene give Andy a hug. It was possible to control their eyes.

"Congratulations," Ivan said in a low voice, and his smile was sincere before he turned to embrace Andy, pat him on the back. Kate watched them, and lightly touched the ring on her finger. This is all good, she told herself.

Afterwards, she walked to a phone booth, put the coins in, and got the courage to call her father. When he answered, she said, "Dad, Andy and I have just gotten married."

Her father was quiet for a moment, before he said, "Congratulations, Kate. Today?"

"Yes, today."

"I hope you will be happy, Kate."

"Thank you, Dad," she said, thinking about the word, *congratulations.* That must be what people say when you get married. Congratulations, and she touched the ring on her finger again while she spoke to her father on the phone, knowing by the tone of his voice he was relieved they had at least married if they were going to live in Nova Scotia.

= 16 =

N SEPTEMBER WHEN HER PERIOD DIDN'T COME, she found a doctor in Greenport. He told Kate she better get her knitting needles out. A curious joy exploded inside her as she took this news to be a sign that everything was going well. The job, the garden, and now a child; all of this seemed so simply started.

"I'm pregnant," Kate told Andy when he got home that day.

The Atlantic wind slapped against the windowpane in the kitchen, and a deep golden sky shone through. Andy just looked at her, stunned.

"I'm pregnant," she repeated, almost giggling.

Walking over, he swept her up into his arms. "That's so wonderful, Kate!"

Now she could show Andy just how much she could love him. Now she would carry his child.

∞

Yet somewhere, deep inside herself, she worried. She had come to Nova Scotia, but now she was going to be a mother. Being a mother was forever; being a mother was about responsibility and bringing new life into the world, treasuring it.

Once Kate woke up in the middle of the night and lay beside Andy with her eyes open. She wondered what woke her. Still stunned she was pregnant, she thought of how her mother's father had died young and how that had hurt her mother. She thought of how her own mother died young and how that had hurt her. Now was she being given a chance to have a different experience? Now could she give birth and raise her own child without terrible misfortune coming to it? She floated in the dream and beauty of a small life.

These questions roused her from her bed, and she put on her robe and went to the bathroom. She looked around and felt something close. It was not a frightening feeling, it was like being in a room and knowing the presence of another being, even though she couldn't see it. She thought she heard breathing or even a small cough. Was it only the sea tapping through the house? Even if it were Basil Tannard, she did not feel afraid. *This will always be Basil Tannard's house*, she heard Sadie say. She thought about spirits returning to inhabit the world they left behind. She thought about their restlessness and longing to be believed. Kate knew she was sensitive to these things. Was Basil trying to tell her something? Some part of her was still that child who danced with the angel. Was she hearing Basil now because she was being given a new chance?

෨෬

The cove lay mirror still the next day when she knocked on Lena's door.

"My, Kate, what a nice surprise! You found me cooking chowder." Lena's white hair twisted on the top of her head. A pink-checkered apron wrapped around her waist. "Come in, please, and I'll make us a cup of tea."

Kate stepped through the door. "Lena, I'm pregnant," she blurted out.

Lena spun on her heels, clapped her hands together. Her eyes widened with amazement.

"Oh, Kate, my, this is cause for celebration!" she exclaimed, reaching out to hug her, a sweet smell of skin mingling with the smell of cod.

Kate burst into tears.

Lena looked at her closely. Her tone was serious. "I hope this is good news. Now, sit, dear Kate, while I make our tea."

Kate took a deep breath and sat down, watching Lena remove the cod from the pan and begin her ritual of making tea. Kate knew telling Lena made this *truly* real. She looked around Lena's kitchen, a place she was coming to know, the plants, the pots and pans, and in the living room beyond, the corner cabinet with teacups, the knitting projects, sewing machine, stacks of material for quilts.

"You're the first person I've told, Lena, aside from Andy, of course." Kate's voice was quiet. "It feels strange, not having a mother now. I called my father but he wasn't home."

Lena rushed around nervously, bringing the teacups—of course Kate's favorite sapphire one with the coral roses—and the teapot, the condensed milk in a pitcher, and the bowl of sugar. Then she sat down across from Kate and sighed. "I'm deeply honored you've told me, Kate. You know how much I wish for your happiness."

Kate hesitated before pouring her tea, breathing in the importance of this ceremony. "I'm so grateful for our friendship, Lena."

"Me too." Lena sipped her tea. Then said, "I will always remember when I became pregnant with Ivan."

"I hope that was a happy moment?"

"Oh, yes," Lena said, sweeping a lost strand of hair behind her ear. "I could *never* imagine my life without Ivan!"

Kate remembered how Lena had told her how much she wanted to leave Slate Harbour, yet didn't because she got pregnant with Ivan. For a moment, the absoluteness of pregnancy overwhelmed her, a woman's body making the decision, the mystery of it going beyond ourselves.

"I can't imagine your life without Ivan, either," Kate said.

"Well, then, Kate, you're going to have to knit!" Lena teased.

"Oh, you're right, I haven't learned yet. Would you teach me?"

"I'd love to!"

And they laughed then, and Lena said, "Perhaps beginning with a small blanket for the baby would be the best way to start… You can get accustomed to knitting and purling, and we can create a pattern." And they chit-chatted about needles sizes, and plies of yarn, the different colors.

Then Lena changed the subject. "If you don't mind my asking you, which room will you put the baby in?"

Her question took Kate by surprise. "Oh, I'm not sure… Our bedroom has a small one off it, maybe there. It's a big house, and there can be noises at night…"

"Do you think it's Basil you hear?"

Lena's directness relaxed her, for how easy can it be to talk about a ghost?

Lena's expression was thoughtful. "No one believed Basil, that a seal saved his life," she continued. "You know, when people experience something out of the ordinary, sometimes they can't manage it. Everyone thought Basil'd gone crazy. Even his wife, Ellen, couldn't believe him, which I always thought was sad. Why would he make up a story like that? He survived more than a week out at sea, not. I guess I do believe *those things* are possible." Her voice grew quieter, and Kate had to lean in.

"Believing Basil made me see the world differently. It helped me survive some very difficult things of my own, mind you..." She sipped her tea. "I remember the memorial service. And then the night he came back, and I think Ellen feared in her grief she'd lost her mind. She asked him where he'd been. He said out on the reef, and he told her about the seal. Well, seals were never popular with us. But how else had he lived? Still, no one could quite believe it. The minister still spoke to him, but others began to avoid him. I remember he'd sit on a log and braid eelgrass, and he'd stare out to sea. I was six years old then. I'd go with the other children and they'd run away, the look in his eyes would frighten them. But I felt sorry for him. One day I walked right up to him and asked him myself. Did a seal really save you? And the way he looked at me, I knew he was telling the truth. Not long after that, he disappeared again."

"What happened that time?"

"His body washed up three days later. I watched them lower his casket in the ground and I saw Ellen stand there in her dark wool dress and everyone knew she would never live alone in that house again. It was the second time they had a service for Basil, mind you. But this time there was his body in the coffin."

She said, "Even when I was a girl I thought there was magic in the sea. How it can take a life and then give it back."

= 17 =

AT WORK, IN A WHITE UNIFORM, white stockings, and white shoes, Kate made beds with Irma Wentzel. Now they were taking care of Mrs. Dauphinee, ninety-three years old, who sat in the corner with her head bobbing against her chest. There was little left of her body but bones and long white hair pulled back in a braid; her small eyes winking. "Oh, my God, thank you," she'd whisper when they carried her from bed to chair. "I found my husband last night, he was waiting for me down at the end of the hall."

Mrs. Dauphinee said this every day when Kate and Irma spread out the clean sheets, and they smiled at each other; yes, indeed, her husband was down the hall even though he had died ten years earlier.

Irma was compact and muscular, a farmer and a fisherman's wife, who woke early each morning to milk their cows, and collect eggs.

Tucking in the bottom sheet, Kate couldn't wait to tell Irma. "Guess what? I'm pregnant."

"Pregnant? Now, Kate, that's a wonderful thing! When are you expecting?"

"In April."

"A spring baby then… How exciting!"

Yet Kate could feel Irma pause. Finally, she said, "What will you do about, I mean, how do you feel about your baby being born in Canada?"

"Oh." Kate hesitated. She hadn't thought about this. "I feel fine about that, now that we have our landed immigrant status."

"I mean, don't you want your baby to be American?"

Kate was surprised by Irma's curiosity. Lena had never even asked. "It's fine. I can make sure the baby will have American citizenship."

"I've always wondered, if you left the United States because you were, well, disenchanted?"

"Yes, you could call it that…"

"No one in my family ever went to college. It seems most Americans have that chance. I must say, you're lucky for that!"

Lucky. Kate felt uneasy, suddenly, making the bed. She heard her father's voice: *You're the narcissistic generation, Kate. You think you can choose anything you want. You don't appreciate the privileges you've had.*

Strange to think Irma would agree with him. Somehow Kate didn't want to be regarded as a "hippie" who had dropped out.

"We Canadians envy the Americans, you know," Irma continued. "On TV, all we get is the American news, not. I probably know more about your country than I know about my own!"

They finished making the bed and lifted Mrs. Dauphinee up from her chair as if she were a small ancient bird, then laid her down on the clean sheets to change her diaper. She was hairless and had tiny muscle-less thighs. They washed her, and when they were done, her legs curled up like the stems of a wilted flower. Irma brushed the white strands of hair away from her face.

"Taking care of these people will help you learn how to take care of a baby, now, Kate," Irma said gently. "The beginning and the end have so much in common."

"Have you seen my husband?" Mrs. Dauphinee asked, suddenly looking up.

"He's just down the hall. He wants you to sleep now," Irma whispered, and tucked the sheet around her. The nurse's aides all knew later that night Mrs. Dauphinee would make the trek down the hall to climb into Ben Whynacht's bed.

"It's all so *simple*," Irma sighed as they left the room. "Whether we're young or old, we do need something warm by our side, now don't we?"

18

T WAS AN OVERCAST SEPTEMBER MORNING, and Ivan drove across the bridge and along the road to the tire plant, seeing Kate's face in his mind all the while, the four of them playing bridge last night, sitting around the table at the Tannard house. He parked in the lot beside the large, dreary buildings and took a deep breath, trying to wipe out that unsettled feeling, bracing himself for the sound of machines and tire-building drums, the smell of rubber. He made his way to the office in the metal-tasting air, his job to make sure those steel monsters spitting out wire and metal shells and casings worked all right. Not always easy. He wasn't sure why he hated his job so much.

He remembered Kate and Verlene talking last night. It made things easier that they got along so well. He knew Verlene was going to want to re-decorate their house just the way Andy's mother had. She'd scan the room: "Where did Mrs. Farrell buy that cranberry wallpaper with *all* the pretty flowers?" Or: "This beveled crystal is *such* a pretty pattern," as her chubby fingers encircled the stem of her wineglass.

Ivan punched in his time card, hung his jacket on the hook. Men in goggles and gloves worked at the various machines spinning out rubber and steel cords. The roar of production.

He'd felt jealous of Kate at first. For years when Andy came to Slate Harbour it was just the two of them. They'd fish in the dory, help Karl repair nets or work on the Cape Islander, go drinking in Greenport. That's how they'd become best friends. Then too, this summer had gotten off to a strange start, learning about Andy's father's murder. How it was affecting Andy, his weird reaction to the fish in the bottom of the dory. He could tell Kate was as puzzled as he was by what was bottled up inside him. How something could set Andy back so quickly, some horrible scene in his mind.

Going to his desk, he opened the notebook to read the notes for machine inspections. Another long day inside this hole, he thought. The eternity of radial tires squeezed like black liquid tubes between those steel drums, that raucous thrum. Sometimes Ivan wondered if the fumes were to blame for his persistent sore throat.

Kate was a beautiful woman. He would always remember how his heart came up into his throat that day she gazed out over the plowed field, both of them standing beside the tractor. How the wind blew softly against her blue cotton blouse and revealed the supple curve of her breasts, and the grace with which she swept her long hair from her face as she stepped over the dirt road towards the house. He'd never seen brown eyes like hers. Usually brown eyes have a surface you can't see through. But Kate's reflected light as if they had water in them. The kind of eyes a man could get lost in.

Private dreams. Across the bridge table Ivan had been careful when looking at Kate. Even now, walking out into the gigantic space where blasts of machine rollers churned around him, he was fighting Kate's eyes.

"Good morning, Ivan!" Buddy, another electrician, yelled out across at him. "Things look pretty good for the moment."

Ivan tipped his cap. "Good morning," he said, putting on his goggles and gloves, wondering about these tires, round and black with their hidden interior that gives them their strength on the road. Is our mind no different than these tires? he wondered; our face on the outside, real thoughts on the inside. When they aren't in alignment, that's when the trouble starts. He couldn't help but chuckle at the thought.

He'd vowed he would never look at Kate again the way he had that June day after plowing. He knew how much Andy loved Kate. He'd witnessed it firsthand.

Like on that night a few weeks ago, when he had walked down to the wharf, looking for his pocket knife he'd forgotten. It was already dark, and the moon hung like a big globe in the sky. Ivan heard a voice like he'd never heard before, deep-pitched, almost singing. He'd walked out onto the wharf, peered around the fish store. And there, sitting together with their feet dangling over the dock, were Kate and Andy; Andy holding a book in the air, black against the moonlight.

Ivan tried to bring Kate into focus. Her head was slightly raised. Were her eyes closed? She seemed entranced. He'd leaned back against the fish house and listened.

I shall wear white flannel trousers, and walk upon the beach.
I have heard the mermaids singing, each to each.

I do not think that they will sing to me.

I have seen them riding seaward on the waves
Combing the white hair of the waves blown back
When the wind blows the water white and black.
We have lingered in the chambers of the sea
By sea-girls wreathed with seaweed red and brown
Till human voices wake us, and we drown.

⚬⚬

In the following silence, a profound melancholy overcame him. He wasn't sure why. He didn't know much about poetry but was moved by what he heard. It bothered him that Andy had never talked to him about poetry. Was it because he didn't have an education like Andy? Ivan realized there was a whole side to Andy he might never know. Often he had come to visit and found Andy reading, but he had never asked Andy anything about those books he read.

All of the things missing in his life suddenly took hold of him. He loved that someone wrote about mermaids. He looked towards the reef that gleamed in the moonlight. Seals lived there, and probably now were sleeping. He heard the poem's last line:

Till human voices wake us, and we drown.

The day after his father's accident, those years ago. Even if he didn't want it, the memory returned. He'd gone to the cave and squatted on a rock watching sunlight streak through the water as the tide came in. Ivan was ready to die when the sea built up around him, and his hands held on to the jagged rock that lined the hollow—hard and cold and leaking water—until his fingers numbed. He didn't care that his boots were filling with seawater, he could only imagine sinking. Letting go of the rock, his hands floated, his body rolled sideways. He believed he deserved to drown that day.

But through the cave's opening, a seal looked straight at him. The tide hadn't come all the way in yet. Ivan saw the seal's dark, flat eyes rise from the water's havoc, then the seal came inside the cave. With its nose, he felt the seal pushing him. Startled by its strength, his back and feet were bumped along the rocks beneath him, the seal pushing and then swimming him from the cave mouth back to the shore. It shoved him up with its snout so hard onto the granite rock, Ivan's face got cuts, and he lay there drenched and gasping out of the reach of the sea.

Ever since that day, Ivan knew he had been rescued. Ever since, he knew that seals could save a human life. But he never told anyone about what happened to him because he didn't want anyone to know why he wanted to drown that day.

Ivan leaned back against the wall of the fish store. He knew his father's accident those years ago had determined his life's course: he would never fish, he would train for a job onshore to make Lena and Verlene happy. Now his days were measured by working at the tire plant, which had no meaning for him. Now he was left with the torment of feeling like less of a man.

He looked back down at Kate and Andy, who were speaking too softly for him to make out the words. Their union was so clear there in the moonlight, the deep things two people can share. Ivan got self-conscious standing there behind the fish store. What if they caught him eavesdropping? He turned and tiptoed in his boots back over the wharf and onto the rocks, and stepped up the path to his house as fast as he could manage, sadness still deep in his chest.

How could the words of a single poem trigger so much emotion? he wondered. Couldn't he go to work and say, *I've had enough!* and walk out? Couldn't he tell Verlene he wanted to go back to school and learn such things as understanding poems? No one in his Tannard family had gotten a college education, he'd never felt worthy of that. Vocational training had to be good enough. At least he was a fireman, that was worthy. Besides, he had to pay the bills.

Buddy's voice broke into his thoughts. "Hey, Ivan! We got trouble over here with this roller!"

"Here I come," Ivan yelled, trying to erase the poem and the moonlit wharf from his eyes. He told himself he had to concentrate and walked over toward Buddy. Whether he liked it or not, this is where he was on workdays. Inside this factory with these damn machines he had to fix.

⹀19⹀

ANDY WAS HOME by himself on Saturday afternoon while Kate worked an afternoon shift. He heard the rumble of a tractor and went out to find Ivan bringing up a load of eelgrass.

"We have this leftover," he called out. "Verlene said Kate asked for more."

"Thank you!" Andy smiled at Ivan, now up on the trailer against the afternoon sky. He'd always appreciated Ivan's thick, dark eyebrows, the curl of his lips that drew a strong line above his chin.

Together they shuffled the eelgrass beneath the tomatoes, easy, just the two of them. He thought of how he'd never felt jealous of Ivan until he'd come here with Kate. Can you be jealous of someone you love? He'd always felt weak next to Ivan.

He remembered, when they were boys, Ivan pointing to a dapple gray rooster, who strutted around the pen among the smaller hens.

"Let's catch him," Ivan said. "I'll show you how it's done."

Confused, Andy watched Ivan coo at the rooster. The bird came at him, beating his wings, while Ivan moved swiftly back and forth, avoiding his attacks. Then suddenly Ivan lunged and caught one of his feet. The rooster flapped wildly, and the hens cried in a whirlwind of feathers, but Ivan grabbed for the rooster's other leg.

A sudden stillness fell over the pen when Ivan held the rooster upside down in the air. Helpless, the bird hung, its wings dropped by its side. Then he set it free again and challenged Andy. "Now see if you can grab him!"

Andy watched the old rooster rush into the corner and scratch the ground. His mind blanked, yet he followed Ivan's order, and plunged to grab him. The rooster, ready for attack, launched at him and Andy could only see a rush of black light. Something dug into his calf, sharp enough to draw blood. He screamed and dropped to his knees and the rooster came at him again, jabs piercing his shoulder. Ivan rushed in and yanked the rooster away.

Andy remembered the silence of the pen then, and how Ivan's eyes had changed. At the time he'd had no way to know how often Ivan had seen his drunken father beat his mother, Lena, seen her terror. Was Andy seeing, in that moment, Ivan's fear of being mean?

"I'm sorry, Andy. God, I'm so sorry. I didn't mean for you to get hurt."

ಬಬ

Now in the garden, their eyes met. Ivan said, "How's Kate these days?"

"Fine, so far. It's early, so keep your fingers crossed."

"You bet." Ivan paused. "Verlene and I've been trying, but it hasn't worked out..."

It was a strange reversal. Now Andy felt a little ashamed. He said, "Oh, something will work out soon, I bet…"

"Yes, I hope so. I don't mean to take away happiness from you, now, Andy. I wish you both the best."

He laughed and pitched a fork of seaweed straight toward Andy, and Andy laughed too, fending off the wet mess. Ivan hurled another handful of grass and Andy threw one back and then they were chasing each other around the garden like boys. Ivan jumped out through the pole beans. Andy lunged, just clipping Ivan's boots, and then rolled onto his back, looking up into the sky, his laughter releasing some large knot that had been tied up deep in his chest.

Ivan came to stand over him, his eyes brilliant as he held out his hand, and Andy let him pull him up. "God, it's fun to horse around, Andy. So goddamned good."

⹀ 20 ⹀

I N OCTOBER, Kate lay on the sofa looking out through the window over the blue sea, its surface flat and windless. An unexpected restlessness came over her as she felt her body changing. She'd called her father and best friend Lizzie to see if they could visit, but they both suggested coming after the baby was born, since Nova Scotia was so far away.

She missed her mother now, perhaps more than ever. Talking to Lena had helped, but she wasn't her real mother. She'd never made peace with how her quickly mother had died, or how little her father had done to prepare her. She remembered how her mother used to love reading fairy tales out loud to her. Even at her sickest, she read out loud to Kate. She must have been in such pain, and Kate couldn't even remember her mother crying. She could only remember her mother lying in bed surrounded by that illness. Then the day when she came home from school to find her even more ashen, having died hours earlier. A ghost of herself. Her father weeping beside her, saying only "I thought they could save your mother, Kate." It was such a different time, when no one could talk about death.

Andy sensed her mood. "Walk with me?"

"Yes, fresh air," Kate agreed.

She got her coat and followed him out the door. Glancing toward the cove, she could see Sadie, wrapped in blankets, sitting on the wharf, rocking back and forth against the shingled fish store.

"There's Sadie in any kind of weather!" exclaimed Kate, waving, hoping Sadie might spot them. But Sadie just kept rocking.

"Maybe she sees us, maybe she doesn't," Andy said. "The rocking warms her."

But as they turned to walk out to the point, her screech trailed them.

Ah ha ha ha, Andy and Kate! Ah ha ha ha!

They waved back at her and went on. The autumn light glowed on western spruce and red maples. At the point, they stood and watched the sea sleeping beneath them. He leaned and kissed her. "Let's go down," he said. "Do you think you can make it?"

She looked down at the trail etched into the fallen cliff face. "Sure," she said.

She balanced carefully behind him, all the while feeling the child inside her. They reached the base and began to walk over the huge granite boulders. Waves churned smaller rocks in a low rumble beneath them. Andy pointed towards a dark opening. "The tide's low," he said. "You can see the cave."

Huge rocks opened like a jaw where the sea sluiced through.

"The one where you and Ivan almost drowned?"

"Oh, we were foolish boys then! It's safe to go in when the tide is low."

She watched the sea sweep in and out of the cave's mouth like a great watery pendulum. Andy took her hand and they walked closer. Foam hissed in the waves around her feet. This could be an entrance to the underworld, she thought. A chill radiated from her spine and into her arms and fingertips as the sea kept clawing through.

"Seals come here," Andy said. "Sometimes you can see them sleeping on the rocks." He leaned over to peer inside. "See?"

Kate squinted in the fractured light. Something turned, a small silken face, on the ledge.

"I see it." Her breath escaped her.

The seal rolled, as if half-asleep, into the incoming waves, and surfaced, seconds later, about twenty feet away. A sleek white face with black eyes looking right at them.

Then it vanished.

"I read, I think in an Irish legend, that seals are drowned souls trying to come back to earth," Andy said quietly.

"Let's go," she said, and they turned to walk back over the rocks.

She thought about having no mother when her baby came. Now her baby would be born in Nova Scotia, and she saw her mother brushing her long black hair with the silver brush in front of the mirror and she heard her mother's voice telling the stories about Nova Scotia.

"I need to go to Cape Breton," she told Andy. "I need to go before the baby's born."

= 21 =

ON A SATURDAY AFTERNOON, after seeing Kate off in a rental car to Cape Breton, Andy drove back to Slate Harbour. The autumn air was cool, and the gold and red leaves filled the air with a dry sweet smell. Crickets sang their change of season song. While he understood her need to go on her own, he still felt bereft. Kate had become his mate, his twin in coming here, his life and blood. And, though living in Nova Scotia had been clear and uncluttered, becoming a father wasn't.

Becoming a father made him think back to his own father; how he would disappear suddenly and no one knew where he was. He remembered his mother sitting in her evening dress alone at the table, waiting for him. Candles were burning. When she came to kiss him good night, he asked, "Where did Daddy go?" and she said, "That's not for us to ask, Andy."

Anger began to boil again. Finally, he could say it—his father had failed him, in not being able to talk about the truth of his life. It didn't matter he was working for the CIA.

What if he failed his own child?

Winding along, he spotted Will's brother, Karl, down on the *Lena*. He remembered how his father loved to go to the wharf to help Karl unload the fish, the two of them so natural together. The way his father would roll up his sleeves, handle the slippery sea critters.

He remembered standing on the deck of Karl's boat that first summer, dressed in Ivan's too-big yellow oilskins. It was the most beautiful morning he had ever seen, with the cove and dark air and the magenta light, dawn a pink line over the horizon. Even at thirteen, Andy knew that going out fishing in the early Nova Scotia morning was remarkable.

"Welcome to your first fishing trip, now, Andy!" Karl yelled out.

No wonder his father loved this place.

They slid past the black rocks out onto the swell of the ocean.

Out on the water, things hadn't gone as easily. He'd found it hard to balance on deck. When he fell across the engine box, Ivan dismissed him with a look. But Karl had given him the wheel and shown him how to keep the Lena's bow lined up with a point of land while Ivan busied himself with the lines.

"The tide's flooding so we'll haul down with it. We'll reset the nets down from the shoals, you!"

Shoals, a word he'd had never heard before.

A buoy bobbed ahead of them. Karl took over and slowed the Lena, and Ivan ran forward and leaned far out to grab it and slip the bowline through. Andy knew he'd never move with that same coordination.

Karl cut the engine. The wind had died, and morning light shone through the green sea and swayed him. He remembered leaning over gunwale to see the anchor line angling mysteriously down into the deep, and he felt as though he were glimpsing something primeval. The stern swung around and a mass of silver fish flickered in the net.

"Andy, get your gloves, boy. We're going to show you how to pick herring!"

He got his gloves then, wrestled his fingers inside them.

Ivan came up and pulled the rope, and Andy joined him. They hauled the net, with herring trapped and tangled by their gills.

"So this is how you shake fish, now, Andy," Karl said. He shook the net and the fish slithered onto the deck.

He didn't know if it was the sea swell or the smell of fish but suddenly he was dizzy and retching over the rail. *Shit*. Weak and pathetic. He wiped his mouth with his sleeve. Karl seemed not to notice.

His throat was in knots while the boat rocked and seawater ran down his aching arms and fish scales smeared his gloves and jacket, but he stood up again and picked and pitched fish into boxes.

"Your oilskins aren't looking so stiff now," Ivan said, and looked at him for the first time that morning.

Later, when they'd finished cleaning up, they let the *Lena* drift while they sat eating sandwiches and passing a flask of rum back and forth. The sun was hot on their shoulders and the alcohol made Andy float.

"Seasickness is part of becoming a fisherman, you," Karl said, then reset his cap over his wiry gray hair. "You'll get stronger."

The sun cast showers of light in their eyes.

Karl looked over at him. "I'm going to tell you something," Karl said. "It's about a dream I've had all my life. It's about the shoals that wakes me up in the dead of night."

"What are the shoals?" Andy finally asked.

"The shallows," Karl said. "Where the seafloor comes up just beneath the surface of the sea. You can't see 'em easily…and you sure as hell try to stay off them. But the rich fishing ground lies right there…"

Karl took a swig of rum.

"I'm coming in from fishing, see, but I can't tell west from east, north from south, because the points of my compass don't register. I try to find the markers for the shoals, but the sky's as black as the sea, and I can't see nothing. I know the shoals are coming like a man can smell the warmth of another human being when his eyes are closed. But the difference is my eyes are wide open. The boat pitches beneath me and I know I've come in by the shoal water. Fear, that's what I call the shoal water, fear that you run aground and let the sea break over you."

"I figure that shoal water is the fear *inside* me. If I can feel the shallows coming in time, I can right myself and get through them."

Andy remembered taking another swig of rum and looking over at Ivan, for the first time not afraid to meet his eyes.

∾

Now he parked the truck and walked down toward the *Lena*. When his steps clattered on the wharf, Karl looked up. "Hi there, Andy! Kate's off to Cape Breton?"

"Yep."

"That's good, not. How long she's gone?"

"Just two nights."

"There you are! Come for dinner."

"That's okay. Kate made me some." Andy smiled, joining him on the deck. Karl handed him some sandpaper. The wind stirred over the cove.

"I was just thinking of the day you first took me out fishing, Karl, remember? And you told me about that dream of shoal water?"

"Yep, I remember."

"I've been thinking about my father. I've been worrying I might not be a good one."

Karl smiled and said, "It's natural. Being afraid when you've never done something before. But you can learn. You're not your father..."

He pulled out a flask of rum and they talked and drank until sunset.

That night Andy fell asleep in the big chair looking out the window toward the sea. He dreamed of the shallows coming. In a dory with his eyes wide open, he tried to call out for help but his voice went hoarse and left him.

= 22 =

KATE, IN A SMALL RENTAL CAR, watched Greenport disappear in her rearview mirror. She was grateful Andy understood her need to go alone. It all seemed so possible, to be driving west across the peninsula, past fields of small dense spruce, and over the causeway. She'd found Baddeck on the map, on the west side of the Bras d'Or Lake in Cape Breton. She could seek out the small brown gabled house on the hill overlooking the inland sea; she'd brought along a photograph she'd found in her mother's shoebox after she died.

The highway rolled in front of her. *Isolated and craggy*, the guide books said.

When she approached the stone causeway crossing the Strait of Canso to Cape Breton, she stopped to read a plaque. It was built in the early fifties, so her mother couldn't have come this way. She remembered her mother saying she'd gone by train.

She crossed and followed the twisting road into the interior, and by early evening Bras d'Or Lake shone like a blue reverie before her.

She stopped for dinner at a small restaurant. Fall leaves shimmered along the shore and stands of spruce coated the hillside. She called Andy to assure him of her safe arrival.

"I've found a lovely B&B to stay in, a room with a shared bath."

"That's great," he said. "I just got back from being with Karl." She heard the alcohol's slur in his voice.

She slept fitfully and woke apprehensive. She dressed and got the photograph from her bag, hoping to show it to someone who might recognize the brown house, and put it beside her place on the breakfast table. Tourist season must be over, as no one else was in the dining room. Silverware and floral patterned china gleamed in the morning light.

A large woman in a blue cotton dress came out through the door, her gray hair tightly pulled back from her round face. "Did you get a good night's rest?"

A slightly different accent up here.

"Oh, yes."

"Would you like a full breakfast of eggs, bacon, and toast?"

"Yes, thank you." She lifted the photograph. "I'm looking for this house. Do you have any idea where I might find it?"

"Oh, my, that's the MacAskill house," the woman said. "It's a historic site now, with its thatched roof and all. Tourists can go there, though it's not in the guide books, thank heavens!"

"Do you know how I can get there?"

After breakfast, she followed the woman's directions, along the lake and up a hill. The woods were scrubby in tangled shadows, and after a few minutes she came to a clearing. On her left, a brown house stood in the sunlight with a gate and fence around it. Spruce woods backed up behind it with a few golden poplars.

Kate got out of the car. There was no mistaking the house. Small and brown, in just the right place in the pocket of the hill. The gate had a sign with *MacAskill House* and the open hours on it. An arbor of red clematis framed the front door. She knocked and a small woman opened it and welcomed Kate in. The receiving room had dark pine paneled walls and an enormous stone fireplace. She saw overstuffed chairs, a wooden rocker, a large pine table with piles of books. In a sun porch beyond it, tall windows faced the still salt lake. The woman told her the house had been built in the mid-eighteen hundreds by the MacAskill brothers from Scotland, and showed her the guest book.

"My mother used to come here," Kate managed to say. "My great uncle married into this family." Pictures of her mother's uncle and his wife and children hung on the wall beside the fireplace. She paused to view them dressed in black suits and white dresses beneath large-leafed trees.

The woman looked with surprise at Kate. "Oh, my, such a legacy."

Kate wished it had been a happier one.

The guest book went back, she saw, for half a century, and she slowly turned the pages.

1933. She scanned the stiff yellowed page and found nothing.

1932. She read the names until she found it: her mother's small printed signature.

Alice Banville

Written with a fountain pen in tiny, blue upright letters.

Her mother, born in 1919, was thirteen years old.

Back to 1931, again,

Alice Banville

Same tiny letters.

Those two summers her mother came here.

She saw her mother then: a child, poised, writing with a pen tipped in her small right hand. Eyes expectant, her left hand must have swept her long dark hair away from her face. Perhaps she had just been running around the house and hiding under the aspen from her sister.

What suffering had built up her mother's dreams of this place?

Kate turned forward through the pages. Now, it was October 16, 1971. She lifted the ballpoint pen and wrote,

Kate Farrell

Her married name, in longhand, now inside this same book with her mother.

She turned away for a final look around the room.

"Thank you," Kate said and went back outside, to climb the hill where her mother had flown kites with her uncle.

The winding gravel road led Kate up easily as if she knew the way by heart, to reach the golden and flat grass where she could rest and her mother may have rested too. She lay on her back looking up at the same sky, imagining the beginning and end of things. It seemed her mother's dying had started right here, in the summer when she had been forbidden to come back.

Kate wanted to steal her now from death for just one minute. *I'm here with your grandchild in this place you loved,* she called out. My lungs have breathed the air in your last footsteps here. I can hear them as I run and chase you. I am laughing under this sky past the walls of the brown house, my sound is your sound and my eyes are your eyes over the knotty pine the stones in the chimney, they can see me and you, the fire and the pain, the tipping point as I run now from the hill past the brown house and over the earth down to the lake

I am swimming you now
in the awkward brilliant light of your signature
I've stolen you away these few minutes
even though a blur of crows interrupts me
with their thousands
you are here, small shadow
that gave me heart, my lungs,
the ground under my feet is yours
and now
mine too

PART II

= 23 =

ADIES. DRESSED IN THEIR BEST, were gathered in the center of the room, all eyes on Kate. Balloons floated from the ceiling. "Surprise!"

Kate, now eight months pregnant, had come for her weekly knitting lesson with Lena. Only last week she'd stopped working at the Harbour House.

"Come in, dear," Lena murmured, smiling. "You know most of us."

Outside, the temperatures were still cold in April, the inlet of Slate Harbor beginning its ice melt. Kate took off her boots and coat, and followed Lena through the kitchen. She recognized most of these women from the quilting circle.

Verlene was the first to come up. "Oh, Kate, what *fun* this is." Her brown eyes roamed Kate's belly, and she laughed. "You look *so ready.*"

"You shouldn't have gone to all this trouble!" Kate said, worrying about Verlene. Over the last few months, when she and Andy played bridge with Verlene and Ivan, she'd go into the kitchen with Verlene to get tea and cake and Verlene would confide that she still wasn't pregnant.

"Come over and sit here," Lena said now, taking Kate to a high-backed chair decked with braids of white and yellow crepe paper.

Kate sat down on the chair's soft cushion. A table to her right was stacked with presents wrapped in pastel colors and "Baby Farrell" written on the cards.

A din of whispering voices.

Sitting on her crepe paper throne, Kate looked across the room at Verlene, the youngest besides herself. She wished Verlene might get pregnant so they could have a baby at the same time. She wondered why she might not be fertile, and studied her tight blond curls and round thighs beneath her daisy-print dress, wondering if something was wrong. Was she romantic enough, or even reckless enough in Ivan's bed?

Verlene smiled at Kate, who blushed, self-conscious that she was imagining her friend making love with Ivan. She shouldn't be thinking this way, knowing some part of her was imagining herself and not Verlene with Ivan.

"Are you hoping for a boy or a girl, dear?" one woman asked.

"Oh, Andy and I will be happy with either one…"

"And how do you like living in the house?" Her tone sounded suspicious.

"I do enjoy it."

Another woman leaned in. "You must feel lonely out there all by yourself."

"Sometimes…"

"And Andy's working with Sherman Smith is going all right, not?"

"Yes."

"But Andy's a man with such an excellent education!"

"Building dories is a fine craft," Kate defended.

"Is your father coming when the baby's born?"

"My father... Yes, I think so..."

"And Andy's mother?" someone else whispered.

Kate grew hot in the fishbowl with these women. Their voices whirled around her. She rubbed the back of her neck and turned to look out the window where the light blazed.

"Kate?"

It was Verlene, pointing toward a cake with Kate's name in the middle of it. Kate looked at Verlene as if she were seeing her for the first time; Verlene, who was so *certain* of who she was in this community with her mother right here in this room. And her grandmother before that. Verlene would never think to move away from here, the way Kate had moved away from New York.

Across the room, Verlene and Lena prepared the lunch, stacking lobster sandwich wedges, cheese slices alongside fresh white bread, arranging celery and carrot sticks, the refrigerator cookies, and the big white-icing cake with her name in the center. Almost painfully, Kate missed Lizzie and now yearned for Verlene to be her best friend. After all, they shouldn't just play bridge together. They needed to see each other more often *without* Andy and Ivan, and form their own friendship. Why had it taken her so long to realize this? Perhaps Verlene could help her organize all the baby clothes she was getting at the shower, she thought, as she began to open her presents: the tiny booties, the miniature ribbed sweater with the lacey border, the diapers, the flannel receiving blankets, and the small patchwork quilts. How could these ladies give her such beautiful things when they seemed—did she dare say this—a bit mean? Verlene could help her understand these things. This would be natural since Ivan and Andy were best friends, and this could solve her deepest worry—if Verlene were hers, she would never be tempted to betray her.

Verlene came over to pass the presents in the open boxes around for everyone to see, her face bathed in daylight from the living room window, coral flushed cheeks, her dense brown eyes.

Kate leaned toward her. "We need to see each other more often, Verlene," she said. "Just the two of us."

Verlene blushed. "Oh, yes! You know, sometimes my hair appointments don't last all day... I could come visit you before Andy comes home. And don't worry about your presents, Kate. Lena and I will plan to bring them over."

Afterward, walking back along the path to the Tannard house, the wind swept about her feet while she folded her hands over her belly. *Verlene will be my friend,* she thought, feeling more prepared now to have a baby in this wild, remote place.

24

NDY LEANED OVER KATE, who lay on the metal table panting. It was five in the morning and neither of them had slept. The room was hot and windowless with a fluorescent light glaring over their heads. He tried to breathe with her, but he couldn't get the rhythm right. He stroked the matted hair from her forehead, and her body writhed beneath a light cotton gown, each contraction a storm he'd never seen before. He wondered if natural childbirth was such a good idea. Her moans kicked at him. He tried to imagine this pain, but he couldn't. "Breathe," he said as she strained, "breathe the way we practiced."

She pushed him away, and cried, "Help me!" He was helpless, on the periphery of what she was doing now. Two nurses circled her bed and examined her; decided quickly to call for the doctor.

"Is everything okay?"

"Everything looks good," one nurse answered, calm in a way Andy thought out of place. "The baby's in the birth canal. Push."

Andy clung to Kate's hand, and this time she let him, this time she looked at him. Her eyes, a deep burning brown. Andy wiped her forehead. "Push," he whispered, believing now he could help her, panting with her, his hands on her belly while her face was a turmoil of tears and confusion. The doctor had come, yet Andy scarcely saw him as he leaned in whispering to Kate; she screaming, her lips bitten, her eyebrows crazed.

Seeing Kate's blood, he saw his father's blood too, and a wave came over him, his eyes smarting, his head going light. He clenched his teeth, hating his weakness, and looked down into Kate's expecting eyes as the baby emerged, tiny, purple, and helpless.

Then he heard it, the first screeching cry.

For a moment everything went still, his eyes locked with Kate's.

"Is the baby okay?" she asked him.

"Yes," he said, scarcely breathing.

And they lay the small boy upon Kate's breast. Andy watched her circle her arms around the warm and tiny breathing body.

And now he was opened up to a whole new universe.

ଊଊ

Hours later, Andy watched Kate sleeping. Though he himself had still not slept. Her face reflected a deep exhaustion and morning light, and now her black hair lay combed around her forehead. They named their son Petey, and he slept in the curve of her arm. Little ancient head, Andy thought, with tiny fingers curled almost boneless and fresh from the water.

Andy scribbled this down on the back of a crumpled envelope, his hands still trembling. Not having slept for twenty-four hours, he didn't want to forget any of this. He stood up, went over to them—mother and child. A deep body smell lingered in the room when he leaned over, slipped his little finger down into Petey's tiny red fist. He pushed slightly. In a reflex, the miniature fingers opened and circled around his large one, and the small heated clasp rose through Andy's arm like a current.

"I will always take care of you," Andy whispered as he gently touched his son on the forehead with his other hand.

He heard soft footsteps, and a voice near his ear: "Oh, Andy, I'm *so* happy for you." Verlene had tiptoed into the room, yet both Andy and the baby jumped.

She bent over Kate, who was still sleeping, and the baby. "He's *so cute*, not. Oh, Andy, he looks *just* like you, and look at him holding your finger." Verlene's tears melted her mascara and trailed in black streams down her cheeks. "I'm so happy."

Verlene had a vase of white roses and a plate full of fudge. Andy knew she was trying to whisper but her voice kept breaking into loud spoken phrases. "I won't stay, I can see everyone is resting. I'll just leave these here. Andy, come to dinner tonight. Ivan and I will expect you around six?"

చ౨

Kate and Petey stayed in the hospital for four days. Andy had started building a cradle in the dory shop, planing and sanding the boards, fitting the joints with precision, and now stayed after work, to finish and rub it with linseed oil. He breathed in the fresh pine. The cradle looked so big, he wondered if Petey would be lost inside it. He lay his hand in it, palm side up, and wriggled his fingers, and smiled. He would have Verlene make a bed of flannel sheets and knitted blankets inside it.

ﻌ

On the day in late April when Andy brought Kate and
Petey home, it was overcast and cold. No clear line was drawn
between the sky and sea. Yet Andy's heart raced as he helped
Kate walk through the front door with Petey in her arms.
The cradle sat waiting beside the cookstove; golden and fire-
warmed, it seemed to radiate the heat in the room.

"Andy, what a beautiful cradle!"

The very words Andy wanted to hear.

Kate trailed her fingers over the cradle top, then handed
a bundled Petey over to him while she rearranged the flannel
bed.

Petey, his red lips twitching, felt like a small bird in Andy's
arms and a sensation of pride rushed through him. Kate took
him then and put him down inside the cradle, where he lay
curled up on his stomach. They watched him sleeping, each
taking turns leaning down to listen for his tiny breathing. Little
eyes shut, russet red cheeks. Andy rocked the cradle, imagining
it a dory holding his son, his small body surrounded by blue
flannel waves, and Petey looked as if he were drifting.

The next days might as well have been the first days; first
days in the life of a new child. Andy felt aware of every detail:
the smell of flowers on the kitchen counter when he returned
home from work, the setting sun laying itself across the linoleum floor. In the evenings, he read aloud from *Moby Dick*
while Kate nursed; a story he chose with the ocean in mind,
those turbulent images he remembered while Kate gave birth
to Petey. Everything Kate did with Petey seemed natural, the

way she supported his head with her hands and wiped the corners of his mouth, and arranged his tiny body around her breast as if the knowledge had been inside her all along.

But for Andy it was different. It was so hard to soothe him, he always wanted to be with his mother. Then too, he was frightened of dropping Petey or letting his head fall because his hands weren't quick enough or accustomed to the smallness of his warm unsettled limbs.

One evening, Lena left them with hot rolls and chowder. Kate and Petey were sleeping. Andy put the rolls in the oven and soon the sweet smell of yeast filled the room. But it gave him a sudden sickening feeling. He sat down at the table, put his head in his hands. The smell soaked through him, made him run to the sink and heave dry air.

Then he saw it: the fresh rolls on the counter of the New York City apartment on the day his father died. The golden contour of their crusted shape. Yet beneath them, there was all that blood on the floor. Why did he have to see these things now? He had a new son, and he was grateful to be alive. He hated this weakness. He wiped his mouth with his shirt sleeve, went to the cabinet, pulled out an open bottle of red wine. He poured a large glass.

The kitchen window rattled from the Atlantic wind. He could hear the waves sweep the shore. After a few sips, a calm washed through him.

After all, his life was happier now.

25

ON A FRIDAY AFTERNOON IN JUNE, Kate looked out to see her father's Oldsmobile sedan. Apprehension filled her as she wondered how he would react to their life here with a new baby. She watched him climb out of the car, the wind matting his gray-black hair. Nervously she picked up two-month-old Petey and opened the door. Her father stared first at her, and then at Petey. Quickly she invited him in, and he kissed her on the cheek as he came through. She was startled by how happy she was to see him, how it welled up inside her chest. She handed over Petey, and her father's eyes teared up behind his black-rimmed glasses. Brown-haired Petey kicked and smiled and her father cooed.

She had always taken pride in how handsome her father was; scholarly, with gray and curious eyes. The same height as Andy, about six feet tall, his shoulders were wide and strong. Her worry about his visit seemed to dissipate with his ease in holding Petey. She breathed in his familiar tweed jacket while they roamed the Tannard house. Verlene had come over to help Kate clean and prepare the guest room on the second floor, and her father admired the flowered wallpaper, the oak bed, and the great window facing the sea.

"Often the fog clears in the evening," she said, proud that the sea was out now, and shimmering for her father.

They had dinner by candlelight; Andy home from work and still in his thick overalls whereas her father wore an oxford shirt and wool vest. Kate had worried how the two of them would get on, her father politely asking Andy questions about his work at the dory shop, though he knew nothing about tools or woodworking. Her father had met Andy only once in Connecticut, and Kate knew he would prefer to have a son-in-law in graduate school rather than building boats in Nova Scotia. But she could also tell that her father was impressed by how articulate Andy was about Canadian affairs and Prime Minister Pierre Trudeau.

Her father said, "You must be glad Nixon has brought the troops home from Vietnam."

Kate looked at Andy.

He said, "I just found out that my friend Tim has a form of incurable blood cancer. He was in the jungle over there where they were spraying Agent Orange. It seems to be related."

"It's been a complicated war," her father said.

Outside, the Atlantic swept the cliffs. Little Petey fussed and Kate's father stood and went to lift Petey into his arms. "Do you know why babies cry at this time in the evening? They cry because the light is leaving. Eugène Marais describes this in *The Soul of the Ape*: how monkeys gather in the evening to ward off their fear of night. He called it the Hesperian depression."

He walked him, singing the Irish lullaby, *Toora Loora Loora*. Petey quieted then, and Kate realized how the Tannard house felt calmed with her father inside it.

Time went by too quickly, and Kate wondered why her father hadn't shown more criticism of their life. They hadn't seen each other for over a year and a half, and on the phone he'd been so distant. Perhaps becoming a grandfather had changed him. For her father seemed to love walking and singing to Petey, or sitting by the woodstove reading while Petey slept, or wandering the cove and going out in the dory with Andy for a quick spin in the *Lena*. He even met Sadie, scrambling from the wharf. *Ah ha ha ha, Kate's father, you! All the way from New York, all the way from New York!*

Of course, Lena and Verlene brought him delicious lemon bars and stayed for tea. "We are all so pleased you have come," they both said. And Kate took pleasure cooking for her father, grinding wheat berries and making bread. She roasted a pork loin she'd gotten from the valley, and made salads with greens fresh from her garden along with her homemade soups. But still she waited for the moment he'd say something disapproving.

One morning, Kate washed the diapers early and wrung them through the wringer washing machine. It was wet with fog outside, so she hung them on a clothesline that ran through the hallway and up to the second floor. They looked like stiff white flags draped through the interior of the house. She remembered how her father had wanted to get her a new washing machine and dryer before Petey was born, but she'd refused, saying how they already had a wringer washing machine. "We try to use as little electricity as possible," she'd said. "We are trying to be self-sufficient and not depend on machines to do things we ourselves can do."

Now she heard his footsteps coming down the stairs, navigating through the diapers. This could be the time, she thought, stepping out to be sure he wasn't getting tangled. He carried a large object in brown paper.

He said, "You should have this now.... I almost gave it to the Goodwill, mind you!"

She followed him into the kitchen. He took off the brown paper and Kate recognized the lithograph she had slept under in her childhood bedroom, NOVA SCOTIA SCENERY clearly written at the bottom. "I never realized this might be part of the reason you wanted to come to Nova Scotia," he said, and Kate heard the sadness in his voice as she touched the familiar black frame lightly with her fingers.

"I admit it made me unhappy when you moved here, so far away."

Finally he'd said it. She thought of Petey and knew how unhappy it would make her if he someday did the same.

Her father sighed. "I know I didn't handle your mother's death very well, Kate," he said quietly. "Somehow—then—I couldn't believe she would really die. The doctors weren't honest with me about how sick she was. So that made it hard for me to be honest with you."

He handed her an unsealed envelope. It looked strangely overstuffed and aged. Tears sprang to her eyes, seeing the small white pieces of paper marked with her mother's stylized printing. She remembered those small little notepads her mother kept around the house, the grocery lists, phone numbers, or notes she'd leave.

"Your mother wrote poetry. I think you might appreciate some of it now."

The room was quiet with Petey still sleeping inside the cradle. Kate had known about these poems; she'd seen some of them strewn on her father's desk. Slowly she leafed through. She remembered her mother's signature in the MacAskill guest book. Her fingers trembled.

"You don't have to read them now," he said. "Just keep them."

"Thank you," she said. And she saw her mother carried down the stairway under the chandelier, and how she'd run to her mother's bedroom window overlooking the street. She remembered the tall brick apartment buildings with their lit windows and the men carrying her mother out the door so far below, her mother's head turned on the stretcher like an image on a small lost coin.

Kate had wanted to call out, *Why did you die and leave me without saying good-bye?* Everything seemed so uncertain, how a day could start and change itself so quickly. She remembered leaning out the bedroom window and seeing the sky way before the starlight left. Would the sun come up, ever again?

ॐ

Verlene came to visit right after her father left. Kate had taken the white envelope of poems and put them in the top drawer of her desk. She'd hung the lithograph on the east wall of her bedroom, out of the glare.

Verlene's brown eyes were dark and curious. "How did your father like it here? He was good with Petey, not!" She laughed.

Kate smiled. "I was surprised by how easy it was. He loved Petey. And he left me my mother's poetry."

"Really? Did you read them?"

"A few."

"Will you read me one?"

"Yes." Kate went to her desk and pulled out a small white note. Her voice trembled.

There are jewels
in my attic
But to wear them
I must climb the stairs

"Kate, that's beautiful," Verlene said, and then, "I know nothing about poetry." She sat back and looked out the window towards the sea. "I feel like I'm always trying to climb the stairs."

"What do you mean?"

"You know, the way I can't get pregnant and all."

Kate reached over and took Verlene's hand.

═ 26 ═

ALMOST THREE YEARS HAD PASSED SINCE THOMAS FARRELL'S MURDER. and Celia Farrell didn't feel up to coming to Nova Scotia to meet Petey. So in October Andy and Kate packed their bags and took Petey to New York.

"I hate the city," Andy complained, as they hit bad traffic.

Yet Kate was glad for the chance to come here.

ⵣⵣ

They found Celia Farrell's apartment dimly lit with half-drawn shades in every window and little food in the refrigerator. Piles of newspapers and documents were stacked on the dining room table and all over the desk and chairs in his father's library.

His mother said, "They're moving *so, so* slowly with the investigation." Her head drooped, she fumbled with her fingers, her depression breathing through her small body. Too frequently she squeezed her eyes closed, and her fine-boned face carried a shadow across it. Her wavy graying hair fell across her shoulders.

Troubled, Andy gazed into his father's library. Walls of shelves filled with books of history, poetry, and maps of the world. As a child he sat here, watching his father methodically press tobacco inside the bowl of his pipe and then light it. He remembered his father telling him, "There are cruel people in the world, Andy. You must stand up for yourself, and not get pushed around."

Celia had gotten a crib and stroller for Petey, and her face brightened when she spent time with her six-month-old grandson. They walked Petey along the New York City streets and Kate looked for children's books in Barnes & Noble and bought Market spice tea, Madras curries, coconut milk, things she couldn't find in Nova Scotia. She even broke down and bought a few colorful tops in Greenwich Village, and coaxed Celia to look for some things for herself. Petey was a good sport wheeling in and out of stores, not too fussy, his eyes staring at the cars, strange people, the honking noises.

The next day, Kate invited Lizzie over while Andy and his mother met with a lawyer about his father's estate. They sat watching Petey play on the living room floor.

"He's so cute, Kate. How brave of you to have a child. I can't imagine it!"

Kate studied Lizzie, her old friend. Tall like Kate, she had short brown hair and brilliant gray eyes. Lizzie had always been smart in school. Nervously they laughed while Petey vigorously shook his wooden rattle.

"It must be hard being in law school?"

"Really hard," Lizzie admitted. "Honestly, I have time for nothing else."

"Thank you for making the time today to see us." Kate knew she sounded timid, as if being around Lizzie made her feel strange, knowing they were going in such different directions. There was no way she could change her course even if she wanted to. Petey reached with his small, chubby hands for his stuffed dog, and she thought of herself hanging his tiny baby clothes and Andy's overalls on the clothesline in Nova Scotia while Lizzie studied books in the Columbia Law School library. Was she jealous of Lizzie? A sudden fear, even though she knew she didn't want to be a lawyer. She surprised herself even further, as if a crack had opened—had she made a mistake marrying Andy? After all, Nova Scotia was his idea and she had just gone along with it. Or was that really true, after all her dreams of going there. Why was she questioning everything now?

"Have they found out anything more about Andy's father's murder?" Lizzie sounded tentative asking this.

"No," Kate sighed. "Nothing's turning up. Andy's mother is finally on lithium for her depression about this whole thing. And now she's worried that Andy needs to see a psychiatrist. She thinks he's *fled* to Nova Scotia, avoiding it."

"What do you think?"

Something inside Kate seized up. What *did* she think? She knew Andy was finally meeting with someone from the CIA. tomorrow. Suddenly Petey fell over and bonked himself, and burst into tears. Kate picked him up to soothe him, relieved, because she didn't want to answer Lizzie's question.

═ 27 ═

THE NEXT DAY, Andy opened the door to his mother's apartment to find a man dressed in a light gray suit, a white shirt, and a blue tie. Slightly balding, his gray hair was carefully combed back from his face. His eyes were round beneath his tortoiseshell glasses, his nose thin, and his lips unusually red. He reached out his hand to shake Andy's.

"Hello," he said, "I'm Peter Phelps from the CIA. I presume you're Andy."

"Yes, I am. Please come in."

They sat in the living room, holding glasses of water Celia Farrell had brought them. Kate had taken Petey outside for a walk.

"I understand that you, and of course your mother, are concerned that your father's murder has not been solved."

"Yes, it's been nearly three years," Andy said.

"Well, the truth is, you're barking up the wrong tree. It's a criminal case that should be handled by the police, not by the CIA."

Andy glanced briefly at his mother, whose expression was tired and anxious. "We know you've thought that. But the police have uncovered no leads. Since my father worked for the CIA., it seemed appropriate that we turn back to you."

"Yes, of course, but his murder had nothing to do with our activities. It was a random act of violence—tragic, of course. But really you should be knocking on the door of your police department rather than ours. Detective Murray is still handling the case?"

"Yes." Andy could only stare at this man, distrust welling up inside him. "Everyone is giving us the runaround. How could someone break into our apartment and kill my father so violently?" Finally, he was able to say what he saw in his mind too often.

Mr. Phelps sat, unperturbed. "That's what I mean. It *was* an act of violence. It's believed that someone was trying to steal something and got into a struggle with your father."

"As you know, my mother has talked at length with Detective Murray, and he and his team have found nothing. No fingerprints, nothing. Somehow the murderer got into our apartment, killed my father with a kitchen knife, and left *without a trace.*"

"Well, you have no other recourse but to keep after the police. Or the FBI. It's not wise for you to suspect the CIA. We are a clean operation, we'd never do anything that…messy. And your father worked for us. He was highly respected by everyone." He paused, and then said, "I'm sorry I never met him."

Mr. Phelps cleared his throat, his eyes penetrating Andy's. His hollow gaze shielded him, the rigid stance of his body. Andy did not believe this man.

"I am looking for help to find my father's murderer! Can't you see how this is torturing my poor mother?" Blood rushed to Andy's face, his anger flooding him.

"I understand how frustrating it must be… I'm so sorry."
Again, the placid face.

"I wish you could hear what I'm trying to tell you." Mr.
Phelps moved slightly in his seat. "Where are you living now,
Andy?"

"In Nova Scotia." Andy clenched his teeth, unhappy about
where their conversation was headed.

"That's far away, a bit difficult to stay on top of things, right?"

Andy stared back. "For personal reasons, I've chosen to live
there, where we have a family home." He did not want to talk
to this man about dreams of starting a new life.

"I suggest you stay with the detective who's been handling
your father's murder and encourage him to keep the case open
as long as it takes."

Andy took a deep breath before he said, "My mother and I
are concerned that this must have been an inside job." He kept
his voice steady while he said what he thought was true.

"I'm sorry you both believe that," Mr. Phelps said curtly.
"You need to understand you are absolutely wrong." He stood
up then. "Mrs. Farrell, I'll see myself out." He bowed his head
slightly towards her, turned, and walked swiftly out the door.
The sound of it shutting sent a gloom into the room.

Celia Farrell put her face in her hands. "What now?" Her
question was muffled in despair.

"We need to make sure Detective Murray is still working
on the case."

Andy sighed deeply, sat back on the sofa beside his mother.
The setting sun through the window cast long shadows over
their laps, down to their feet, and onto the Persian rug. His

heart beat slowly, in their silence. He did not know how long he could keep this up, this search for what happened to his father. He knew it was destroying his mother, and he was trying to figure out how it might not destroy him.

Was his father was a hero? Maybe. Perhaps his father had disobeyed an order because he didn't believe in what he was being asked to do. Or perhaps he had discovered something happening during the war that no one wanted to hear. Maybe that was why he got killed. *The fucking Vietnam War.* Andy wanted to put a face on the man who came to kill his father. He wanted to know how much this man weighed, and the color of his hair. He wanted to look him in the eye so the man had to see his own evil reflected back on him.

He went to grab the bottle of wine he'd bought earlier.

≡ 28 ≡

THE DAY AFTER THEY RETURNED FROM NEW YORK, Andy went into work and found Sherman looking over papers at the workbench.

"The orders are down." Sherman looked straight at him, his eyes full of concern. "I just got another cancellation. The business is changing Andy. I don't think I can keep you on."

He swallowed hard. "Okay."

"You've done a good job. I'll hire you back as soon as I can."

"I appreciate how much I've learned from you, Sherman."

Andy packed up his tools, wondering how a grown man could feel like crying.

"Tell Kate I'm sorry, with the baby and all. And I'll help you get the papers for unemployment. Things might improve, not."

ର

Kate stood up from the rows she was planting and wiped her hands against her overalls. A cool midday breeze blew over the point.

"I've been laid off," he said. "The work's run out."

Helplessly Andy watched surprise fill her eyes.

"Oh," was all she said before she came over. She hugged Andy then, sighing. "Oh, this will be hard on you."

After dinner they put Petey to bed and sat at the kitchen table with glasses of wine. Kate said, "Perhaps we should go back to New York."

Andy looked down at his hands, his biggest fear thinking she might say that. "Don't you like living here?"

"Well, I feel isolated sometimes. Tourists come in the summer, and it's busy, but for the rest of the year, it feels... desolate. And if it's hard to find work..." Kate ran her fingers around the base of her empty wineglass, then got up.

"I hope you'll give me some time to figure things out?" Andy asked.

She seemed to ignore him. "Coming?" she asked, sweeping her hair behind her shoulders. "I need to get some sleep and Petey wakes up early. We can talk more about this tomorrow."

"In a minute."

Instead he opened another bottle of red wine, poured a full glass, and walked the living room floor. He sat in the rocker that faced the ocean and lit a cigarette he'd gotten from Ivan. He blew out the smoke. He'd sensed since the trip to New York that Kate wasn't happy coming back.

His deepest wish was to make her happy here, for they had a son now.

He thought about Kate's comment on summer tourists making the area feel busy. What might tourists like?

A bookstore. The thought shone like a light in his mind.

He remembered his mother wishing for one when she was here. A voice inside him said this clearly. Why didn't he think of it sooner?

He poured himself another glass. This calm that wine brings, he thought, swirling it. He inhaled deeply, then swallowed, feeling it flow down his throat with ease, going somewhere close to his heart. A sensation of richly grown grapes crushed beneath a bright sun along the verdant hills of an old country—perhaps France or Spain—and his mind was traveling now. So simple, he thought. Like floating on his back in a river.

No, I cannot give up living here now, not now.

ౠ

The next morning, Kate, holding a squirming Petey, looked at the empty wine bottle beside him. "You never came to bed," she said.

"What?" he said, startling.

His head hurt and the light from the window was too bright. He was slouched in the chair and his mouth was dry. He stood. "Let's start a bookstore," he said.

"Start a bookstore? With what money?"

"Remember I told you my father left an inheritance I can have when I turn thirty. Maybe my mother could give me a loan now and I'll pay her back."

"But your mother is already letting us live here. It seems… too easy."

He didn't like the tone in Kate's voice, as though she were losing respect for him. He wanted to prove to her that starting a bookstore was worthy. He would do research and convince her there was a need for it.

Celia agreed to the idea right away. "You know I'd always wanted a bookstore nearby those summers we came to Slate Harbour," she said. "It feels right to help you and Kate out now."

Already Andy could see the sign over a large window: Farrell's Books. Red ochre letters on an earth yellow background. But he also heard the undercurrent in his mother's voice: *Andy, I'm trying to help you now because you haven't gotten off to a good start.* It bothered him that she said it that way, as if he'd already failed at something.

29

KATE SAT IN THE ROCKER BREASTFEEDING PETEY, feeling the draw of his young appetite. The sea sang outside the window and the simplicity of motherhood was comforting to her now. Though she wished she wasn't so apprehensive about Andy starting the bookstore.

She wound the silky brown hair in a circle on the top of Petey's head, worrying that she hadn't made good decisions. Even if she wanted to return to the States, she didn't think she could now, without Andy, who was even talking about becoming Canadian.

She rocked, looking down at Petey, knowing she'd better apply for his passport soon. Whether she liked it or not, she *was* American and changing her citizenship could never change that.

So this, she did know. But now in the house looking out across the Atlantic, she wished she could know other things more clearly. Her confusion felt like a tide moving in and out over her heart, and she remembered how she had been too ashamed to talk to her friend, Lizzie, about it.

She stared at the sea, its crosscurrents whipping up the entrance to the cove. She felt trapped. But she had to *be here*, and help support Andy's desire to start a bookstore. This was the best she could do, maybe *all* she could do right now, given Petey.

Is this what happens when you have a child with someone? That you wish and pray that everything will be all right?

Yet Kate knew, even though Andy was smart and capable, there was something else that was dark and troubled. And it wasn't just about his father.

Those times Andy went out with Ivan and came home drunk in the night. "We're just having a little fun, Kate," he said, even after he woke her up vomiting on the bathroom floor.

She worried about the alcohol, but she couldn't talk to him about it, she wasn't ready to go *there*. Because she didn't understand how alcohol could creep up and take hold of someone. Yet she could smell it and touch it with her hands when she let herself lie beside him in their bed and she knew it was making her afraid.

— 30 —

VAN WAS DISTRESSED THINKING THINGS MIGHT NOT
WORK OUT FOR ANDY AND KATE. He'd told Andy he'd
gotten used to seeing the lights on in the Tannard house. But
he couldn't tell him he'd imagine Kate wandering through the
old rooms, tucking her long black hair behind her ears while
she nursed her baby; or that he imagined the white skin of her
breast, her nipple's deep shade.

Shame from seeing Kate this way got mixed up with the
house he knew by heart. Sometimes in the night, he'd walk out
to the field, still seeing his own life there as a boy; those times
he'd fled into its dark and lumbering shape, and how the house
had watched over him.

He stopped by Will's store. "Yep, it's a bad sign if Sherman's
orders for dories are down," Will said, sitting amidst his store's
provisions: canned food lined up, halibut hooks, twine, a
freezer full of cod. Fog from the outside blocked all views from
the windows. Miserable at the tire plant, Ivan still dreamed
about being out on the sea. He knew he inherited this straight
from Will.

He remembered summers as a boy, when the sun was a hot
ball of fire in the sky and the water moved in long blue folds
beneath the wharf.

"We are building a little house, see," Will had said, showing him how to drive the nail. The lobster trap was a half-cylinder cage made of lath and fish netting, a door with leather hinges at the top, netting with a large metal ring at one end.

"The lobster crawls in through the ring, see, eats the bait in the kitchen, and then goes off to take a long nap in the parlor. He doesn't even know he's trapped in his own house, you!"

Chuckling, Will would give Ivan a quick look. "But the little ones, Ivan, they are called the tinkers, and they're small enough to get back out of the ring."

And Will would bring his hand out from the ring as if his hand were a small lobster, and he'd cry out, "The tinker gets free!" and he'd play with Ivan, and Ivan would play with Will, both of their hands moving together as if they were tinkers swimming along the silt bottom ahead of the sea light, their tails spread out like fans.

But now his father, in the store and sitting on the stool behind the counter, said, "There's no point fishing. The catches are dropping. Those new trawlers with their fancy sonar can locate the cod and wipe them clean out, you!"

"They can't kill off *all* the cod," Ivan protested.

Will's gray eyes lit as he flattened his fingers on the counter. "You think man can't destroy the sea bottom? Yes, I believe he can, you. Man is destructive! Even the lobster industry is hurting! Now when the fishermen haul in their traps, a lot of them are empty."

"Maybe the inshore fishermen need to get together. Protest."

"Yeah, maybe they should." And Will looked at Ivan as if to challenge him to do such a thing. "You don't have to be a fisherman yourself to protest for their rights, you know."

Something in the way Will said this made Ivan mad. He turned and left the store.

The next day after work, Ivan stopped by Andy and Kate's house. "Glass of wine, a beer?" Andy asked.

"Thanks, a beer would be much appreciated," Ivan said. He saw Kate with Petey in the rocker, the sea churning in the window behind them. The evening sun lit her hair and cheekbones. Ivan wondered if it was possible for Kate to look more beautiful now than she had before. Her eyes were wide and brown, and her lips shone as she smiled at him. Again, a helpless longing rose inside him. Women are changed after childbirth, he guessed. A pang of sadness struck him as he looked down at them. Petey, wrapped in a light yellow blanket, yawned and squirmed in Kate's arms. For all that Ivan hoped for a baby of their own, it frightened him to think of how helpless they were. "He's so tiny," he said.

Such innocence, he thought. He might as well have walked into a space of pure sunlight, everything was so clear. *Never would he betray this young family.*

"Would you like to hold him now, Ivan?"

Caught off-guard, Ivan felt himself blush. "Oh, my. My hands are far too clumsy!" He turned then, relieved to find Andy walking back into the room with a beer. "Here you go, Ivan."

Ivan smiled back at Kate, taking the beer. "Next time," he promised.

They sat and talked about Andy's plans to go look at buildings for the bookstore, and Ivan said, "If I go with you, maybe I can give you some tips, you."

The following Saturday they went to Greenport and set out in search of a suitable store. They walked the streets laughing and telling jokes while Ivan poked the blade of his pocket knife into the foundation posts checking for rot and beetles. Sherman at the dory shop gave them a tip about an old outfitting store, only a block down from the main street with a nice lookout to the harbor, tall windows, and high walls for bookshelves. The price was right too, though it needed a fair amount of remodeling.

"When I have some spare time, I'll help you get this place in order," Ivan promised.

ဇဇ

Kate, holding Petey in her arms, eyed the building cautiously. "It sure needs a lot of work," she said. "This is a huge undertaking, Andy."

"I know. But I think I can pull it off."

Ivan watched Andy kiss Kate on the forehead and sweep back her hair. He whispered, "Please believe in me, Kate."

She looked up into his eyes. "Okay, Andy. Okay."

Within a few days, Andy arranged to buy the old store. He made plans for rebuilding the interior with new shelving, rewiring for lighting, painting, and replacing the glass in the storefront windows.

For many weekends in a row, Ivan helped Andy tear out old cabinets, re-plaster the walls, paint, and put up shelving. They drank beer and Verlene brought sandwiches and soup. On the days Kate visited, Verlene loved to hold Petey. Sometimes Ivan felt protective towards Verlene. But if anything, holding Petey seemed to cheer her up.

"Oh, just look at his *tiny* little lips, you!" And she sang and cooed and little Petey giggled and kicked his legs and Verlene pranced around the store holding him close to her cheek.

How selfless Verlene could be, Ivan thought. Though he still couldn't help the way he watched Kate, in a simple gesture when she bent over to put Petey back into the basket, and arrange the blanket around his face. He turned away, still puzzled by this attraction.

Boxes of books had already begun to arrive. Their brown, square presence made him curious. He remembered that poem he'd heard Andy read to Kate down on the wharf that night. He stopped for a moment, looking at Andy.

"Do you know of a poem, Andy, let's see, one that might have a mermaid in it?"

Andy seemed surprised. "I didn't know you liked poetry, Ivan."

"Well, I thought you might be surprised, you!" He grinned, knowing Andy could never imagine what it felt like to be undereducated.

"Hmmm. Can you tell me more? Where did you hear it?"

"Well," Ivan cleared his throat, "I heard the poem recited once, maybe in school. Maybe one of my teachers, you know, read such a poem. There were waves and such, and something about drowning at the end." He was startled by his own lie.

"Drowning…" Andy said.

Ivan had always admired Andy's face when he was pensive. The intensity of his clear, gray eyes. His dark black hair.

"I wonder if you're thinking of "The Love Song of J. Alfred Prufrock." Are you familiar with T.S. Eliot?"

"No..."

"I'll look," Andy said, heading to the back of the store.

A light rain spattered against the storefront window, and Ivan felt like a spy. Andy must know he'd heard him read this poem to Kate. He'd never forget how hearing this poem made him feel.

After a while, Andy returned with a book and turned a few pages and began to read out loud. His voice deepened as if some part of him became the poem itself.

I shall wear white flannel trousers, and walk upon the beach.
I have heard the mermaids singing, each to each.

I do not think that they will sing to me.

I have seen them riding seaward on the waves
Combing the white hair of the waves blown back
When the wind blows the water white and black.
We have lingered in the chambers of the sea
By sea-girls wreathed with seaweed red and brown
Till human voices wake us, and we drown.

"Yes, that's the one," Ivan said, his voice very low, a pit forming in his throat. Startled by how well Andy read, he couldn't help but feel jealous of Andy now; jealous of his education and of his being Kate's husband and having a child. A grown man, he almost felt like crying.

The rain was hard against the window.

"Would you like to have this book, Ivan?"

Andy put the small book into Ivan's hands. *The Poems of T.S. Eliot* written in gold script on blue leather.

Wiping his eyes, Ivan looked down at it. With his dry muscular fingers, he tried to open it, turn the clean stiff pages. Seeing the words made him light-headed. "Maybe you could give me a few poetry lessons, now, you?" he managed to say.

Andy laughed. "Well, yes, I could."

Ivan nodded, wondering what he had gotten himself into. It might be hard to read these poems.

"Hey, you're my first customer, Ivan!"

"But I didn't buy the book. Here, let me." Ivan dug in his pocket for money.

"Nonsense. It's a gift, Ivan. For all the help you've given me."

They were boys again, standing in the cave. They were exchanging their favorite piece of pyrite. Ivan worried suddenly that Andy might not always be in his life. He was surprised this worry overcame him now, especially since he'd just felt jealous. But Ivan knew Andy had shown him something different; coming here to live and doing something entirely different from where you came from. He wondered, *Would I ever be able to do that? Change my life as Andy has?* He was still at the tire plant and hadn't gotten the courage to quit. He'd talked to Verlene about wanting to, perhaps go back to school, but she questioned him, asking how'd they support themselves.

He put the book down carefully beside his jacket. "So let's get back to work, you."

— 31 —

ANDY MADE A LARGE SIGN WITH RED OCHRE letters—Farrell's Books—painted on an earth yellow background, and hung it perpendicular to the storefront's windows.

That first year, while Petey napped in a basket in the back of the store, Kate helped set up the oak display tables. She hung pictures of old schooners and book covers on the wall, stood back, surveyed what she'd done. Then she planned the nautical, mystery, and romance sections, got Andy to help her move the shelves around to create good spaces. They were at home in this world of books and figured selling both new and used would give them a sense of what people liked. While it didn't give them a large income, it was a start.

Before long, Farrell's Books became a landmark in Greenport. People came from all around to see the new book business located between a ship-supplies outlet and the foundry.

Exhaustion filled them. They worked hard every day, making some mistakes with orders and having to send large boxes back to the publishers, but Andy got better at ordering: C.S. Forester's Captain Hornblower series for readers like Will, knitting and quilting books for Lena, novels, and even poetry for Ivan, who was beginning to read Elizabeth Bishop.

Sea adventures, gardening, romance, Agatha Christie, science fiction, Babar. Though Kate and Andy could worry about the business making it, they took pleasure in the bookstore becoming a favorite destination for tourists, businesspeople, captains, fishermen, teachers, children.

The days passed with the strong North Atlantic seasons: the long winter when the cove iced over and blizzards kept them home, with a brief spring and fall on each end, and a short, golden summer. In storms, the sign rocked back and forth like a wooden sail, but Andy had secured it well enough that it managed to hold fast.

∾

When little Petey turned one, Kate got some relief by putting him in day care while she worked at the store. Being there by herself gave Andy a break too. An English major, she became inspired to select novels and non-fiction stories her customers might enjoy. She wrote Lizzie that she felt like she was using her brain again, and enjoyed the contrast of digging in her vegetable garden to planning good book selections. Andy and Kate took turns picking Petey up or dropping him off, and after making dinner, bathing, and putting Petey to bed, she fell asleep beside Andy, no longer tormenting herself with *had she made the right decision?* Working hard made her too tired to worry, and it seemed the more they did, the more they took on. In the summer, they enlarged the garden, and Andy in his spare time built a chicken pen. Kate watched Andy frame the structure while she weeded and planted and harvested alongside, and he built the frame, the shed roof, the boxes for the chickens to lay their eggs in, with little doors opening to the outside. A fine little home for the twelve hens, Kate thought, and Petey screamed with joy when they collected the first warm eggs laid in the hay, and Kate scrambled them for breakfast with savory herbs, basil, cheese, and mushrooms, and Petey, walking now, jumped up and down as he searched for more eggs and watched the birds strut with their bright red feathers through the pen, he running and cooing alongside them through the chicken wire.

ന്ധ

"My mother is coming to visit," Andy told Kate one day. "She wants to see the store."

Kate was not happy about this news, for Celia Farrell had been calling Andy too many times, still with no leads about his father. Kate had grown weary of the whole mess and how it was affecting Andy. It was in late October, and the first frost had iced the fields and roads, turned the maple leaves red. Andy picked his mother up at the airport, and since she didn't want to be in the Tannard house, she stayed at a B&B in Greenport. When she first came into the bookstore, she looked dazed, as if she'd lost her way. Gray wisps of hair had escaped from her bun, small pearl earrings glowed from her ears. She was wrapped in a worn fur coat. "Oh, hi, Kate," she said vaguely, hugging herself. "It's so much colder here than in New York. So now look at this," she exclaimed, her eyes scanning the store.

Andy walked her through, while she chanted, "Oh, my," over and over, wandering and pausing, clicking her lips with a slight hum, her fingers roaming the surface of books. "Your father would be proud of you," she said, her voice high pitched. Kate could tell she was trying to be supportive, and that the lithium had calmed her, though Celia's finely chiseled face had gotten reddish and puffy, and a strange light had taken possession of her eyes.

She was only going to stay three nights. Petey, one and a half, charmed her in the children's section where Celia sat on the floor and read picture books out loud to him. Kate overheard her say, "I came to see you too, dear Petey. Not just the bookstore." Moved, Kate went to kneel beside her. "Your generosity has made it possible for us to start this store. Won't you come out to the house? To see how we fixed up Petey's room? He'd love that."

Celia's eyes wavered toward Kate. "How about on my last night," she answered quietly.

The wind blew hard over the point when they arrived in Slate Harbour. Celia wrapped her fur coat tightly around her as they approached the Tannard house, looming larger than ever into a troubled gray sky. The sun played tricks with the clouds over the sea, casting dapple gray light in and out of the windows as they came inside.

"Oh, you've kept the house nicely," she mused, ending up beside the great window where the sea light mirrored the lack of joy in her face. Petey ran up to her, hugging her leg. Now her eyes brightened. "Come to my room!" he cried, and they disappeared while Andy and Kate got the roast chicken ready, set the table for dinner. And later while eating, Kate watched Celia examine the crystal glass she drank her wine from, and touch the edge of the porcelain blue plates she had chosen those years ago, her long pale fingers reaching out, and she wondered if she could remember at least one or two dinners with Thomas Farrell that might have been wonderful. Compassion for Andy's mother overwhelmed her, sensing her decline on the lithium and her discomfort in the old house.

Later, after they put Petey to bed, Kate lifted her wineglass towards Andy's mother. "Thank you for all you've done for us."

Their eyes met then.

"I'm sorry, Kate. How you've had to deal with so much... confusion...over Andy's father. I'm sure that's not been easy for you." She paused and looked around. "I was never really happy here. It was Andy's father who loved it."

Andy poured them more wine and they sat in an uncomfortable silence for a few minutes. Already Andy's eyes had gotten glassy.

Then Kate got up her courage. "Was one of the reasons you were unhappy... Well, have you ever felt another *presence* in the house?"

"Oh, you mean Basil Tannard?" She laughed. "Yes, I heard him... He never liked me though..." Her voice trailed off, and she looked out the darkened window, the hum of surf rambling beneath the cliff.

Kate cleared her throat. It never occurred to her that she was lucky *not* to be afraid of Basil Tannard. "Strange," she admitted, "I really don't mind, hearing him."

Celia gazed at Kate. "How wise of you, Kate. Not to be afraid."

After Andy returned from taking his mother back to Greenport, he sat in the living room looking out toward the sea. Light sank from the room though the house was filled with Celia Farrell's brief visit.

Kate came in. "Aren't you going to turn on some lights?"

"I like it dark right now," he said. "It soothes me." Kate noticed he had a bottle of wine by his side with a glass in his hand.

"I'm going to bed," she said. "Will you come?"

But Andy only poured more wine into his glass. "Not yet," he said.

"Andy," she said emphatically. "You're drinking too much."

But Andy sloppily brushed his hand through the air. "Not tonight, Kate. Don't worry about me tonight."

Kate, at a loss, sighed deeply and walked back into the dark hallway of the house.

$= 32 =$

THE NEXT DAY, while Andy was taking Celia to the airport, Ivan came into the bookstore. Outside the day was fresh with sunlight drifting in through the window.

"I thought I'd check to see if the book Andy ordered me had come in," he said, smiling.

"Yes," she said, bending to get it beneath the counter. Her cheeks still flushed around Ivan, which bothered her, like they did when they looked at each other across the bridge table. That heat of attraction. She rang up the cash register, and felt Ivan watching her. She wanted to shield her unhappiness with Andy from him.

"Also I wanted to pick Andy's brains about organizing the inshore fisherman to protest the scallop draggers. He's smart about stuff like that..."

"Yes, he is," she said, faltering. "He'll be back around two... He's taking his mother to the airport."

They looked at each other then. Kate glanced nervously at the clock.

"You look beautiful, but sad today," he whispered, his eyes searching her face.

Kate was unable to speak, wondering if she were imagining things. She wanted Ivan's comfort and she looked around, to see if anyone was in the store.

Ivan reached out and touched her hand. "Kate?"

She looked at him then and nodded towards the back of the store. In her fantasy, they walked quickly back and stood against the tall bookcase, out of view from the front door. Kate turned so that Ivan could hug her close and kiss her deeply, she wanting the reassurance that living didn't always have to be so hard, and she might even let him lift her dress and stroke her naked skin with his fingers, Ivan pressing even more deeply against her, his hands kneading her breasts. Her body longed for this comfort.

We're doing this, she thought, a deep part of her organized world bursting apart.

"Yes." He inhaled, his breath warm on her neck.

But the front door opened, startling them, and her fantasy burst apart. Kate had to turn her eyes away from Ivan to gather herself and greet the incoming customers. Ivan still stood in front of her, collecting his book.

"Can I help you?" she asked the visitors, her voice trying to shake itself free of her fantasy.

Ivan tipped his cap while she helped the other customers. "See you soon, Kate. Thanks for the book, and take care, you." *Take care, you*, resonated through her body, and within moments, he was out the door.

Kate knew she was in trouble, that terrible confusion coming back. What was wrong with her, her fantasy world consumed by Ivan? She was unsettled, worrying about losing touch with Andy. But did this explain her greatest fear—that she was capable of betrayal, and not only would she betray, but it would be with Andy's best friend. How could she prevent herself from self-destructing, her worst enemy—her own body—waiting for some kind of longing she could not control. Was she *that* unhappy?

Not only that, she knew she still loved Andy. But he was such a mess, and she felt terribly for him. He was the one who needed her now.

Was it possible to love two men at the same time?

Yet she might be pregnant. She didn't want Petey to be an only child like she had been. To experience that loneliness without a sibling like she had.

33

KATE LEARNED SOON AFTER THAT SHE WAS EIGHT WEEKS ALONG. When she told Andy, she felt the news of pregnancy temporarily lift them out of their turmoil, giving them something to look forward to. Time passed quickly in the blur of winter.

On a Saturday in February, usually the bookstore's busiest day, Lena offered to watch Petey while Kate worked. The winter storms created large banks of snow along the streets. Ivan and Verlene came in, and the wind blew the door shut behind them.

Verlene yanked off her hat, fluffed up her curls. "Hat hair," she groaned, as she hugged Kate. She backed up, patted Kate's bulging tummy. "Oh, how cute you are when you're pregnant!"

Kate, now six months along, smiled.

"How charming your store always is! Speaking of which, do you have anything about hair? I need some new ideas for my clients. I know I should go to Halifax for some brush-up classes, but you know how the time goes."

Ivan tilted his cap toward Kate and grinned. "Hi, there." His voice—still that longing inside her. Yet Kate was pregnant with Andy's child, which had settled her, and she watched as Ivan leaned over the display table and touched the books in a way that made her remember, even if she didn't want to, those fantasies about him.

"I'll order one, Verlene. I know we should have something."

Verlene's face grew serious. "Thank you," she said, and looked around the store. "I really would like a book to read too, you know. A romance maybe."

The phone rang and Andy went to answer it. She led Verlene to the romance section. A shrill of young voices scattered from the children's section.

At a distance, she could see Andy on the phone, looking agitated.

"When is your *exact* due date?" Verlene asked.

"Oh, May tenth," she said.

"That will be almost two *perfect* years between your babies."

"Yes," said Kate, seeing Andy hang up the phone.

Who was it? she mouthed toward him.

My mother, he mouthed back.

Celia Farrell's state of mind had only worsened since October.

But now, as she leaned in towards the Harlequin series, she heard Verlene whisper: "I can't have children, Kate. They finally figured it out. The doctor told me yesterday. Something about how my uterus is strangely curved up."

She reached over and put her arm around Verlene, breathing in the sour-sweet fragrance of Verlene's hair, feeling the thick wool of her brown coat, this woman who couldn't have what she most wished for in the world. "I'm so sorry, Verlene."

She almost wished she could give her this baby she carried.

Verlene grabbed a Harlequin romance. "This one looks good," she said, smiling, and wiped her eyes, and Kate walked with her to the counter.

Later, Kate asked Andy about his mother's call.

Andy's voice was distressed. "She's checked in to the psychiatric hospital, Payne Whitney. Perhaps, finally, something will help her."

Yet while Andy spoke, Kate could only think about Verlene.

= 34 =

KATE KNELT ON THE TILE FLOOR, bathing Petey. Pressed against the enamel, she could feel the baby kick inside her. She was happy about having another child, but she was still worried about Andy. She wished she could work more at the bookstore. Or was this her way of wishing away that slow dark mood welling up around him?

Andy surprised her, appearing in the bathroom doorway. She turned to look at him. His lips were curved into a half-smile. He'd brought her a bouquet of irises and red roses.

"What's this?" she asked.

"It's just a thank-you. The store has been open for exactly two years, Kate," Andy said. "I know it's been a lot of work and I couldn't have done it without you." When he leaned to kiss her, his lips were warm and tasted like wine. She smelled it on his breath more than usual, and it unnerved her. She bent her head, not wanting to ruin the gesture of his gift.

She forced herself to say, "Thank you, Andy. They're beautiful."

Petey splashed his little fist, getting them both wet, and they laughed watching him, his body plump and rose-colored amid his fleet of blue plastic boats. His hair was now dark brown and curly, and his eyes bright gray.

"Here, I'll dry him off," Andy said, reaching over Kate to pick up his wet and squealing son.

Upstairs, they tumbled together on the mattress. When Petey was dressed for bed, they lay back against the pillows and took turns reading *The Runaway Bunny* and *Goodnight Moon* until Petey's eyes were heavy.

Later, they sat in the living room, Andy's flowers brightening the small table by the window. The night was so still that Kate could hear the Atlantic breathe its waves beneath the point, but the sound did not calm her. Andy sat across from her, his elbows on his thighs, his hands folded together and his head bowed down. This was the position that shut Kate out; Andy staring down into a cavity of air.

"I worry about you." The words came out and she felt enormous relief. She had tried before, but this time she hoped she could break through and reach him. Maybe the flowers gave her hope. She leaned forward, trying to look at him.

"I'm sorry," he said.

"It's good your mother is at Payne Whitney."

"Yes."

"Nothing new from Detective Murray?"

"No," he said.

"You are depressed, Andy," she said. She tried not to panic. His depression sat with them like another human being.

"Yes," he said, again simply.

Kate remembered when she first saw Andy, how she'd been attracted to something different in his eyes, as if they'd seen something most people never see.

He said, "I wish there was something I could do to help my mother. I feel guilty about living away." He got up and walked to the window. He put his hands on his waist, looked out into the darkness. "There's a lot of suffering," he said. "The soldiers coming back from Vietnam. Tim dying. I am not the only one suffering."

"Yes."

"They're ashamed. No one welcomes them back."

Kate wasn't sure what to say. She breathed. "Yes, there is a lot of suffering."

He turned and looked at her. "Yes," he said.

"Andy?"

His eyes seemed clearer.

"Are you in danger?"

"No, I'm not," he said, sounding certain.

"Andy, you're drinking too much."

"I know. I'm sorry." He came over to where she was sitting and took her hands and pulled her up against him. His chest was warm and his lips were wet and she wanted to cry.

🙰

Later that night, Andy and Kate woke with a start. Outside their window, a huge orange glow shone from across the cove. Getting out of their bed, they pressed their face to the glass. "Oh, my God!" Andy exclaimed. Arms of fire reached up into the cold black night, there was a distant sound of sirens. Looking closely, Andy said, "It's the barn across from Flossie Mossman's house, up the rocks from Ivan and Verlene's. I've got to help!"

Andy raced to put on his shirt and trousers.

"But you're not a trained firefighter." Kate was frightened.

"Ivan is, he'll be there. I know he'll tell me what to do."

= 35 =

VAN HEARD THE PAGER GO OFF AND JUMPED OUT OF BED. He looked out the window, and there up the hill, he could see Flossie Mossman's old barn in flames. He jumped into his bunker gear and ran out the door. Verlene called after him: "Be careful, Ivan!"

He approached the barn slowly, feeling the heat come in swells over his body, the flames an inferno in his eyes. In the distance, he heard the sirens, wondered who'd been the first to see it. Since being a fireman, Ivan was that boy familiar with fire, the boy who burned the cardboard boxes for Lena behind the store, using lath from old lobster traps for starters in the fire pit. That rush of adrenaline, fire easily out of control.

But this fire in front of him was growing gigantic, the flames climbing through the limbs of the old barn, snapping them with their devouring heat. He saw the fire trucks pull up, men jump out to get water towards the blaze. Voices shouted commands.

Just then, Andy came up beside him, startling him.

"Andy, what the fuck, get out of here! This is dangerous, you're not trained!"

Andy stared at Ivan with a look of fear and embarrassment, the skin of his face reflecting the waves of fire. Helpless, he turned and ran back.

Within seconds Ivan was working with the other firemen surrounding the barn, making the plan for containing the fire. The barn was twice the size of any neighboring house, one hundred yards away from Ivan's. They worked all night trying to put the fire out, wetting the land and roofs of houses near it. They knew they'd lost the barn, but there were no animals, only hay and stored goods. Nothing explosive. The posts and beams gradually caved in on themselves in orange embers while the villagers watched at a distance. It took the night to burn down, a beast exhaling and finally giving itself up, and by morning there was only an enormous charred rectangle where the barn had stood. Smoke sizzled from the debris of it, along with a breathing sound only sudden emptiness can leave.

Ivan was so tired when he got home that he crashed in bed, hardly speaking to Verlene. He slept fitfully, the fire trapped in his eyes and his mouth, its smoke caught in his throat. He dreamt he was the boy again, burning boxes for Lena behind the store, the boy who didn't see Will that night because he'd run away.

36

T WAS ALL A BIT MESSY WHEN THEIR SECOND CHILD, Craig, was born. There was so much laundry, and hanging tiny shirts and diapers on the line, though Kate always loved the fresh smell of dry cotton when she brought them in. Thanks to Lena's help, the garden did get planted, yet Kate worried about the weeds and the mulch that hadn't been spread. Ivan promised he'd bring some eelgrass up from the beach and Kate was looking forward to that.

Andy tried to help with the new baby, though he found it hard to get up at night when Craig cried. So Kate'd get up and sit in the rocker in the dark, the baby's small warm head cupped in her hand, trying to convince herself that having these children could make their lives healthy. After all, can't the world become clearer with the demands of young lives?

And then, with Ivan's encouragement, Andy decided to join the fire department. "I need to have the training," Andy told Kate. "We're vulnerable here, and I want to know what I'm doing if anything like a fire happens to us."

"But you're running the bookstore without my help right now. Do you have the time?"

"I'll make time." Andy paused, and then said, "It might help me if I'm busier."

He looked at her then, and Kate didn't know what to say.

So they got into a pattern: Kate staying at home while Andy ran the store; Kate doing the cooking, the dishes, picking up the scattered toys, cleaning the house. Many nights Andy was out. Every Tuesday he did training for the fire department. On top of that, he helped Ivan organize the inshore fishing protests that were building up throughout the province. Everyone knew the times were hard for the inshore fishermen, and that the failure in fisheries management was preventing the cod fishery from thriving. Karl's catches went way down, and both Andy and Will stepped up to buy shares in the *Lena* to help Karl out.

Yet Kate, in her own world, was tired. She was growing apart from Andy. When Payne Whitney contacted Andy to say Celia's mental health was worsening, she found herself encouraging Andy. "Perhaps you should go to New York and check in on your mother. It's been a while since you've seen her."

"Yes, I suppose you're right. You won't come, with the boys?"

"One of us needs to look after the bookstore. Also, the trip would be very exhausting with a baby..."

"But we've just hired Kenny now, who can relieve us."

Kate knew she was seeking time to be by herself. Solitude with the children without worrying about Andy. Somehow life would feel simpler.

She'd been honest with Andy, at least, that she didn't want to go. But she knew this made Andy nervous, when he walked over and put his arms around her, his breath warm in her hair, saying, "I need you, Kate."

I need you. Something inside her was changing, not liking these words.

≈ 37 ≈

FOR JUST A MOMENT, the world careened. Kate, Ivan, and Verlene floated around him. They were playing bridge.

Then Kate said something to him.

"Huh?"

"It's your turn, Andy," she said, looking grim.

Why does she always have to look *so grim?* he asked himself. The cards blurred in his hands.

"Maybe we should call it a night."

"Let's play!" he said, even though his eyelids drooped like loose rubber. He heard Kate being angry and slouched farther back into the chair.

"Can you hear me? Let's go home."

He felt the strength of Ivan's arm before going out the door. On the path, he swayed, knowing Kate was ahead of him headed towards the house. He tried to catch up and ran clumsily. But the rocks twisted beneath his feet and he fell. He lay looking up at the sky that was black with stars. He couldn't call out Kate's name. Finally he hoisted himself up and made it home.

But once inside the house, he couldn't climb up the stairs. Falling on the steps, he heard Kate cry, "You're drunk! Goddammit! You're turning into a drunk!"

Petey came out from his room, crying. Kate rushed to pick him up. Andy hid his face, not wanting his son to see him.

"Sleep downstairs! Don't come near us!" she cried.

Andy rolled back down the stairs and somehow got to the living room sofa, where he collapsed in a groaning heap.

38

THERE WERE NIGHTS WHEN KATE WOULD WAKE UP AND SEE THEIR BEDROOM DOOR OPEN. Strange, for she knew they had closed it. She'd get up to close it then, the air dense with salt and no light from outside. Yet once it closed there seemed to be a brightening or even a shudder on the other side.

She guessed it was the ghost of Basil Tannard.

She stood in the kitchen one afternoon while Petey and Craig were napping, watching the low sun spread its blond light in the field. Something flickered out of the corner of her eye. She thought she saw a man dressed in gray pants and shirt slip around the corner of the house. She ran outside and saw nothing but the wide empty field.

But she had that feeling someone was close by. She wondered if Basil was trying to give a warning.

Over the point, the sea played its eternal keys of waves.

═ 39 ═

K ATE HEADED OUT TO SKERRY POINT with baby Craig
wrapped in a sling to her chest. Jubilant, Petey ran alongside her. The summer sun had burned off the fog and
Kate longed for some fresh air to wash away the sleepless blur
of the night before and her disappointment in Andy. Now as
she walked the point's path, Craig's small damp body against
her chest, the wide-open sea seemed to play with her senses.
Petey kept running out of her reach, making her afraid.

"Petey!" she cried, "Don't go too far ahead!"

How easy it was to feel fear, she thought, imagining Petey's
split-second fall from the cliff. Even though the walk was
to enjoy the brightening sea. Black-backed gulls flew lazily
through the windless air and the tall field grass brushed her
legs. She wanted to be calm, but she wasn't. Everything put her
on edge now; she yearned to believe that she could still love the
man who was the father of her sons.

Petey ran back to her, a mischievous look on his face and a
scrunched-up wild rose in his hand.

"Mommy, I pick a flower for you!"

Kate smiled. "Thank you, Petey," she said, taking the bent
stem, leaves, and petals. As she reached for his hand, his little
fingers entwined with hers.

From somewhere, a sound suddenly came up between the rock and water.

Kate turned. "Petey, listen," she said, almost whispering.

Petey's eyes grew large, and he looked in the same direction.

The sound of a human voice rose up the cliff face. Almost like a drift of light as Kate listened; and she began to hear a song, its long notes ascending in the offshore breeze. Out on the water, a dory was coming back in from the sea, its bow plowing a small wake in the cove. She squinted, for it looked like Will's boat but it was not a man who rowed it. Petey stepped ahead on the path, pointed his little finger. "Yela!" he cried, because he couldn't say "Lena."

There was Lena, singing as she rowed inside the rock shoulders of the cove. Her silver hair tied in a bun, she wore a sleeveless white blouse and plaid cotton skirt, and she might still have her apron on. Had she just left her chores in the house, walked down to the wharf, climbed in the dory? Kate had seen Lena out rowing before, but not for a while, and she rowed as if the dory was a golden leaf upon the water, her arms pulling the oars smooth, each stroke a salty rhythm slicing the sea. Clap and pull; and clap and pull.

And with each stroke, Lena sang a melody. No words, only a choral slow repetition of *whooo, whooo, khoooo*—a pure Gaelic sound that haunted the sea with its bellow; a pipe tune perhaps. *Aahhhh oohhh, whooo khoooo.* With the water and sky so blue that there could be no difference between them. *Aahhhh oohhh, whooo khoooo.* Only this, risen up.

Kate stood on the cliff, transfixed. They were somewhere out of time. Even little Petey stood still, and Craig slept inside his sling, tiny lips twitching. They were not that far away from Lena, who rowed maybe fifty feet across from them. It must have been the offshore breeze that brought the musical notes so deep inside her ears that Kate remembered the first time she saw Lena rowing in the dory, that first day coming to Slate Harbour. And as she watched her row, her strong arms lifting back the oars, she wished suddenly for Lena's advice about her own life. After all, she'd told Lena the good news when she first moved here, but how could she tell her the troubling news? Was she too ashamed?

"Mommy, why are you crying?" Petey called, startling her before she wiped her eyes.

"Because the sound of Lena's voice is so beautiful," she said, regretting that Petey had noticed.

40

THE NEXT DAY, Kate went to visit Lena for her knitting lesson.

"How are you?" Lena asked. "Are you getting enough sleep? You look tired, Kate."

She'd left Petey at day care in the basement of the Anglican church. Craig was sleeping by Lena's cookstove, in the same basket Petey had when he was a baby. Now Kate was learning the cable stitch.

"It's better now. I can get four hours straight sometimes. And I've learned to take walks, which helps clear my head. Petey and I saw you rowing in the dory yesterday. You were singing!"

Lena laughed. "Yes, I do that from time to time." She didn't seem embarrassed.

"What's the name of the song?"

"'The Mermaid Song.' My mother used to sing it in Gaelic, which I never really learned. So I just hum the tune. But I know the story."

Out on the waves in a storm
Desperate cold, and far from land
My love for you remained true
Although you were a mermaid.

"When I was a little girl," Kate said, "my mother told me a fairy tale about a little mermaid. How the mermaid's love for a prince made her sacrifice herself to walk on pins to be on land with him."

Lena kept her eyes on her needles, her expression thoughtful. "And how are you, Kate, *really?*"

Kate kept her eyes down. "It's not easy right now. We are too busy, with the boys and the store and all."

Somehow that was all she could say, as if a door had crashed down inside her chest, blocking her voice and making her afraid. She longed to cry it out—*Lena, I'm miserable!*—and yet she couldn't lift her voice up, she couldn't lift her courage up, and she didn't know why. She was the one who was walking on pins now.

"Kate, I will take you out for a row sometime soon, not." And Lena's invitation soothed her.

41

ANDY DECIDED TO GO TO NEW YORK, and Kate knew, as she waved good-bye, how much she was looking forward to being on her own.

Later that night, her father called. She told him she was sorry not to have been in better touch, but things had just gotten too busy.

"Is everything all right?"

"We're getting used to having two children and running a bookstore," she said. "Andy's headed to New York to visit his mother."

What she really wanted to tell her father was that she was terrified by *what was happening* to Andy, and her feelings for him, and that she was relieved he was away. But, just as with Lena, she couldn't say *that*. Instead, she told him about Nicole, their babysitter who was helping out while Andy was gone. And a new person, Kenny, from Halifax, who loved books and wanted to work for Farrell's Books part-time, so Andy hired him. She looked out the window as she talked. It had just rained, and the clouds were pulling away from the sun and cast a reddish-gold light across the water and through the spruce, singeing their tips. Kate paused for a moment, seeing this beauty in the natural world and feeling her own dichotomy in it.

"That sounds good," her father said. "You know, Kate, I've been thinking. When I come this summer, how about we go to Cape Breton together, look up your relatives?"

"Hmmm," Kate said, drifting off, not knowing what the summer might bring. How could she tell her father that finding her mother's signature in the MacAskill house was so private in her mind, as if she'd taken it with some light and wind and leaves that smelled like cinnamon from the house and beach of Bras d'Or Lake, and turned it into something secret that could not be disturbed? Something bright and small and magical. And ever since, she could bring it back in her memory whenever she needed to. Her relatives might tell her things she didn't want to hear and spoil it.

"Can I make reservations in Baddeck in mid-August?"

"I really don't want to go back to Baddeck," she said.

"I thought you wanted to meet your relatives..."

"I've changed my mind. Really, all I wanted was to see the place where Mother was happy... And I've done that already."

"Oh," he said, and Kate realized that *he* was the one who wanted to go to Baddeck, so he could learn more about her family, even if the stories weren't happy ones.

"I'm sorry," she said. "Andy's gone and I must be tired. Perhaps we can talk about it another time. I can't wait to see you, Dad. We'll have so much to do just being here with the boys. You're welcome to stay as long as you want."

She knew, when she hung up the phone, that her father might guess something was wrong. But now, even more, she was worried about *what* was really wrong. She knew *she* was part of the problem. Why did she have to be so powerless?

What had happened to her—the part of herself who had danced with the angel as a child, and why couldn't she find any of that magic now? What was she wrestling with? What would a normal person do?

The house grew quiet after she had put her sons to bed. She looked through the window toward a half-moon that was brilliant above the point.

She'd ordered some journals for the bookstore and brought one home. Rising from the chair, she got her pen and went to the table to open it. The first page stared blank and bright towards her. Did she dare mess it up? A peppery fragrance rose from the paper. Perhaps with the first words down, she could discover something. Some peace settled within her, even though her hand was shaking as she began to write.

I am glad to be alone now. The sea reflects only a half-moon of myself. I wonder, to become full again, what do I need to do? At least I am beginning to ask the question.

42

THE NEXT DAY, she took Petey and Craig to the beach just down from Skerry Point. Kate had Craig in a backpack and Petey went ahead down the steep path from the bluff. At the bottom, they climbed over granite boulders strewn along the shore.

The seals lay out on the reef in the sun, the closest ones being about sixty feet away. They lifted their heads, sniffed the tidal air. Huddled together, they'd stretch over the rocks surrounded by the ragged water. Golden rockweed ebbed and flowed beneath them.

Petey and Craig were always excited to see them. A large seal—Kate guessed a male—drew up his two front fins and pushed his chest in the air. Slowly, he slid from the rock and sank beneath the surf, and when he reappeared, his head arched above the water less than ten feet from where they were standing.

The seal looked straight at them, his eyes black and soft when the light flickered. Petey jumped up and down excitedly, holding his breath, as if that would make the seal stay there, just over the water. But of course, the seal turned and dove again.

The three of them stared from the shore, laughing, playing this game they loved to play, sweeping their arms through the air as if they were swimming, so that when the seal appeared again, this time much farther out, they pushed back their hair as if it were as wet as the seal's. Finally, Kate's heart was beginning to feel light.

A shout came from inside the cove. Kate looked over and saw Ivan standing on Karl's wharf by the *Lena*.

"Hi there!" he yelled.

They waved. Sunlight played on the water. They watched Ivan board the *Lena*, start up the engine and back her around, aim her out the channel. He motored up close to where they were standing beneath the point. The smell of gas mixed with the salty air as he slowed the *Lena*, her hull white and solid on the windless sea. With one hand gripping the wheel, his fisherman's eyes lit up, he waved in the watery light before calling out to them, "I'll bring you a haddock if I get one!" Petey yelled "Yay!" just before Ivan sped up the Cape Islander, and Kate smiled at him, her heart tangled up with desire. And Ivan smiled back—just at her, and not at the boys—his thick hair swept partly over his eyes, and even the distance over the water could not block out his gaze.

തെ

Verlene called and invited Kate and the boys for dinner that night. "Ivan got a haddock," she said, "and we want to share it with you."

"How about you come over here, so I can put the boys to bed when they need to?"

"Okay, but I'll cook it at your house *my* special way," she said.

So they came over with the fish and scalloped potatoes, and Kate prepared a salad while Ivan wrestled with Petey in the living room. Craig leaned against a pillow, almost sitting up, giggling beside them.

"Do you miss Andy?" Verlene cast a quick glance at Kate, squeezing lemon juice over the haddock.

"Actually, I can say this just to you, Verlene, but I'm enjoying some time to myself."

Verlene's eyes narrowed, as if surprised by her honesty. She said, "You work so hard, I barely see you anymore."

"I wish things were a bit easier, too," Kate admitted.

"You mean with Andy?"

"Yes, I guess that's true. He's having a hard time."

"I've noticed he drinks a lot, Kate." Verlene's voice was matter-of-fact as she grated pepper over the potatoes. "I know it must be hard, with his father and all…"

"Yes. Something *has* to change." Then, on impulse, "Verlene, would you cut my hair?"

Verlene stopped and looked at Kate, bewildered. "Oh, Kate, I have always loved your hair. Why would you wish to cut it?"

"I am so tired of it. I think the weight isn't helping me now. I look in the mirror and my hair does not cooperate with how I'm feeling. I think I'm getting lines in my face and I need a— brighter look."

"I don't think you know how beautiful you are, Kate." Again, something in Verlene's voice sounded sad.

Kate flushed, embarrassed. "I want a change, Verlene. Can you cut it?" It didn't matter if she was attracted to Ivan, she needed Verlene's friendship more.

"Okay. I'm sure I have some openings next week. How about you call me at work and we'll make an appointment?" Verlene spread the scalloped potatoes around the fish. "Maybe Andy just needs to get help, you know what I mean? From a doctor?"

"Well, perhaps. Did you know that his mother is in the hospital?"

"Oh, Kate, I didn't realize that. Too much stress? For Andy too?"

"Yes."

Verlene slid the fish and potatoes into the oven. Then she stood up and faced Kate. She said, "Encourage him to go to a doctor. You *can* help him."

Kate was self-conscious standing there, getting advice from Verlene.

Then Verlene continued. "I know I'm lucky to have Ivan, Kate." Kate looked at Verlene's plump arms, imagining them naked beside Ivan. "Really, it's luck, you know what I mean. Luck to have met such a man."

"Yes, you are lucky, Verlene," Kate said, a pit forming in her stomach, suspecting that Verlene knew she was attracted to Ivan.

Verlene straightened up her back a little bit more. Her eyes were brown and moist. "He's *my* husband, Kate, and I'm grateful for it, and I wish you the same."

"Yes, Verlene," Kate said—and she was ashamed now to be crying, and even more when Verlene came to put her arms around her.

෴

Later, just as Verlene and Ivan were leaving, Ivan lagged behind. He turned, whispered to Kate.

"I have a friend who has a small cabin outside of Greenport. Perhaps we can meet there sometime, and talk? You seem unhappy."

"Coming Ivan?" Verlene called from outside.

"Oh," Kate said, surprised though joyful that Ivan was reaching out.

When he turned to close the door, Kate's heart thumped inside her ears, ringing. "Now what do I do?" she asked herself.

— 43 —

WHEN ANDY RETURNED from his visit with his mother, he told Kate:

"We know one of the security men who watched our apartment was a double agent and let the murderer in. The killing was deliberate and planned, even though they tried to make it look like a random act of violence. The CIA knows why my father was killed. They're covering it up because my father knew too much about the secret missions in Vietnam and refused to follow an order. So someone took him out."

They sat by the large window facing the Atlantic, and the wind gusts whipped rain against the glass. Upstairs, the boys were sleeping.

"How did you learn this?"

"An agent from the FBI contacted my mother, but wouldn't let his identity be known. The problem is they can't *prove* who the murderer was."

"Do you or your mother know what order your father refused to follow?" Kate asked.

"No."

"This is what you've suspected all along, isn't it?"

"Yes."

"Are you trying to find that security man who let the murderer in?"

"We keep running into dead ends. The CIA probably changed his identity."

Andy looked at her with that distress in his eyes. "I need to find a way to move on, Kate."

"Yes," she said, realizing how much Andy needed her support. Again, she wondered if she could give it. She looked at him, his eyes darkened, his hands clutched. He was still handsome, though, with his black hair combed back. Perhaps those days being on her own had given her some strength. "You really need to get some help, Andy. It's too hard on you. Please go to the doctor, and get a referral for a psychiatrist."

"Okay, I will."

44

KATE WAS RELUCTANT to talk with Ivan about meeting with him privately, still believing she needed to stick with Andy. His invitation, though, was an opening that soothed her mind; a small stone shined up by the sea that she carried inside her.

One afternoon, she brought the boys to the bookstore. It was an early afternoon at the beginning of fall. Andy was sitting by the cash register filling out order forms, and looked startled to see them.

"Daddy!" In seconds Petey was on his father's lap. Kate held Craig, a wriggly six-month-old.

"My boy!" Andy exclaimed, though he was obviously distracted.

"Daddy, can I have some?" Petey whined, spotting a 7UP can resting on the counter. He jumped down from Andy's lap, grabbed the can, and shoved it to his lips.

"Petey, don't!" Andy shouted, taking the can away. Petey, who had already taken a gulp, looked fearfully back at his father, 7UP trailing from the corners of his mouth.

"Yuk," he sputtered.

"Petey," Kate said. "That wasn't a good boy to take Daddy's can in the first place." Wiping Petey's mouth with a Kleenex, she watched Andy take the 7UP can to the bathroom. She smelled alcohol on Petey's lips.

"That was yucky stuff Daddy was drinking," Petey said, wincing.

She took a deep breath. "Let's find you a book," she said.

"But Mommy, that stuff was *yucky!*"

Andy came back out, and sat down. Kate didn't want to look at him; she tried to breathe evenly, settling Petey with a Dr. Seuss book. The store seemed very quiet. Then with Craig still in her arms, she walked back over to Andy. "Ivan said he would bring manure for the garden tomorrow."

"Great," he said, turning slightly in his chair.

"Verlene asked us to play bridge tonight."

"Okay."

"What was wrong with the 7UP?" she asked, moving closer. Andy frowned and didn't answer.

"What was in the 7UP?"

"Rum," Andy said wearily.

"Rum?"

"Yes." He stared at the paperwork in front of him. "A buddy brought some in and gave me a little."

"Andy, while you're working at the store? This *must* be affecting our business."

"I'm sorry," he said quietly. "I'm sorry Petey got it. It's not affecting our business, everything is going well."

"Andy, I'm trying to stay calm. It's wrong to drink in the middle of the day, for God's sake. Have you told your psychiatrist that you're drinking while working in our store?" Andy had been seeing Dr. Russell for the past month.

As she spoke, she could smell the alcohol and see it in Andy's eyes, but she also felt paralyzed. He'd promised he would get help, and finally, they'd had some sweet times together over the last weeks, even making love. She had been relieved she hadn't strayed towards Ivan, but now she was brokenhearted.

"Kate, I don't want you to worry."

She stared at Andy. "Watch the boys for a moment," she said, and walked out the back door looking for the garbage bin. Dark and plastic, it stood up against the shingled wall. Walking to it, she took off the cover and looked inside. Rum bottles were mixed in with paper, their glass necks leaning toward her. Her head ached, she lost her breath. Blindly she ran back into the store, past Andy—her eyes full of tears—and came to the children's section to fetch the boys. "I can't stand this anymore, Andy!" she cried, even though someone else had come into the store. Now she did not care if someone heard her. "Your drinking is ruining our lives!"

She pulled both children with her out the door.

45

THE NEXT DAY, Dr. Russell peered out of his office and motioned for Andy to come in. Andy entered and sat in the soft beige chair facing the doctor's desk. Dr. Russell sat down, pushed back his gray hair with his large hands, and looked at Andy with quizzing blue eyes. His face was serious, unsmiling, and his cheeks seemed flat and pale.

"How are you today, Andy?"

"I'm okay." Jittery, he wiggled his knee, holding his cap in his hands.

"Is there anything that happened this week you'd like to talk about?"

"Not too much. The store is going well, more people are finding us. Someone drove all the way from Canso."

"That's good." Dr. Russell sat quietly looking at Andy, waiting for him to speak.

Andy sighed. "Well, Kate and I aren't getting along too well."

"Why do you think that is?"

He could hear Kate yelling at him about being a drunk in his mind, but he couldn't track it.

"Well, I think she is resentful being stuck at home with Petey and Craig."

"Do you think she'd like to work more at the bookstore?"

"Oh, yes." He took in a breath. He didn't want to talk about his drinking with this man. An invasion of his privacy. After all, alcohol was his elixir, the place he could go safely and calm himself.

"Can you make that happen?"

"Well, it's all about getting help with the kids. Petey likes day care but Craig is still pretty young."

"What are you feeling toward Kate?"

"Anger," he said, surprised by the emotion rising up.

Dr. Russell took a deep breath. "Anger. Why?"

Andy looked nervously out the window, blinking his eyes. There was no view of the ocean, only the flat and lifeless rooftops of other buildings climbing up the hill from Greenport. "I don't think she loves me anymore."

A dull thud beat in his heart.

"And that makes you angry?"

"I guess so, yes."

"Why do you think she doesn't love you?"

Andy sighed deeply, almost a groan. "Maybe my depression's been too hard on her. She always puts me on the defensive."

"Is there a way you can open up to her, so she feels *let inside* by you?"

Andy was quiet for a long time. "I'm not sure *how* anymore. I think she has decided that I'm hopeless, and that I have disappointed her."

"Disappointed her in what way?"

"Kate took a chance to come with me to Nova Scotia. Not that she didn't have her own reasons, because she did. But living here has been a disappointment to her. Maybe she's not satisfied… I think she's in love with my friend, Ivan."

"Really?"

"Yes."

"Have you asked her?"

"No."

"Why?"

"Because I'm afraid of what she might say. I'm a failure in her eyes. I'm not sure…" he said, almost choking, "I can't really blame her."

Now, in his mind, he did see himself drinking. He put his head in his hands as if he were holding his greatest fear.

"But you've started a bookstore. You're a volunteer fireman, you've helped the inshore fishermen with their protests. Seems to me you've done pretty well."

"There's something missing. There's something *terribly* wrong," he moaned through his fingers.

"She knows you're here working with me trying to make sense out of a very troubling crime? A crime that has hurt her as well as you?"

"Yes, she knows that."

Andy hadn't thought about the crime hurting Kate.

"Are you telling me everything, so that we can make progress?"

"Yes." Andy cleared his throat and looked up.

"You mentioned that she might want to move back to the States?"

"Perhaps."

"Would you do that for her?"

"I'm not sure."

He felt very sad, saying that. He realized, for the first time, he might not want to do something for Kate. He didn't like her attacking him about the drinking. He wanted to separate *that* from his relationship with her. He didn't know what it was about drinking, why he had to keep coming back to it.

They were silent for a very long time. Andy began to feel claustrophobic beneath Dr. Russell's gaze.

"I can't help you, Andy, if you don't open up to me."

Andy bent forward and put his head back in his hands. "But how can I when… I loathe myself so much?"

Dr. Russell leaned forward to hear him.

"What makes you loathe yourself?"

"I just can't explain what *it* feels like," he moaned, clenching his teeth.

"What is *it*?"

"I know I need to change *it*, but I don't know how."

"Change what?"

"Me."

Andy couldn't speak anymore. He just couldn't speak anymore.

=46=

KATE DREAMED she was rolling inside the trough of a gigantic gray wave. Drenched in the turmoil, she was trapped by the sea's steely arm. Curled up and shivering, she reached out her fingers to touch the water. It was soft and heaving, a contrast to the danger she felt.

Suddenly the wave exploded and she was hurled into a wild sky, her arms spinning, then crushed when hitting the shore. She lay there naked on small rocks, rockweed pouring out of her mouth. She tried to cry out for help but she couldn't.

Kate woke up terrified, looking around the room. Her fear of leaving Andy and his grief and the alcohol consumed her. She'd ask to see Dr. Russell, but she was told that was unprofessional, that he could only see Andy. Kate guessed Andy wasn't talking to him about his drinking.

After the incident in the bookstore, she'd told Andy to sleep in the guest room. Now she wondered where he was, and she got up and walked quietly down the hall. The guest room door was open, and she saw Andy asleep on his back, his face very calm. Light even gathered on his cheekbones. A profound sense of foreboding overwhelmed her. Basil Tannard? Yet she did not hear him.

= 47 =

VAN WENT DOWN TO THE FISH STORE to sort through
Karl's old nets because Lena wanted some for planting peas.
The air was still, and he heard a noise out at the wharf's end.
In the evening's purple light, he saw Kate sitting alone. The
temperature was warm, and she wore a white sleeveless blouse
and shorts, and her long legs hung over the piling's edge. Ivan
stood and let his eyes travel on her skin. Her head hung down
and her black hair fell over her thighs.

He took one step forward, tempted to walk down. But then
a muffled sound drifted up from the wharf. Kate's shoulders
moved suddenly, her face turned up.

"Help me!" she cried out into the sky.

Startled, Ivan drew back into the corner of the fish store
and looked at her through the small window. He wished he
could comfort her. His eyes burned through the dirty, blotched
glass down the weathered boards and for one instant, his eyes
were his hands and he caressed the back of her neck. Then he
lifted the weight of her thick, black hair and gently kissed her
shoulder, and her skin smelled of vanilla.

But Kate kept on crying.

လလ

The next day, Ivan drove a load of compost to Kate's garden on the tractor. He saw her cry out, but he couldn't hear her until he turned the engine off, and jumped down. And she stood there, a bright figure in the field of his eyes.

He tipped his cap. "Look at all of you so happy to see compost!"

Kate said, "Let me get some shovels and we'll help you unload."

"Nope, let me do it, now. You guys might get some of this all over you."

He watched her put Craig down on the grass. She swept back her hair, her white T-shirt different from the one she wore last night. But her shorts were the same.

Then Petey tackled him, giggling, and he chased Petey around the edge of the garden. He could feel Kate's eyes on him while she called after him, "You never let us do the heavy things, Ivan!"

Ivan stepped back, catching his breath.

"Okay, Petey, I got work to do," he said, walking back toward Kate, to grab his shovel from the trailer. Embarrassed, Ivan felt desire swell under his jeans. Was she thinking the same thing, he wondered, smelling the fertile black compost as if it could be an act of sex between them.

Their eyes met then, but this time they did not shy away.

Ivan swallowed. A gust ripped around them.

"I'll be right back," she said, and turned with the boys and walked to the house. For a moment, Ivan put the shovel down, gazing over Kate's garden. How much taller the corn was now.

He looked toward the house, listening for Kate's voice and the boys' laughter; but everything was quiet.

But then Kate came back outside without the boys and walked right up to him. Her hands reached to hold his face and she kissed him deeply on the lips, really, the world turning upside down there on the field, Ivan's desire filling him up while she pressed against him. They held each other hard then, very close, while the gusts still drove around them. Ivan could feel Kate's heartbeat, her breasts, her small quivering muscles. "You deserve to be happy," he whispered to her, and they kissed and rocked each other, for minutes with all their clothes on, their feet planted on the garden soil, Ivan rubbing Kate's thighs into his own while he wept, a man no less weeping as he came helplessly against her inside his jeans, the image of Kate crying on the wharf still in his eyes.

"I love you, Ivan," she said, before she pulled away, and Ivan cried, "I love you, Kate," and they stared at each other, both of them breathing as if they'd just been running.

"Can it be enough right now that we *know* this? It's all I can give right now, Ivan," Kate said, eyes streaming. Her black hair blew high away from her face.

"Yes, Kate, yes," Ivan said, watching her, understanding. And she turned and walked back over the field and into the house, their desire spent at last, effortlessly with the sound of crows breaking over the point.

=48=

ANDY AND WILL were on the Lena cleaning up after fishing. Though Karl was still the main person who took care of the Lena, Will and Andy helped out as much as they could, since they'd bought shares in the boat.

At the end of the wharf, Sadie, wrapped in her old cloth, stood and lifted her arms. *Ah ha ha ha.*

A cormorant opposite her stretched out its wings to dry.

Andy swigged rum and watched her as Will ranted.

"The modern bottom trawl is a steel mouth with five-hundred-pound weights scraping away the sea plants. The government doesn't listen to the likes of us inshore fisherman."

"Perhaps the protests will help. And then you fishermen can build a strong lobby," Andy said. "All the companies care about is money. I read how those modern trawlers can locate where the fish are with sonar and clean them out."

"I'm not sure how to build a strong lobby, you," Will muttered, coiling the rope. "Maybe I should join Ivan in some of his protests." He looked up then. "Go on home, Andy, I'll finish up," he said.

"No, let me help you clean."

Gulls were beginning their scavenging swirl over the *Lena.*

"Nope, you go on home, not. Take a few for you and Kate."

"What's wrong?" Andy asked.

"You're getting careless. Both Karl and I have found the *Lena* poorly moored in times past."

They were quiet a moment.

"You might not listen to me, Andy, but you need to know the drink will kill you." He pointed to his mangled face. "This ugly skin is the best thing that ever happened to me. Something intervened, not."

Andy, ashamed, said nothing. He put the bottle down.

"I started fishing at eleven years old, you. I was barely strong enough to do the work. I was rushed up fishing straight away, not. I can't remember when *that dread* started. Each day was different and you never knew what was going to happen. Nobody spoke about the danger, because that was our life, see. It always began early in the day, when I drank too much. Usually, I'd go out to drop the buoy. Then take a look around. Get the bottle." He pointed to the rum bottle. "It starts that simply, doesn't it?"

"I guess it does."

"I didn't like it when Lena called me a drunk." Will rubbed his face with both calloused hands. "I was in the hospital for three months. They took skin from my thighs and stitched it on my face. When they took the bandages off, I didn't want to look in a mirror, you. But I do remember that for the first time I could see what I had done... to Lena and Ivan..."

Andy stared at the rum bottle. He still thought of those times Kate called him a drunk. He wanted to believe that he could quit drinking anytime, that was what he told himself even if he didn't have the courage yet. It wasn't anything he needed to talk about with Dr. Russell. He just talked to him about his depression, not about *drinking*.

"I asked Lena if she thought the Lord burned me up. That's when Karl gave me the money to start the store, see. Your father, he bought the house, that's where the money came from."

Andy's head grew light, not because he didn't know this. But hearing it now from Will made him see things differently. "You got a second chance, Will," he managed to say.

Anger took hold of Andy then. Maybe there was a reason he drank. Why shouldn't he drink—maybe he just wanted to drown everything out. His father was a good man and perhaps tried to stop a war. His father bought the house that gave Will a second chance. But Andy's father didn't get a second chance. Where was justice in that? Or in Tim's death in a pointless war? There could be no God who watched thousands upon thousands die in a senseless effort. What God would let that happen?

Grief overcame him. He had two sons now, in this terrifying world. How could he keep them from harm?

— 49 —

KATE'S HAIRCUT APPOINTMENT with Verlene was at three o' clock. She decided not to cancel it. She left the boys at day care and walked up the street, seeing the gold-painted script on the window, Haircuts with Verlene. The sun was bright after some rain, and the smell of salt from the harbor was crisp and clean.

When she walked through the door, Verlene looked up from her desk and gave her a knowing smile. Kate followed obediently and sat in the appointed leather chair, fully exposed in front of the large mirrors, in the benign scent of soap and water.

Verlene stepped up behind her and spoke softly, "Now, let's take a look."

The two of them, in contrast now: Verlene's dyed blond curls and red lipstick, Kate's black hair and pale face. Verlene exuded a natural confidence in the way she stood up so straight—the very opposite of what Kate was feeling, her shoulders slouched and afraid to look at herself, ashamed. Verlene seemed to sense this, and she held Kate's head up like a clay bowl, her hands warm and strong in the way they fanned her scalp. Verlene studied her with her clear brown eyes.

"How much do you want cut?"

"Shoulder length," Kate said. "I still want to put it up when I garden."

"Okay, let's shampoo," Verlene said, drawing an apprehensive breath. Kate followed her to the far end of the room and put her head back on the cold ceramic sink. Verlene released a stream of warm silky water all over her head, squeezed on the shampoo and massaged her scalp, strong and deep with her fingertips and sometimes her nails, with the fresh-smelling suds. Kate looked up. Verlene's eyes were serious and bright. Kate squeezed hers tightly shut. Verlene was strong and steady and not shy, and Kate guessed Verlene knew she'd almost made love with Ivan.

Verlene rinsed the suds with just the right temperature, then wrapped the white towel around her head and guided her back to sit in front of the mirror. Small lightbulbs framed them: Kate's thin lips and arched eyebrows, Verlene's plump lips and furry brows.

In an instant, Kate changed her mind. Now she wanted it *all cut off* into a pixie style. She wanted the weight off, the layers off, her past life off, her mother dying when she was only eight years old, marrying Andy and having children with him way before she had any idea about what that meant, *off*, loving Ivan, *off*, she wanted it *all cut off*.

"Short, Verlene, cut my hair short," she said.

"Short?"

"Yes. A pixie style that I had when I was young. Do you know how to do that?"

"Yes, I know how to do that."

Verlene looked hard at Kate before she took her brush and combed out her long wet strands down equally on both sides, just beneath the jawline, then cut evenly all the way around Kate's shoulders.

She paused then. "You're sure?" They looked at each other in the mirror. Two women loving the same man.

Kate nodded yes.

Verlene seemed to understand, because when she got the right size scissors, she worked hard—that was the nature of her—shaping the cut lines for each layer, the hair falling like black seaweed on the floor, and her jaw was clenched while she cut and styled and combed and then dried her hair with a blow-dryer, and they both watched in the mirror as if they were waiting for someone they hadn't met before, a different Kate who would walk around the corner, Kate with a pixie, now looking almost like a young boy, still beautiful with her high cheekbones and deep brown eyes, but now her long hair was lying, lifeless, at their feet.

Kate rose and smiled, relief filling her chest. Maybe now everything was going to be all right and she wouldn't betray her dear friend, Verlene.

"Thank you, Verlene. You have talent to give me such a fine cut."

"You're welcome," Verlene said, drawing in her breath.

Kate got her coat, and paid, and walked quickly out into the street.

Because now, her feet were light and might carry her into the day more easily.

— 50 —

OOKING UP FROM THE BOOKS ON HIS DESK, **Andy** paused for a moment, studying her. "Wow, you never mentioned you wanted to cut your hair. It actually looks…quite…nice."

She heard his voice slide. Then she said quickly, "I had to have a change. I'll get the boys and meet you at home. I hope you remember that Lena invited me to go rowing tonight?"

"I do. Of course, I'll be home with the boys."

Later that evening, Kate walked down to the wharf. The lowering sun cast long shadows on the water.

Lena smiled to see her. "Kate, your haircut looks just great, you! You look….younger…"

Blushing, Kate moved her fingers quickly through her hair, hoping she'd dressed appropriately, wearing a long-sleeve cotton shirt, jeans, and sneakers. "Thank you, Lena. I haven't really rowed much, after all this time being here."

"No worries," Lena said. "I taught myself when I was about your age." She looked beyond the cove's mouth where the sea waited. There was no wind to speak of, only a haze blurring the horizon.

The dory was tethered at the wharf's end, and Lena stepped down the ladder and into the stern.

Kate followed, and Lena pointed for her to sit amidships. "That way you can watch me row." Gulls passed above them as Lena pushed the boat from the wharf and set her oars.

"When I was a girl, no woman went out alone in a dory. We kept the house and garden, and it was only the men who went out on the nervous water. Okay, so set your oars in the tholepins now," Lena said. Kate noticed that Lena was dressed the same when she'd first seen her row, in a white cotton blouse and a flower print skirt.

Kate awkwardly worked to get her oars from beneath her seat and set them. "These oars are long!" she said, tightening her clasp around the splintery spruce.

"Okay, now with both hands push forward, oars up. Drop the blades in the water, lean back, and pull!" And Lena began to row.

Kate's oars tangled unmercifully with the water.

"Oh, yikes!" she called out.

But Lena kept very slowly repeating: "Lift forward, down, pull, and back; lift forward, down, pull, and back" until the rhythm of her words moved with the motion of her body and the oars did too—a hypnotic stroke inspiring Kate—and finally she fell in rhythm with her oars and the water and Lena, pulling with all her might, feet pushed against the ribs, hands clutched tight; and the dory, a heavy boat, began to move more swiftly out from the cove and onto the sea.

"Lena, I've got the swing of it now!" she cried, and Lena began to sing her Gaelic song and they rowed toward the reef in the ebb tide.

With the evening sun on their backs, they rowed past the cliff and the Tannard house, and Kate imagined the boys sleeping there alone with Andy, and grew tense.

Then Lena stopped singing and called back to Kate: "You know, the first time I took a dory out by myself, I put a gouge in her watching seals by the reef. I took the boat out behind Will's back and he never figured it out, and I sure wasn't going to tell him, you!"

Kate could hear defiance in Lena's voice that might have been new to her then. Now Lena seemed almost childlike in her exuberance.

"Being out on the water helps you see things differently, not. That's why I love to row!" and she began to sing again— *Aahhhh oohhh, whooo khoooo.*

But as they came closer to the reef, Lena stopped. "Let's rest a bit," she called back, pulling up her oars and setting them. The swollen sea grew deep around them. Kate drew up her oars too and looked at the reef not far off.

"As we get closer to the reef, you can see the seals sleeping," Lena said, pointing. "Some may follow us as we row, not."

Kate was quiet, looking for signs, remembering watching the seals with Ivan.

Then Lena said, "Will talked to Andy the other day, did he tell you?"

"No, he didn't," Kate answered, worlds away. It was still Ivan's voice she heard in her mind. *You deserve to be happy,* he'd told her.

"You know, Kate, that night Will burned, Karl said a wailing sound woke him up. A singing cry, like a woman's. Karl thinks it was a seal crying, and he got up and ran down to the cove just in time to save Will. So now, all these years, I've believed it was a seal who saved Will. Just like a seal saved Basil Tannard those years ago."

Kate was quiet then. She gazed over the reef where she imagined the seals might sleep inside the caves of volcanic rock. She imagined the seals going there to keep company with sea urchins, crabs, and starfish; sea turtles and lobsters. They would eat their dinner of mackerel and halibut, then fall asleep on beds of dulse and rockweed. She was watching for the light that might catch on their whiskers and shine from their wet black eyes.

Lena had turned to face her.

"Listen, Kate... You must *do* something before it's too late. Andy's an intelligent man. I believe he can change."

Their eyes met then, the sea slapping against the dory.

"What should I do, Lena?" she asked, her shame gathering inside her. She knew she couldn't tell Lena she loved Ivan and was trying not to. She knew she couldn't be with Ivan and also help Andy. And what about Verlene? "Andy's been seeing a psychiatrist and that isn't helping."

A little wind came up, her own confusion.

"Take the bottles away," Lena said. "Get rid of them so there's nothing left for Andy to drink. I wish I'd done something like that for Will, but I didn't. I was jealous of the sea, I really was. I believed the sea took Will away from me. I see now that it isn't just fishing that makes people get *that way*."

Kate clasped her hands together, relieved that Lena could talk about *that way, that alcohol.*

"I'll try to find the bottles, Lena. I'll take them away," Kate said quickly, though this seemed too easy a solution. Yet she'd be ashamed if she didn't try this. She looked around her, surprised by the beauty of the evening. The sleeping seals on the reef, the blue bowl of the sky. Even with the small breeze coming up.

Then Lena asked her: "Has Andy ever…hurt you? Hit you, I mean."

"No." Though it felt as if he had, this ongoing misery.

"That's good, Kate. I know people lose all their power with the drink. It makes them someone they're not, you."

"Lena, I'm miserable with Andy." There, she'd said it. Kate put her head on her knees, and Lena patted her gently.

"Know I'm here to help you. Let's row back. I'll teach you that song, you."

And Lena turned around and set the oars and began to row. And Kate followed her lead, all the while thinking *this is Ivan's mother* and they moved through the water back towards the cove, and Kate got a ray of hope as the August sun began to set and ignited her oars as they swept over the darkening ocean.

— 51 —

WHEN IVAN SAW KATE WITH HER NEW HAIRCUT, he wondered if she looked like a tomboy. Still beautiful, but maybe more playful, liberated somehow.

He remembered their time on the field. Should he feel some guilt toward Andy or Verlene right now? But how can you feel guilty about love when it's so pure and still so *secret*? He loved both Kate and Andy, but they were two different kinds of love. He wondered if Kate would ever meet him at his friend's cabin. He knew, with this wish, he was crossing a line.

Now what would he do about that?

These thoughts swirled through Ivan's mind as he lay in bed with his back to Verlene. Her eyes were closed and pink plastic rollers covered her head. He made sure no part of his body was touching hers as he tormented himself with why the big decisions of his life were made with so little thought. He'd even become an electrician because Lena had wanted that for him. Yet he could only blame himself for this. Now he could only dream about Kate. What was the unnamed thing Kate had brought into his life? He knew his feelings for her had more to do with his desire to change his own life, but he couldn't see how that was possible.

Ivan heard the early morning crickets singing from the grass when he got into his car. A strong westerly was ripping up the charcoal sea with whitecaps. He smelled the salt water from the paved road.

The fishermen in the village were going out in their boats; they were smelling the sea itself, out on the water where the wind was fresh and the gasoline engines rapped and there was excitement about what the day might bring.

But this morning he was headed for the fish plant. The supervisors had called him in as a consultant for an electrical upgrade, but he was skeptical. Especially since there were rumors of the plant closing.

The fish plant was a group of low, flat buildings that stretched inside the curve of the harbor. Huge wharves for docking the steel-hulled trawlers reached out into the water to the east of the buildings, and to the west unrolled a wide parking lot. He parked as a shift was letting out. Streams of men and women flowed from the doorways: cutters, and packers wearing jackets and hard hats, women with netted hair, cotton uniforms, and aprons.

At least he and Verlene had escaped working at the fish plant. Verlene had been a secretary here when he met her, but then she decided to take an eight-week hair-cutting class in Halifax and open up her own business in Greenport. She'd told him that on their first date, over a piece of sponge cake at the counter in the Greenport drugstore. They were both eighteen. He'd admired her for that. He'd driven her home that night, and instead of getting out of the car, she'd taken his hand and slipped it up under her skirt way beyond her stockings and he knew then he would marry her. It was so simple the way they had good sex at the beginning; her plumb willingness to let him touch her body in a way that had stirred him for a long time.

After his meeting at the fish plant, he drove the gray road back to his job. He looked at his watch. Not quite lunchtime. He could visit Andy briefly at the bookstore. Because, on top of all those other thoughts he had, Andy was worrying him. There was something about Andy that reminded him too much of Will; way back somewhere in the pit of his childhood.

He drove back toward Greenport, the sea on his left and the long, rolling fields on his right. His eyes shifted from the paved road to the fence line running past him and the time came back to him those years ago when Andy and he were both sixteen. Karl had always come up with lots of chores to keep the boys busy, and one day he'd sent them into the woods to cut tall, thin spruce trees. He'd wanted a fence built up through the field on the point, and the June day was gray and cold when they'd walked through the woods, and Ivan showed Andy how to choose the right trees for fence poles.

"We have to take the tall, straight ones that aren't too thick, you," he said.

They walked and eyed the trees. When they found a good one, he'd showed Andy how to chop down the tree with an ax, how to peel the bark. They worked until their hands smelled of spruce and they brought back the skinned poles.

Later they dug holes along the field edge and set in the thicker poles for posts eight feet apart. The earth smelled sweet and warm as they worked the freshly thawed ground.

"Got to build fences while the ground is still wet," Ivan said.

Laying poles against the posts, they drove in the nails one after the other, hammering in rhythm. The wind blew against them, filling their lungs, and they stepped back to admire their fence that grew like a low web across the field.

"I feel good when I'm doing this work," Andy shouted to Ivan while the wind blew harder. "I love this land and this place and this wind! I love you too, Ivan!" Andy cried out, laughing.

Ivan had never before heard those words said from one man to another. Stunned, a sixteen-year-old boy, he shot a quick glance over at Andy, and kept on hammering.

Ivan walked through the door at Farrell's Books. Andy peered out from behind the back shelves. "This is something that doesn't happen too often," Andy said, greeting him with a smile.

"Well, I got a chance to do something different today and thought I'd stop by to see you. I like getting away from the tire plant."

"Come on, let's sit over here. No one's in the store right now." Andy led Ivan to the back of the store.

There was that scent Ivan always loved in the bookstore, a dry smell of hay stored in a barn. He wondered about another poetry book, though he was still reading Robert Frost. He settled into a wood chair, leaned back, and ran his fingers through his hair. He sighed, trying to settle his nerves.

"How's it going, now, Andy?"

Andy avoided his question. "Coffee?" he asked, pointing to an electric water kettle.

"No, thanks," Ivan said.

"How are things with you, Ivan?"

"Oh, same as usual. Doing the job. Working inside with machinery and tires and no daylight." He laughed, appreciating how he could say these things to Andy, no one else.

Andy settled his hands unsteadily on his knees.

"I've missed seeing you," Ivan said.

"Yeah."

"Anything the matter?" Ivan grew hot as he tried to be casual, pushed his fingers through his hair again.

Andy shrugged his shoulders. "No, not really. The store's been busy. It's stressful sometimes, two kids, Kate, all the paperwork here."

"Kate?"

"Oh, she gets on my case a lot. I don't handle it very well." Andy looked down at the tips of his fingers pushed against each other. "Why are you asking me about Kate?"

Ivan tried to open his mouth to say what he was thinking, but no words came. Instead there was a deep clench in his gut, and for the first time, he felt his own cowardice. "I'm really enjoying Robert Frost," he said instead.

Andy looked right at him, the expression of his face uneven. "I'm trying to quit, I just want to tell you that," he said.

"Quit?"

"Listen, Ivan. Maybe you can understand what I mean. It's not a big problem, I don't want you to get me wrong. But I'm trying to give up drinking."

"That's good, you." Ivan nodded.

"I know it's why you came to see me."

"Though I was too coward to bring it up myself, not."

Andy was quiet for a moment. Then Ivan cleared his throat and said, "The problem is, other people suffer from the drinking..."

"What do you mean?" Andy asked.

"I...saw...Will," he said, each word a brick from his mouth.

"What?"

"I *saw* Will that night he burned, down there. I didn't go down. I didn't help him."

Ivan put his head in his hands and everything went silent. He wanted to lie down somewhere, get over this dizziness. He wanted to confess, not only about Will but also that he wanted to make love to Kate. He could barely feel Andy's hand on his shoulder.

"Thank you, Ivan," Andy said.

Abruptly they stood up, looked at each other, Andy's gray eyes penetrating Ivan's. Ivan said, "There's no judgment, you."

Andy nodded.

"See you soon, not."

52

HAT NIGHT, Andy announced to Kate that he was going to stop drinking. "If you could cut your long hair, I can stop drinking. I want to win you back, Kate, I really do." She looked at him, not sure what to think.

It was late summer, now: Andy and Kate standing together at the end of Skerry Point watching their two boys roll over one another in the dry summer grass. Petey, four years old, and Craig, two, chased each other in dizzying circles. Craig, darker than Petey, with bright black hair and blue eyes, pushed his chubby body against his brother's lean one, trying to knock him over. Petey, with brown curls blown over his eyes, patient with the confidence of being taller and older, raised his arms high up in the air.

Andy and Kate laughed out loud, a few happy moments. They still enjoyed taking these walks together, admiring the garden. Kate knew, whatever was happening, she did not want her boys to lose their father. She lived with these two things inside her: Andy, her husband, and Ivan, the man she dreamed of.

Beyond them, the golden field fell against the Atlantic.

Often on Sundays, they took the *Lena* out a short distance from the cove. The boys wore life jackets and laughed in the wind and loved it when Andy let them fish from a rod. Kate's father, who visited each summer, enjoyed fishing with his grandsons too.

Times like these got measured by the growth of the boys. Last year Kate would never let them get anywhere near the cliff edge. But now while they played, she could see the boys change while the physical world around them did not: the cove's scrubbed stone, the slow growth of spruce, the distant reef. The boys were a fast-forward reel in front of her eyes; their youthful bodies in T-shirts and jeans that faded and grew too short every year while the point over the Atlantic stayed the same.

Andy's volunteer work for the Greenport Volunteer Fire Department was going well, his practicing every Tuesday night at the fire station. Kate watched him leave with his bunker gear, hard hat, and boots, and noticed he was happier when he returned home. "I like working with people," he told her, putting his pager down on the table. Sometimes she went with Verlene to play bingo, hosted by the fire department at the Greenport Center to raise money, and Kate enjoyed watching Andy and Ivan socialize with the other firemen.

Throughout, Farrell's Books prospered in Greenport.

And Ivan and Kate watched each other, remembering their time on the field. From time to time they'd let their eyes meet; their bodies brushed against each other in the kitchen, after they'd played bridge. A sensuous heat in the air. "I really like your haircut," Ivan would whisper. They knew they were in an unknown period, Kate trying to be supportive of Andy and not being deceitful to Verlene. Ivan doing the same. And yet every once in a while, they checked in with each other—in their eyes—to reassure each other of hope, that love can come in different ways. Now in the way they were being, they were showing the restraint of love. But one time, Ivan did remind Kate about his friend's cabin.

Among their poetry and philosophy books, Kate had discovered Thomas Merton, his deep spirituality and attraction to Asian thought. She read his book, *The Way of Chuang Tzu*, and became fascinated with the timeless wisdom of the Tao. She then ordered Lao Tzu's, *Tao Te Ching*, and began to crave learning more, to achieve her own sense of balance. Perhaps in studying this meditative work, she could learn to find her way. She wrote in her journal almost every day and knew that as long as Andy stopped drinking, she would stay with him to raise their boys.

And Andy tried to stay away from drinking. Even though *alcoholism* wasn't a word much used in Slate Harbour or Greenport, he did order books on the subject for the bookstore. He even went to a few AA meetings in Greenport, and *Twelve Steps and Twelve Traditions* lay on his bedside table.

=53=

CRICKET SONG. Andy lay on his side in the field listening to the small percussive notes of late summer. The sun was setting lavender and gold. He breathed in barley, goldenrod, and asters, their dry overlapping stems big and close to his eyes. He was thinking about how much he loved Petey and Craig. He was thinking he wanted to be present for his sons, not far away like his own father had been.

"Dad, I found one!" Petey ran toward him through the grass, then knelt beside him, panting. Andy sat up.

"Look. Do you see it?" Petey opened his hands carefully, like a shell.

Andy peered in and caught the flicker of a shining black back. "You got a cricket," he said, grinning.

Petey looked at him, his gray eyes triumphant. "It's a big one."

"You going to keep him?"

"Can we?"

"Maybe if you keep him, the summer will last longer."

"How?"

"I don't know. It was just an idea. Maybe if he keeps singing, the summer will just go on."

"I like summer," Petey said.

"Me too."

In the kitchen, they found a glass preserving jar, a metal lid, and white gauze. They put bits of green grass and sticks and leaves in the bottom of the jar. Petey shook the cricket into its new home. They watched it through the glass, its body short-winged and black, climbing down the green stems. Its thin hind legs bent at steep, long angles.

Petey said, "Do you think he minds being in a jar?"

Andy said, "I'm sure he'll be fine for one night. Maybe even two."

They took the jar up to Petey's room and set it on top of his bookshelf.

"Now what?"

Andy looked at his watch. It was almost five. "I should make dinner before Mom and Craig come home. But you can go out again."

When Petey was gone, he went to the glass cabinet in the living room. He reached to the top shelf and felt behind a row of leather-bound classics, pulled out a whiskey bottle he'd hidden there, and carried it toward the kitchen.

Down from the staircase came a song, pure and clear and percussive, a tiny drum of late summer. He stopped, holding the whiskey, knowing he should be doing something different.

Just one more, he thought.

He went to find a glass.

54

KATE STARED OUT THE WINDOW DOWN THE DRIVE and watched the grass blow in shadowed waves against the lowering sun. Dinner was hot in the oven and Petey and Craig were playing in their room. Kate knew Andy was slipping. She saw it in his bloodshot eyes, and the Listerine didn't fool her. That panic began to come inside her chest again.

And yet, she had slipped too. At the bookstore when Ivan came in one day, she said she'd meet up with him at his friend's cabin.

She'd taken Petey and Craig to day care. A deep, insatiable longing she didn't understand drove her to the small building back in the woods. She'd followed his directions and driven into a parking lot, and then climbed stairs over a muddy cliff. They had an hour before he had to go to work. Ivan had lit the little woodstove. They'd peeled off their clothes and made love, barely talking, only letting their bodies hold each other like small animals in the wild, unjudging forest, and they breathed inside and out of each other as long as they could.

But when Kate got home, she surprised herself. Now, when she looked at Andy, she was the deceiver. It was as if she'd just broken off a huge part of herself that believed she was good. A skewed division inhaled her body and made her sleepless with night sweats and dreams.

She had to tell Ivan she couldn't meet with him again. Not because she didn't love him, but because she didn't believe in herself.

So days later, all of this was racing in her mind while Andy's car came up the drive. It pulled to a stop and Andy climbed out with his briefcase. Kate stared as it swung by his side, looking too heavy.

She bolted out the door and down the steps to meet him.

Andy looked up, startled.

"Andy, you're late," she called out.

"Not very," he said, looking confused.

"Andy, let me see your briefcase."

"What?"

Kate walked up to him, put out her hand. "Let me see your briefcase."

"Why?" he asked, backing up.

"Because I want to see what's inside it."

Andy kept stepping backward but Kate followed him.

"Let me see it!" She lunged to grab it, but Andy took off, at a dead run through the fields. Kate ran after him, close behind, her legs churning beneath her.

At the cliff edge, Andy swung his arm back with the briefcase, then swung it forward. His father's old leather briefcase flew through the air like a large rock, lumbering into the sky and landing on the face of the cliff with a hard thunk, rolling down lopsided from end to end but still not opening, as though its latch were as strong and as tight as the grip the alcohol had on Andy. Kate and Andy stood on the cliff edge and watched it—the unbreaking grip—until it came to a stop in between the slate and wheat-colored sand by the water.

For a moment they stood in silence, hearing only the sea and the wind. The sky seemed immense with only a few clouds.

Kate, too, saw her own betrayal lying there by the sea. She said, her voice more crushed than hard, "Andy, we're both done." And she turned and walked back up through the field to the house where Petey and Craig were still looking through the window.

Later that night in the living room, after the boys were in bed, Andy spoke. "Kate?" His voice was dull in the darkness of the living room. A moon was rising in the east.

"Yes."

"Can you still love me...at all?"

For a long time, Kate did not answer, and the only sound was the waves outside, pounding beneath the point. "I don't know..." she said finally.

"Are you going to leave me?"

"I can't do this anymore, Andy. We're both living in hell."

"There are times when I don't drink."

"You've said that before."

"It's not that easy...to quit for good."

They were both quiet.

"Kate, I'm going to stop. This time I mean it."

"You need help to do this, Andy."

"Perhaps I do."

Then a pause.

"But I know I can do it."

Then Kate got up the courage. She needed to tell Andy about Ivan. "I've betrayed you too," she said finally. "I made love with Ivan. Only once." As if the *only once* could absolve her somehow.

A moment of shock blazed inside the room. As if the darkness and rising moon erupted into one single light that was foreign yet absolute. Abruptly Andy stood up and went to stare out the window. He put his hands on his waist and straightened up his back.

He took a deep breath before he said, "So we've both betrayed each other then." His voice was slow, dry, and angry.

"Yes," she whispered, feeling the tears swell in her eyelids. Her head ached, and she wondered which was worse, betrayal or honesty.

Andy turned. "I'm glad I've been sleeping in the guest room," he snapped at her.

And he walked with heavy steps up the stairs and slammed the door behind him.

55

THE MOON WAS UP NOW and the sea was a silver field through the window. Too beautiful for the war of raging emotion inside her.

She lay on the sofa in the living room and blinked in the moon's brightness.

She didn't know what was coming and all she could feel was consuming pain.

She wanted to remember falling in love with Andy, that first time seeing him at the protest, the strong outline of his face and his startling eyes. She noticed his full lips then.

Why did they need to break each other's hearts? What had come into their lives to tear them apart? Andy hadn't even gotten that angry at her. Had he known? Had he just been waiting to see if she would tell him?

Turning her back to the moon, she pressed her hands against her face. She wanted to cry and her eyes were burning. But instead, sweat gathered in her fingers and she could not cry. She was empty.

There was a sensation, a tap on her shoulder. It startled her so she sat up quickly.

A sound from somewhere.

Feet moving slowly across the floor.

Though she couldn't quite see his eyes, she felt them.

Basil Tannard.

Was he really in the house?

She wasn't afraid.

Was he trying to tell her something?

She wanted to hear him.

PART III

56

DESPITE EVERYTHING, Andy wanted to keep his word and stop drinking for good. His head split and his hands couldn't stop shaking the first day he really didn't drink. A wild current ran inside him, shattering his concentration.

He could feel Kate watching him in the bookstore. The daytime around him ached with the light that lay over the bookshelves. They didn't talk.

The second day, he stayed home in the guest bedroom with the shades drawn and drank fruit juice. Sweats, fever, and chill, terrible dreams...he didn't know which was worse, the thought of being without Kate or this terrible illness. Was it addiction? He'd never used that word before. Or was it the thought of Kate and Ivan making love that made him feel so sick?

He could hear the commotion of shuffling feet, Petey, Craig, and Kate going off to day care. He could hear them asking, "What's wrong with Daddy?" His head throbbed.

Once, when they were away, he went to the bookcase to find the rum still there, but he put it back. Even though the hurt he felt about Kate and Ivan was almost killing him.

Seven days went by. Finally, he could return to work at the store. His eyes stung when he looked at the books. He could still feel Kate watching him. They did not speak, and even though they were in the same place, they were on separate continents. He expected nothing good to happen between them now. He had completely given up; all he cared about was not taking a drink. To prove at least *that* to himself.

When people came in and spoke to him, he watched himself as if he were in a play. When no one was around, he stared out the windows and drank Coca-Cola. He thought about how nice it would be to go out on the water. He always felt better on the sea.

He still thought about the rum bottle in the bookcase that blinked like a beast in his mind. But he didn't go near it. He realized, as if for the first time, it was poison.

A few days later, Craig woke up with a high fever.

"I need to take Craig to the doctor," Kate told Andy. Andy had just come downstairs and could feel Kate looking at him, wondering if it was safe to leave Petey with him.

"Yes," Andy reassured her. "I will be fine with Petey."

"How are *you* feeling?" she asked. Again, those brown penetrating eyes. He was surprised she cared enough to ask him.

"Pretty terrible," he admitted.

"Headache?"

Andy nodded. "I'll get outside while you take Craig to the doctor. Petey and I'll do something fun."

"Okay," Kate said, studying him. "You still haven't had a drink, have you?"

"No."

He watched Kate through the window when she got into the car with Craig, her short black hair whipped back from her face. Now he wondered if he still loved her, his wife who'd made love to Ivan. He didn't want to imagine it, their two bodies locked together. But he was too pent up to get angry, he just stuffed it inside, this truth he'd guessed at.

There was a strange rattle in the kitchen, a shaking window loose in its frame. He turned and watched Petey building a large fort. "Good job, Petey." He tried to sound cheerful.

Suddenly Kate came back into the house. Andy turned and saw her watching him. "I worried that I might have left a burner on," she said, glancing at the stove.

Andy looked at the upright knobs, knowing that was not why she'd come back.

"Everything is fine," he assured her. "Petey and I will be fine."

"Andy," she said.

"I'll be careful," he said.

"Please," she said. Trying to cover the anxiety in her voice, she said brightly, "Petey, have fun with Daddy."

"We will," Petey said, still playing with his blocks.

Andy waved good-bye to Kate as she went back out the door. Then he turned his attention to Petey, who looked at him quickly. "Come play with me?"

So Andy got down on all fours and stacked blocks with Petey.

"Daddy, can we go out on the *Lena?*"

"I'm not sure that's a good idea right now," he said.

"Why?"

"Well, because your Mom has taken Craig to the doctor and we should be here when they get back."

"But we could just go out for just a little..."

He looked at his five-year-old son. He wanted to believe he could be in control and do something fun. He wanted to believe he could get away from the pain of his life now. Petey looked at him with such hope in his eyes.

"Well, we can go for just a short bit."

"Whooppeeeee! We're going out in the boat!" Petey cried, jumping up from the living room floor.

Andy poured one more cup of coffee, stirred in honey and cream. He took three aspirin to knock out his headache. Then again, the bottle in the bookcase; he knew he had to get rid of it. So he went into the living room, reached up behind the books, pulled out the bottle. By habit, he unscrewed the cap, and took just *the smallest* swig, barely any at all, the golden brown liquid in his mouth feeling like an old friend. He licked his lips and sighed. Better in my coffee, he thought, putting the bottle under his shirt and returning to the kitchen.

Petey was waiting. Quickly Andy poured just *a little* more rum in his coffee, drank the whole thing down. He was surprised by how much better he felt. He wondered if it was the aspirin kicking in or the alcohol.

He returned the bottle behind the books, then came back to the kitchen. He congratulated himself because he had resisted drinking very much, he had only taken a few small sips. He promised himself later that afternoon he would get rid of the rum bottle once and for all.

"Let's go!" he called to Petey, and he dressed his son in warmer clothes, got their oilskins from the hooks on the wall.

Andy found some paper and a pen and wrote: *Petey and I went out for a short ride on the Lena. Home by two. Andy.*

Fresh air, sunlight, and a high blue sky. A joy came over Andy he'd not felt for a long time. "Hey, Petey," he cried, "maybe we can even jig for some halibut!"

Petey—with his lanky body and curly brown hair—walked with his father down the rock slope to the water, their yellow oilskins clutched in their arms, and the *Lena*, tethered to the wharf, waiting for them.

"Petey, I've had some trouble getting the engine started, so wait on the wharf for a bit, please."

Andy stepped aboard, balanced himself to the boat's sway. Then he lifted the cover from the engine box. Karl had given it a new coat of paint, a red ochre color, so the cover had a sticky feel as Andy leaned it against the gunwale. The engine was taken from a 1975 Chevrolet Impala, its metal housing exposed, greasy black in the box. He looked it over and then moved forward to turn the key in the starter. The engine coughed, then started right up, startling some gulls. "We're in luck, Petey," he called out.

Andy got Petey's life jacket and helped him jump from the wharf into the stern.

Petey sat beside him as he headed the Cape Islander out of the cove, and the sea ran beneath the boat while sunlight caught in its wake, and all Andy could feel was the gladness to be going out to sea.

Sudden short gusts came up from the southwest as they moved past Skerry Point. Andy turned, remembering that he had left the cover off the engine box. It leaned against the gunwale, solid beside the fast-moving water just over the railing. Distracted by the increasing wind, he looked out across the choppier water. His head began to throb again and he felt the nagging wish to have a drink. He gripped the wheel and felt the jabbing pain of Kate and Ivan's betrayal. Yet in some distorted way, he felt he deserved it. The sky was so blue and the sun was so bright, with only a hint of clouds in the far distance.

57

K ATE LOOKED AT THESE SAME CLOUDS—their pure white edges—on the blue horizon when she came back from Greenport and drove down the road into Slate Harbour. She got out of her car with her arms filled with groceries and Craig walking alongside her. She'd gotten antibiotics from the doctor and was eager to get Craig back to bed.

Kate looked down toward the water. The *Lena* was gone, and Kate knew right away that Andy and Petey had gone out.

"Petey!" yelled Craig, running toward the house.

"Daddy's probably taken Petey out in the boat," Kate answered as they walked inside.

"I go too," Craig whined, and Kate, putting her groceries down, read the note that lay on the pine table. *Home by two.* Kate looked up—the clock on the stove read one.

Craig whined again. "I wanna go…"

"Hey," Kate said, picking him up and trying not to show her concern. "You're sick. Let's have some soup and a nap."

"Okay," Craig said, the freckles on his face standing out when Kate kissed his cheeks and tried to make him laugh. She held him tight, thinking of how much stockier he was than his brother. Feeling him close, she felt the stab of telling Andy about Ivan.

Kate put Craig down and went to the kitchen window. The sun shone down brightly on the rocks, and the wind blew strong, wrinkling the water beneath the wharf. She wished the *Lena* were tied there and that Andy hadn't taken Petey out.

She looked back into the living room where Craig was lying on his back beside the wood fort Petey had built, tracing shapes through the air with his fingers. Beyond him, through the bay window facing the Atlantic, whitecaps began to tear up the blue surface of the ocean.

Kate's eyes turned back and fell on the blue coffee mug in the sink. She walked over, picked it up, and smelled the inside. But the mug had been rinsed out and there was no scent of alcohol. She tried not to panic. They'll be okay, she thought, breathing in easier, and she put the mug down and heated up some soup.

"Okay, you little monkey, soup's ready."

She went to pick him up and hug him, his small chest hot and damp under his red T-shirt. She scanned the sea but still the *Lena* was nowhere in sight. To the northeast, the clouds were building up—charcoal and dense—and she had a feeling the wind might change. She put Craig down and took him to the table to have his soup, and after that, to his room for a nap. "You'll feel better soon," she said, putting her hand on his forehead. Then she came downstairs and seeing the sun and strong westerly blowing along Karl's fence that bordered the field through the window, she tried with all her might not to worry.

The phone rang and it was Ivan. "Is Andy there?"

Her heart stopped. They hadn't spoken since she'd told Andy; since she'd told Ivan they couldn't meet up again.

"Oh, no, Ivan, he's taken Petey out on the *Lena*."

"Really?" He sounded surprised. "I thought I saw the *Lena* go out. Are you okay?"

"Well, I'm not, really. Craig is napping now—I took him to the doctor, he's on antibiotics, and I left Petey with Andy. Andy wrote a note saying they'd gone for a short spin on *Lena*, so now I'm worried."

Ivan paused for a minute. Then he said, "I'll be right over."

That desire. It was still there, lying in wait for Kate. She knew, when she put the phone down, seeing Ivan would be hard, that looking into his eyes, the same thing would happen, her confusion and longing for him. Again she scanned the sea for the *Lena* but it was nowhere in sight when Ivan's knock came at the door.

"Would you like me to go out and bring them home?" Ivan asked, standing in the doorway. His voice was so quiet, and his eyes penetrated hers.

"No, I think it's okay," Kate said. "Andy promised they'd be home by two."

They looked at each other. The clock that read 1:15.

"Where's Craig?"

"He's napping upstairs."

"Kate, I..." Ivan said, walking toward her. He lifted his hands, and she let him come into the kitchen, knowing what was inevitable as she let Ivan lay her down, shoving away the blocks all too quickly on the rug, his hands on her breasts, both of their jeans pulled down, the speed with which love can upend two physical selves in an act of union, the rhythmic beat of breath, skin in its longing, they were powerlessly alone there by themselves on the floor for these very few minutes, finally with no words or reasons, only the wind and the sun outside while they spoke out for each other—"I love you!"— desperate and without reason, both of them knowing that nothing made any sense anymore except for this deep longing, and the call for a happier life, Kate amazed that this could still come to be even though she had said no, and now no one saw them or knew the depth of their own private storm.

58

THE LENA HAULED THROUGH THE GROWING WAVES. Andy and Petey stood together behind the windshield, laughing as the salt spray misted their faces.

"Can I steer?" Petey asked.

"Sure." Andy stepped back so that he could get Petey in front of him with his life jacket on, and placed Petey's two small hands on the black plastic wheel.

The Cape Islander's bow pitched heavily as they moved farther out onto the open ocean, and their bodies jerked together while rolls of waves beat against the hull. Andy knew they shouldn't stay out long. He gripped the wheel harder with his right hand and put his left arm around Petey. "Hold on now," he said, smiling down at his son, wishing he could ignore the change of weather. Petey looked up at Andy, his eyes ignited by the wild air.

"Daddy, what makes an engine go?"

"Well, gasoline mixes with air inside the cylinders of the engine," he began, distracted by the spume hissing along the side of the boat. He started to turn the wheel to bring the *Lena* around and head her back toward the cove.

"What is a cylinder?"

"A cylinder is like a box. So when gas gets lit by a spark inside this box, the gases burn and push on parts called pistons inside the engine to make them move. And this motion turns a wheel, or a propeller…"

Just then, he felt the wind come fiercely. He looked at the shoreline waving like a thick black line, and he thought about Kate, imagining her coming home and finding his note. Were they really finished? Remorse and anger filled him, knowing he'd gone to that rum bottle today, even though he'd scarcely had any. Damn, got to get rid of that bottle, he chided himself. But even more, he knew he couldn't go back to being that hopeless drunk there, on that black line, in that underworld of lies where no one can tell the truth. Was he really addicted? And is that what drove Kate away? He couldn't go back to being the man whose wife loved his best friend, a pain that stabbed him so deeply in his heart he could barely see now. But he knew Ivan loved him too, and Kate had said *only once*. Didn't that mean he could change and make things right?

The wind had shifted direction. Now it came strongly from the northeast and far out on the horizon, the clouds were building up deep gray over the blue water. He watched the waves, trying to maneuver the *Lena* to go downwind with them. "We'll be home in a jiffy," he called down to his son.

But then, he looked over his shoulder and saw a large gray mass slowly come toward them. At first, Andy thought it was the crest of a gathering wave, but then as he watched it, it looked like another boat the same length as the *Lena*. It was coming quickly behind them, and he flashed on the old sea story of a boat apparition that comes in a time of danger. Did he see two fishermen aboard, waving? Their sou'westers were on. Andy breathed easier, thinking they were not alone out on the spitting sea. But his relief was broken when he saw he was not looking at the hull of another boat, but at the foaming rim of a huge, gray wave that was rising above them. He gripped his hands over Petey's on the wheel and aimed the bow directly away from the rising wall of dark water.

"Hold on! Petey, hold on!" Andy cried.

Petey arched his head back against Andy's chest, his eyes—young and trusting—filled with the color of the wave that was turning into a gray-blue ceiling above them. Andy leaned over and clutched Petey, he put his head so close that he felt his son's cheek and his hot, terrified breath, and he wrapped one hand around Petey's life jacket and the other around the steering wheel and they were in slow motion—for this was the split-second vacuum of the wave—and he pushed Petey forward hard against the wheel with all his weight.

The wave crashed down—a blue thunder of water. It churned them like stones in a torrential haul, as if he had no weight or no matter and Andy could only feel Petey being sucked away—his small hands and thin arms, birdlike bones in that last second—into the chute of blind air, and hard water, and choking salt.

Andy, thrown hard against the railing, found himself sprawled over the gunwale. His eyes blurred. He could barely breathe, and he looked out over the water. The ocean heaved in wild jerks, but it was still blue and the sun still shone on it.

The engine was silent. Slowly—in the absence of sound—he regained his senses.

"Petey!"

He pulled himself up and tried to balance himself to the pitch of the boat. He turned around. Petey lay diagonally across the engine. His arms and legs twitched, his head over the edge of the box. The boat rocked fiercely as Andy lifted him up, smelling the burn of Petey's life jacket. Then gently, he laid Petey down onto the washed surface of the deck. Petey's eyes were closed as if he were sleeping. His face was pale yet strangely at peace.

Andy bent over him. "Petey!" he cried through the wind. Salt water rushed up and down the deck around the base of the engine box and under his lifeless boy.

Andy checked his life jacket. It was burned only on the outside where it had landed on the engine, and maybe this had saved his life, Andy hoped. Some blood flowed from the underside of his head, and Andy lifted it and touched a small gash on the left side of his temple. A sweep of water carried Petey's blood through the hull of the boat.

In a panic, Andy stood up, tore off Petey's jacket, then knelt and searched for breath. He did feel it slightly.

He took off his wet cotton shirt and carefully wrapped it around Petey's head.

Somehow he managed to re-start the stalled engine and aim the *Lena* back to Slate Harbour.

— 59 —

KATE AND IVAN LAY SHIVERING while they held each other on the floor. Some clicking sound—that same rattling window—provoked Kate to get up from under him, look out. She could see past Karl's house to Will and Lena's store. The *Lena* still wasn't back.

Suddenly, Lena came running from the store. Kate knew instantly something was wrong. She ran to the dormer window that faced the channel. The sun glared through the wind stirring up whitecaps. Then, in the torn-up lines of the sea, Kate saw the *Lena* coming swiftly back in, her bow pitching heavily and Andy waving his arm wildly from the cabin.

Ivan was right behind her. "Oh my God, Ivan!" she cried, buttoning her pants. "Please watch Craig!" She ran out the front door and down the slippery gravel path, her eyes fastened on the Cape Islander moving into the calmer waters of the cove. Andy still waved in distress from the boat.

Karl was the first on the wharf.

Karl!

Andy's cry was hysterical from the *Lena*.

The Cape Islander circled around fast and came in alongside the pilings. Andy cut the engine, threw Karl the bowline.

Petey's hurt! Oh, God, Petey's hurt!

The wrenching words rose disembodied from the boat.

Call an ambulance!

"Where's Craig?"

"He's with Ivan."

Kate could barely see Andy against the water, a dark form in the wind and light. Karl secured the bowline, then quickly raced to the stern. Then Kate saw Andy's face white with terror.

"I'll call the ambulance," Lena shouted out.

"Thank you, Lena!"

Kate paused then. As if praying for time, she didn't want to turn her eyes to the *Lena*. Maybe she could find that temporal space where she could change anything she wanted in the world, so she wouldn't have to see what had happened.

Kate watched Lena take off at a dead run up the hill and knew in one fleeting moment the dread of what might be true, but Karl was here and maybe that was a good sign, because Karl had saved Will those years ago, so maybe there was an angel here in this cove at this moment too.

Where's Kate?

She hadn't turned yet, but she did hear Andy's voice.

Kate?

Karl stepped up and took Kate's arm. "An ambulance will be here soon," he said softly.

Everything seemed still, although she knew the wind was blowing. She finally turned and stepped up to the *Lena*, and she saw the blood that washed along its deck. The bow and stern see-sawed against the incoming waves and Kate shivered, wrapped her hands tight around her. Karl's arm still held her.

For a moment, all she could see was red washing up and down with the motion of the boat and her head grew light while the wharf and the boat and the rocks swam around her. But after a few moments, things slowed down and the engine box in the center of the boat took shape in her eyes. It had no cover, and Andy knelt alongside it on the deck. He was stretched over Petey, and Petey's legs lay out beneath him, and the wind caught Petey's hair that was loose from the shirt wrapped around his head. Kate wanted to get closer, but she was paralyzed now with Karl still holding her. Maybe there was something she could do, maybe find a blanket, but she saw that a blanket was already over Petey just above his knees and she worried—something was exploding inside her—should she interrupt Andy, who was whispering to Petey?—but she called out anyway, "Petey?"

Kate, came his wrenched voice again, *I'm keeping Petey warm, oh God, Kate, where's the ambulance, oh God...*

Kate saw Andy's hand wrapped tightly around Petey's hand, and she wanted Andy to save Petey from wherever it was he was going, and she knew she shouldn't have left him with Andy—*oh God, how she knew she shouldn't have left Petey with Andy!*—and she tried to jump on the deck of the *Lena,* but she was too nauseous and Karl pulled her back, he said the ambulance is coming over the hill—how could it come so quickly?—and it took her some moments to register the sound, at the same time Karl's arm was tight around her, and the ambulance swung down over the rocks, it bounced and turned around and the men rushed out—"Over here!" someone shouted—and they came with a stretcher and they spilled onto the deck of the *Lena*. The men unclasped Andy's hand from Petey's and gently pushed Andy away. Kate saw the blood-soaked shirt around Petey's head and she smelled the burn of his life jacket when they lifted him up—his eyes closed under a tuft of fallen hair—and they carried Petey away from the boat on the stretcher.

Then Kate heard Lena's voice from somewhere say, "I will watch over Craig now, Kate," and she heard herself calling back to her: "Thank you, Lena, I think Ivan is with him," and she looked back to see Andy come up the hill, and someone helped both of them climb into the ambulance—there seemed to be a lot of people around now—and she heard someone inside the vehicle say, "It's the boy's mother and father," and the doors slammed shut and the ambulance spun off with its whine-whir over the rocks.

In the ambulance, Kate saw Petey's head wrapped in a white sheet. His eyes were closed but he looked strangely peaceful. His lips quivered slightly.

"Where's he hurt?" she asked numbly.

"We're not sure," the paramedic said. "We think it's a brain injury."

The bumpy road unwound like a long gray corridor beneath them.

She lay her head on her son's chest and wept.

When they got to the emergency entrance of the hospital, a nurse led Kate and Andy as they followed Petey on the gurney, down a long green hall and through another pair of swinging metal doors. Two doctors and nurses crowded around Petey, slipping him onto a metal table. Kate forced her way through.

They took Petey's blood pressure and slipped an IV into his arm—the needle a cruel silver jab through his young white skin. Nausea choked her, the smell of disinfectant and the slow pulse of the machines now monitoring her son, who lay on his back while they removed the sheet. She saw Andy's cotton shirt stained with Petey's blood now, the shirt she'd washed only yesterday, the shirt that used to be blue. The pit in her stomach finally made her retch. A nurse held her and wiped her mouth while they washed Petey's face and forehead, exposing a small gash on his left temple. His mouth was open yet his eyes were still closed.

"Mrs. Farrell?"

Kate nodded.

"Mrs. Farrell," the doctor said, "your son is unconscious but breathing. His heart rate is normal. We're putting him in intensive care"

"What?" she asked.

The doctor's large dark eyes met hers.

Then Kate leaned over her son, so that she could kiss the edge of his lips. She needed to be sure, she wanted to feel his breath.

"Petey, I'm here, and everything is going to be okay," she said softly. "Don't worry, I'm here with you..."

And then, the doctors and nurses rolled Petey away.

When she looked up, Andy was on the other side of the room. Their eyes met.

ରେ

She heard the lap of waves, thunderous in foam on the sand, small particles of stone hauled through the old gut of the sea. They pounded in her now, waves and stone, and her head split in the motion. Her eyes opened and she minded the light, wanting to throw off her gathering consciousness.

She lay on a line of chairs while the four white walls closed in around her.

Petey.

She wanted to slip back to the time when she took her keys out of her purse to go to the doctor with Craig and let Andy stay at home alone with Petey. Petey would have come with her when she took Craig to the doctor. That way Andy could not take Petey out on the boat, and Ivan wouldn't have come over.

The memory hit her, a ton of bricks—she and Ivan were making love while her own son Petey was being hurled into a hideous accident out at sea.

Her mind blanked.

Everything she had done up to this point had been wrong. Leaving Petey was wrong, loving those precious minutes with Ivan while Craig lay sleeping upstairs was wrong.

Petey's face was fixed in her eyes, more real than the day around her. This was proof enough that he stood at the end of that corridor between life and death and with all her strength she tried to reach out and bring him back. He sat playfully on the edges of light beams through the room.

Yet he eluded her. He kept disappearing just when she thought she had found him. He raced around corners and down the hills towards the sea, and Kate saw the grass and the rocks through his liquid body.

Sitting up, she realized she was in the hospital waiting room. She had been sleeping on the chairs, and her neck hurt. Looking over, she saw Lena sitting and dozing, and Andy too.

"Where's Craig?" she called out.

Lena jolted out of her doze. "With Verlene and Ivan," she said. "Don't worry, Kate, they will take good care of him, you."

"I think...I better call my father."

"Would you like me to?" Lena offered.

"Oh, I will, Lena. But I'm not ready for him to come."

☙

The doctor and nurse led Kate into Petey's room. She saw his sleeping face and a machine with a green line showing his heartbeat. A breathing tube came out of his mouth.

"Your boy, Mrs. Farrell, is in a coma," the doctor said quietly.

Kate rushed to Petey's side. "He looks...so calm."

"Yes, he does," the nurse agreed, rustling around, organizing cords and tubes.

"Do we know anything?" Kate asked. "I mean, about when he will wake up?"

"No, unfortunately we don't. He's suffering from an injury to his brain, and it's hard to tell the magnitude of the damage."

"Where's Andy?" Kate heard herself ask this through the dim air of the room.

"He's here," Lena said, coming up beside her. Kate hadn't realized that Lena was in the room with her. "He's not too good..."

"Oh..." said Kate vaguely, looking down at Petey again. She didn't know what time it was, she didn't know what day it was.

☙

The next morning, when Kate woke up on her cot, Andy was slouched in the chair beside her, his eyes open. Her mind blurred. She was still so raw and empty.

They looked at each other for what seemed like a long time.

"Tell me what happened," she asked, finally.

"The sea got rough. We were coming home." Andy spoke as if he coughed out each word. "I was standing at the wheel with Petey. He was in front of me and I was standing behind him."

Blackness washed through Kate's eyes while Petey lay in his bed beside them.

"I was looking off to starboard; I knew the wind had changed and we were in for bad weather. I tried...to get back. But the wave came..."

"The wave?"

"A freak wave came out of nowhere..." Andy choked, pushing himself on. "The wave knocked us both out, I lost Petey from my arms, the water threw him into the engine."

"The engine?" Kate's voice descended.

Andy broke down, tears streaming down his face. No sound came from him for a long time, until he said, "I left the cover of the engine box off."

The words beat inside Kate's head. She stared at Andy in the pale hospital glow.

"I forgot. I'd intended to put it back on, but I didn't want to leave Petey."

"Were you drinking?"

"I took a tiny swig of rum before we left. Barely anything at all."

Kate tried to even out her breaths.

"I left you with Petey. You promised to take care of him."
Tears leaked out of her eyes, rolling down her cheeks already chapped from crying. "Why did you go out on the *Lena*, for God's sake?"

Her voice was loud now, anger flooding her.

Andy looked away, said nothing.

Just then, the doctor came in. First she heard his voice, which was calm. Then she looked up. He said it was good that Andy had wrapped Petey's head up on the boat and had gotten him to shore so quickly. His skull was not fractured, and while there was internal bleeding, the gash was not causing much swelling. He did have a hematoma. Being in a coma is good at this point, he said, as it will give the brain time to work out its trauma.

The doctor looked mostly at Kate while he gave this information.

Andy sat up straighter in his chair. They all looked at Petey; and the doctor leaned over him, checked his pulse, and listened to his heart.

"There's still no idea how long he will be in a coma?" Andy asked.

"No," the doctor replied.

"Will he…be different?" Kate asked.

"Perhaps, it's hard to know. Every case is different. I'll check on him often," he said. He paused then and looked at both Kate and Andy. "I'm sorry you both have to go through this," he said. Then he looked at Andy. "You did the best thing you could have done for your son out on that boat," he said, and then he left the room.

∞

Later, when Kate woke up beside Petey's bed, she felt a soft weight over her that made her look down. The quilt, Fisherman's Reel, was spread over her, the red triangles and squares intricately joined. Verlene and Lena swam in her head, the memory of their voices over the quilting frame in Lena's kitchen. Now Lena had put Fisherman's Reel over her exhausted body, and she lowered her hand to feel its cotton, the threads like the hands of the women in Slate Harbor trying to comfort her.

There were whispers. Kate looked over towards the door and saw Verlene, who smiled, her hair blonder and curlier than ever. "Can I get you anything?" she asked.

Again, everything was wrong.

"No, thank you, Verlene. Where is Craig?"

"He's with Lena. They will come in and see Petey this afternoon."

Kate could see the tears in Verlene's eyes.

"Thank you, Verlene."

Kate looked back down at the quilt again, and she saw the bright red reels spinning over the whiteness. All she could do now was wait for Petey to wake up. He looked so peaceful, she thought, remembering Petey playing baseball out on the field, swinging his plastic bat low. Andy threw the ball towards him, and he hit it and ran to first base. Petey had such fast legs. Once he ran too fast over the field toward the promontory, fell in the tall grass, and scraped his knees. But he got up laughing and kept running on ahead.

— 60 —

AFTER FOUR DAYS IN THE HOSPITAL. Kate needed to find the rum bottle Andy drank from before taking Petey out. She needed to go to the house. Andy had been in and out, and she knew he was staying with Will and Lena. She called Lena for a ride home. When Lena dropped her off, she didn't look happy. "I'll come back in an hour, Kate. I'm worried about you being alone in that house. Craig's with Verlene."

"It's something I need to do," Kate said, getting out of the car.

She walked up to the house, pushed through the door, and walked through the kitchen into the dining room. Her heart was racing and she knew she was having trouble seeing things clearly around her.

She felt Andy's absence from the house, and she looked briefly at the floor where she had lain with Ivan, surprised to still feel any sweetness there. But the gray afternoon light was too bright in the room and she anxiously walked across to the glass cabinet where her stoneware blue dishes were kept. She bent down to open the bottom doors, where she'd previously found the bottles of liquor before throwing them all away. The doors clicked opened with that familiar sound. The shelves were empty and smelled of pine. But their emptiness gave her no relief.

She turned to face the living room, her breathing quickening in her chest. Her stomach hurt while her eyes fastened on the books in the shelves and she walked toward them, her feet unsteadily navigating the rug and bare floor. She reached for a collection of leather-bound novels—Dickens and Tolstoy in fine gold print—and she yanked a group down into her arms. They were heavy, so she let them fall to the floor, the volumes twisting open at her feet. The scent of dusty paper clobbered her, so she swept her arm behind more books and pulled them towards her, letting them fall with a clumping sound. She swept the rest of the books from the shelf, and then went to a higher shelf and swept those books too, they were hard and heavier and they bruised her legs as they fell down against her. Then she got a chair and went to the top shelf, where she pulled again, and when these books fell, she saw the rum bottle.

It stood alone on the shelf, a faint layer of dust on its dark glass.

She stared at the label of Myers's Rum in stylized print, sugarcane bushes and white oak barrels filled with Jamaican molasses painted beneath it. A man walked there holding the cane stalks as if he had no awareness of danger. She grabbed the bottle's neck and shook it, the dark glass trying to hide this rum slosh.

She got down, put the bottle under her arm, walked out the back door, barely feeling the wind that blew the door shut and threw back her hair. The late afternoon seemed flat and gray over the water, and Kate walked down the path over the rocks toward the shore below Skerry Point. She avoided looking toward the wharf where the *Lena* was tied, and out over the ocean where Petey got hurt. She looked only towards the tide that was low and the golden rockweed that lay in clumps along the shoreline. Kate went close to the water, and when she knelt down she barely cared that the rockweed cushioned her knees. She took the bottle out from under her arm and raised it over her head.

She smashed the bottle down onto the rocks. The glass shattered in all directions, while the alcohol flowed into tide pools and thick strands of seaweed around her. Staring at the broken pieces shining on the rocks, she was surprised by how quickly the ocean swallowed her pain.

She tossed the bottle's unbroken neck into the salt water, grateful for the sea's strength. But now her strength was gone. She could only fall against the rock. Curled up, she put her head onto her knees.

She did not know she'd cut her hand. She did not know a seal watched her.

≡61≡

VAN'S HEAD HURT IN THE DULL GRAY WEATHER, and he chewed the pork chops Verlene had left in the oven. Out of the corner of his eye, he saw someone at the base of the path to the Tannard house. He put down his fork and leaned forward. The person fell, then remained still.

"Someone needs help," Ivan said out loud, looking closer, worrying it might be Kate. He got up from the table and grabbed his jacket and hurried out of the house and down the road. The cold offshore breeze blew as he ran over the rocks and grass and through the backyards of houses for a shortcut to the point. When he reached the top of the path that led to the water, Ivan looked down and saw Kate curled up against the rocks. He stepped down the steep incline, his eyes fastened to her. Stones clattered from under his feet.

Kate looked up.

"Oh, my God, now..." Kate's face was blotched from crying. Her hair lay pasted to her head.

Ivan stepped down closer.

Kate recoiled as Ivan came beside her. "Go away, Ivan!" she cried into her knees.

Ivan touched the top of Kate's head. "Come with me now, Kate," he said softly.

Kate stayed curled, her body shaking.

"Take my hand, now, Kate," Ivan said, and he bent over, reaching for her arm. Kate, still coiled tight, stiffened as Ivan tried to pull her towards him. Finally, sensing her distress, he lifted her from the path, his arms circled around her, and she smelled of salt and rum when he pulled her to his chest. Still crimped up, she made no move to resist.

When he reached the top, he put Kate down in the grass with the wind blowing around her. She lay back, and carefully Ivan studied the cut in Kate's hand and was relieved it wasn't deep. He got his handkerchief, wrapped it around the wound. He couldn't help but see Kate in the grass, and then again on the kitchen floor, her black eyebrows over her closed eyes, her eyebrows in the shape of crescent moons.

"Petey hasn't woken up," she moaned.

Chilled by her grief, he put his arm around her and guided her as best he could across the field's knotty ground towards the Tannard house.

62

VAN CALLED FOR LENA to come over when they got back in the house. No one knew for sure where Andy was, but they all knew that Andy wasn't the one to look after Kate now.

"I need to see Craig," Kate said, putting her head in her hands. In minutes, Lena came through the kitchen with Craig, who looked shocked seeing books scattered all over the living room floor.

"Glad you're here," Ivan whispered, and he leaned down towards Craig. "Take good care of your mother, now. Okay?"

Kate's and Ivan's eyes met then, just before he turned and went out the door. In her exhaustion, Kate no longer feared showing her love for Ivan in front of Lena. Still feeling his heartbeat through his shirt when he'd carried her from the rocks.

"Mommy!" Craig cried, throwing himself against her.

Kate hugged Craig tightly, feeling his little and breathing chest. "Hi, Craig," she said, bending to kiss him. Through the window, clouds broke up in the sky and spilled light over their faces. Kate saw more than ever how Craig had the same curved lips as Petey's.

"Mommy has an owie?" Craig stared at Ivan's handkerchief around her palm. Though Craig was only three, he was old enough to know her wound had something to do with the shock of these last days.

Kate lifted him up into her lap. "Mommy has a small cut on her hand," she said quietly. "But it's not bad." Craig studied the handkerchief, then looked at Kate. "Mommy, can Petey come home now?" he whined.

Kate's heart wrenched. "Not quite yet. But we can go see Petey at the hospital together."

Craig twisted his head up towards the ceiling, rolled back his eyes. "But *when* is Petey coming home?"

"I don't know *when* Petey's coming home. He's in a coma, Craig..."

"What's *coma*?"

"A coma is when the brain goes to sleep."

"Oh, he's sleeping!" Craig's eyes were hopeful. He thumped against Kate's chair. "Let's wake Petey up. I want him to come back *now*, I don't want him to sleep."

Then Verlene came into the kitchen with a casserole, and Lena whispered something to her.

"Mommy!" he cried, eying Verlene and Lena suspiciously, fearful they would take him away. "Will you build blocks with me, Mommy?"

Kate motioned to Lena and Verlene that everything was fine. Craig jumped down from Kate's lap and ran past the disheveled books to the box of pine blocks in the corner. Kate went to sit with Craig on the braided rug, and together they stacked the different shapes.

Craig's eyes were determined. "Petey will come here to sleep."

"Good idea..." said Kate, guarded.

"I build it all by myself."

Craig stacked the blocks, varying in size, some long and narrow, square or triangular.

"Petey's bed!" he said proudly, stepping back, the mass of blocks caught in sunlight. "He can come home *now*, Mommy!" And Craig jumped on the rug with such excitement that the rug slipped beneath his feet and shook the blocks crashing down.

"No!" Craig yelled at the blocks. "No!" He threw himself over the collapsed pile.

"Craig..." Kate tried to pick Craig up, but he kicked out his feet and pushed her away.

Kate's voice was firm. "Come here, Craig."

Finally, he crawled over to Kate, and she lifted him up onto her lap while he clung to her, and she rocked him close while he cried. Her eyes scanned the scattered blocks on the rug, and again she saw herself lying there with Ivan, and she cringed, knowing her life was immutably changed.

තිරි

Kate said, "I knew when I first met Andy there was something wrong."

The living room was dark. Lena sat in the other chair. Blocks were still scattered on the floor.

Kate choked, barely able to speak the truth. "I loathe Andy for this accident. Lena, I have to tell you that. But I loathe myself too—I never should have left Andy alone with Petey. I never should have stayed with Andy this long."

"You were trying your best, Kate."

"Andy has too much sadness, Lena. I married his sadness. God, look what's become of us..."

"You know, Kate," Lena said. "When we're young, we think we know what we want. We try something out with the best of intentions, even though it might turn out to be a mistake. You're so young, Kate. You will have time to work through this tragic accident... I do believe that love carries us through these terrible things."

Then Lena began to hum. And Kate couldn't help but think of what had happened to all the men who lived in this house. The suffering and death. Basil Tannard. Andy's father. Andy. And now Petey.

AFTER LENA WENT TO BED, Kate lay down on the sofa in the living room. She could sleep more peacefully here, where she had slept so many times. She blinked in the night's brightness.

Turning her back to the window, she pressed her hands against her face. She had cried all she could and now was empty. Maybe, at last, she could sleep.

She put her head down.

A sound came from somewhere. Feet moving slowly across the floor.

Though she couldn't quite see his eyes, she felt them.

Was he really in the room?

She wasn't afraid. She'd experienced this before.

But this time he was closer.

He took her hand. She looked up.

Basil, is it you?

His eyes were kind and watery, a pale luminescence tracing his body. He lifted her to come toward him. She heard the tune that Lena sang.

He was taller than she'd imagined. He turned her.

She dreamed while they danced, his form growing dark against the sea light outside the window. She was afraid she might lose him.

I believe you, Basil. That a seal saved your life.

Again she felt him in the room, and Basil came and turned her, more closely now.

If they had believed you, Basil, would you have lived?

She could see him smile. He said, *I'll show you.*

In her dream, Basil led Kate to the shore, sank them both deep inside the water. Kate could feel her body change when the cool sea streamed into her eyes. They sped over the reef and out into the vast blue universe, and they were fish, swimming through sunlit stones. The seafloor scattered beneath them until a current snaked up, hurled them onto the reef. Kate could not feel the razor-sharp rock, she did not bleed. Basil beckoned her towards the cave's dark mouth. They climbed inside, knelt on a bed of eelgrass. Kate fell forward, her cheeks warm in the sticky salt bed prepared by the seal. Sea light spiraled on the walls, and though she could not see the seal, she felt her presence. She could sense the seal's heart, her liquid eyes. And Kate could feel her strength.

⸗64⸗

VAN DIDN'T KNOW WHAT KATE MIGHT HAVE TOLD ANDY.
All he knew was he needed to see his friend. He went to Will
and Lena's to find him.

Andy was at the kitchen table when Ivan let himself in to
sit across from him. Andy looked up, his gray eyes bleary and
wet, and said nothing.

"I'm sorry, Andy," Ivan said, his heart beating in his throat.

They sat in a long silence. Andy hadn't shaved and his face
was darkly shadowed.

"Maybe you could use some food, not."

"No."

Andy pushed his mug away, and with some effort, stood up
from the table. He shot a wild look at Ivan before he walked to
the window and stared out across the Atlantic. "I can't stand
living with this nightmare, Ivan." He leaned forward, pushed
his knuckles hard into the windowsill.

Ivan hesitated a moment and then walked towards Andy.

Andy swung around. "Stay away, Ivan." His whole body
shook.

"Andy, you need some sleep now..."

"Fuck you, Ivan, you get some sleep! I know you slept with
Kate."

Ivan stood motionless, not knowing what to say.

Andy edged along the windowsill, then turned and ran out the door.

Ivan hurried after him. The sun had risen higher and brightened the tall summer grass. A strong wind came from the east as he ran behind Andy down to the wharf. When their feet hit the clattering boards, Andy turned.

"It's not good for you to come down to the *Lena!*" Ivan yelled.

"My son's in a coma and I can fucking come here anytime I want..." Andy said, his voice breaking.

"Andy, you're tormenting yourself." Ivan leaned in close and put his arm around Andy. Andy stood with his head down. His body smelled strangely sweet and warm.

The gulls swirled over the wharf, the sun heating their backs, drawing the salt from the boards. The water lapped in a gentle beat against the Cape Islander, and Ivan looked past Andy. He could still see the stain of Petey's blood, but Ivan knew that Karl had washed the boat down, so maybe it was just in his eyes or in the paint. The engine sat without its cover and the boat rocked sideways with the engine box in the middle as though it were turning on an axis and all the rest of the world was still.

"What happened out there, Andy?" Ivan asked, his voice was slow and considered.

"What does it matter?"

"It matters."

Andy struggled to speak. "The wind was too strong when I took Petey out. But I didn't want to disappoint him, he wanted to go. I wanted to go too." He shot a quick look at Ivan. "Then a bit offshore, I knew we had to turn back. After I brought the *Lena* around, this roller swamped the boat..."

"It was the wave, then?"

"The wave shook the boat and got Petey from me. Petey was thrown into the engine, just like that. I left the cover off."

"But what if the cover were on? Petey could still have hit his head."

Andy glared at Ivan. "Don't try to make me feel better, Ivan. You don't know *a single thing* about what this feels like. This *guilt*."

"I do know something about it, Andy. I walked right past my own father when he was burning that night."

രുരു

It was a night like many other nights, those years ago.

Lena was leaning over the sink as though she were sick. "You are a drunk, Will."

Will just stood there, his sodden face; the alcohol, the cod, the grease.

"Don't call me a drunk!" he cried, and—in one split second—grabbed her by the shoulders and shook her—*Don't call me a drunk!*—and Lena's head snapped back. Then Will hit her once, then twice in the face.

Ivan ran into the room, sprang at Will from behind. His nails dug deep into his father's skin. "Stop hurting her!" he cried. "You've hurt her too many times!"

Will stiffened, let go of Lena, and turned. Ivan punched him twice, hard in the face, then watched Will turn, stagger towards the door. Opening it, he stood for a moment and faced the black air outside. He was crying as he heaved himself through.

Ivan went over to his mother. He touched her shoulder.

"I'm okay," she whispered.

He turned and ran out the door.

He followed the path to the Tannard house as he had so many times before, his heart pounding while he climbed through the old window, avoiding the shards of glass, his eyes wrestling with the dark to find the old crate. Perhaps roll a cigarette, listen to the whir of bats and the sea. But on this night he was too restless and didn't stay. Instead, he walked back towards his house and heard someone talking down on the shore. The voice floated up from the inky cove in disjointed, muffled notes. He walked down closer. The lights of the fish stores reflected on the water like strings of fire across the inlet. He saw a man's head and back bent over the rocks. Was he talking to himself or singing? Was it Will's voice? A thin stream of yellow light circled up the man's arm. Was it light from the fish stores reflected on the water? It moved in a stroking orange wave up his arm. Ivan heard the slurred words, then the man slapping himself.

He ran then. He ran back up the hill to his house, through the kitchen, and up the stairs into his room. He slammed the door behind him and crouched by his bed, breathing fast, wondering if Lena had gone to bed. She must have because he hadn't seen her in the kitchen. Everything would be all right if he waited long enough.

ಬಬ

Ivan said to Andy: "Maybe something makes us blame ourselves for these things. Maybe we try to make sense out of the violence and the only way we can do that is to blame ourselves..."

Andy just stared into the water, saying nothing.

Ivan said, "I know you'll hate hearing anything positive right now. My whole life, I've blamed myself for that night. For not going down to help Will. I learned later that he'd dropped his cigarette on himself. But the strange thing is, Will's accident was, in a twisted sort of way, the best thing that ever happened to him. To all of us."

≡ 65 ≡

KATE HURRIED TO THE BOOKSTORE. When she saw the "Closed" sign on the door, she guessed Andy had asked Kenny to put it there. Unlocking the door, she went inside, the moist sea air following her into the musky smell of books. Breathing deeply, she looked at this familiar place where she and Andy had worked so hard. A huge stack of mail rested on the counter and some boxes were piled beside it.

Who would take care of this now, this business of books and mundane bills? This world should have stopped.

She knew there was a book they'd ordered, *Oceanography, Exploring the Planet Ocean* by J. J. Bhatt. She aimed for the science section, got down on her knees, and pulled it out, but she could find nothing listed in the index for rogue waves. She even leafed through the wave section.

Rogue wave.

She had to get *information*, as if facts about a rogue wave might soothe her, convincing her of the unpredictable turmoil of the sea. She felt like a detective, as if finding this might offer her some relief from the rage she felt toward Andy. Quickly she left the bookstore and locked the door, the key sounding loud as she turned it. Fog had moved in to Greenport and the deep bellowed horn sounded through her body. She pulled the hood of her jacket over her head, walking down the streets, remembering how the fog had unsettled her when she first came to Nova Scotia, making her feel blinded. But now she was grateful for its great watery veil that protected her from being seen. Petey's accident was big news in the town and she didn't want to answer questions.

In the library, she fingered through the card catalog: *Waves and Beaches: The Dynamics of the Ocean Surface* by Willard Bascom. Scanning the shelves, she found it, a paperback dense and small, part of the Science Study series. She read on the back cover:

> *Is there anyone who can watch without fascination the struggle for the supremacy between land and sea? The sea attacks relentlessly, marshaling the force of its powerful waves against the land's strongest points. It collects the energy of distant winds and transports it across thousands of miles of open ocean as quietly rolling swell. On nearing shore this calm disguise is suddenly cast off, and the waves rise up in angry breakers, hurling themselves against the land in a final furious assault.*

She studied Willard Bascom's face, his intelligent, scientific eyes. He *knows*, she thought. Then she turned the pages to chapter IV: *Waves in Shallow Water*:

> *As these various waves approach the shore and move across shallow water they react in special ways. They reflect, diffract, and refract—which means that they are turned back by vertical obstacles, spread their energy into*

the water...and bend to fit a gradually shoaling bottom. The great low waves of the deep sea may move up an estuary with an abrupt steep-front... Shallow-water waves have just as complicated characters as deep-water waves, and they are likely to be more interesting, because it is in shallow water that they most affect mankind.

Getting out her journal and pen, she wrote beneath the pale hum of the library's fluorescent lights. Her hand was shaking and made her writing crooked. She looked over her shoulder, and no one was around except the clerk at the desk. She got up and brought the Encyclopedia Britannica to her table.

Rogue waves are an open water phenomenon, in which circumstances cause a wave to briefly form to become far larger than the "average" large wave in that time and place. The basic underlying physics that makes rogue waves possible is that different gravity waves can travel at different speeds, and so they can pile up at random. Once considered mythical and lacking hard evidence for their existence, rogue waves are now proven to exist and are known to be a natural ocean phenomenon.

According to this hypothesis, coast shape or seabed shape directs several small waves to meet in phase. Their crest heights combine to create a freak wave.

Waves from one current are driven into an opposing current. This results in a shortening of wavelength, causing shoaling (i.e., increase in wave height), and oncoming wave trains to compress together into a rogue wave.

It seems possible to have a rogue wave occur by natural, nonlinear processes from a random background of smaller waves. In such a case, it is hypothesized, an unusual, unstable wave type may form which 'sucks' energy from other waves, growing to a near-vertical monster itself, before becoming too unstable and collapsing shortly after.

"Kate?"

Startled from her concentration, Kate looked up. Kenny stood at the far end of the table, his blond hair waving over his questioning blue eyes.

"Oh, Kenny," she said, flustered from being seen. She put her hands over her notes, her eyes still drenched in the hollow of waves. He walked a few steps closer, and sensing her distress, whispered, "Is there anything I can do to help you and Andy?"

A flow of people began coming into the library, and Kate realized she should leave this place. She wiped her eyes as if to free herself from the notes she'd written.

"Thank you," she replied, breathing in and letting Kenny see her exhausted eyes. "Can you look out for the bookstore? I mean…check the mail. We could come in and sign some checks if we need to…"

"Sure, of course. Do you want it open for a few hours during the day, perhaps?"

"Oh, do you have the time?" Her voice strained to ask this.

"Yes. I have the time to help you and Andy out in any way I can." Kenny's voice was sincere, and Kate noticed he included Andy every time he offered help.

And then he said, "I'm so sorry about Petey…"

The murmuring of people was hurting her ears now and she had to leave. "Kenny, will you walk me outside please?" she asked, as she noticed a few people staring, many recognizing her from the bookstore. She put her hood over her head, closed the books, and gathered her journal and pen. Kenny took her arm and guided her carefully out the door. She realized again how real Petey's accident was, and now that the world knew it, she was being forced to know it again too.

— 66 —

VAN CAME BACK FROM HIS NIGHT SHIFT at the plant and climbed into bed to sleep in the early morning. Soon after Verlene got up to go to work, a knock at the door woke Ivan up. He rubbed his eyes and staggered from his bed to the kitchen door. Will stood outside in a sweep of rainy air. Ivan shivered, seeing his father's face.

"What is it?" Ivan asked.

"It's Andy. He's down on the rocks. He needs help." Will's eyes penetrated Ivan's.

"Where?" Will turned and pointed down beneath the house, and the fog pulled back, showing the rocks that stretched along the shoreline.

Ivan dressed and went quickly from the house down towards the shore. When he got close to the water, he saw Andy curled up, half on the rock and half on a bed of seaweed. His khaki pants were gray with dirt, and his shirttail flapped in the small breeze.

Ivan stepped up close. Andy's hair was matted against his head, and his beard—unshaven since the accident—lined a dark, irregular pattern over the lower side of his face. A rum bottle was cradled in his arms.

"Let's lift him, now," Will said.

Ivan crouched beside Andy, the water close and lapping at his feet. He reached out to Andy's shoulder, but Andy didn't respond.

Will got on one side of him, Ivan on the other. Andy groaned with each move but he didn't resist as they hauled him up from the shore.

= 67 =

VAN DROVE FROM SLATE HARBOR, the road twisting through the rocks with the bends he knew by heart, the grid of the village disappearing behind him, the wharves in the cove, the houses up on the rocks. He knew taking Andy to the detox center in Halifax was the right thing to do.

Andy hadn't resisted being taken off; he hadn't even asked where they were going. Like a child, he'd followed Ivan and Will to the car after Verlene had made the call to admit him.

Ivan looked over at Andy, his head bent back on the car seat, eyes closed, mouth open. The motion of the car had put him to sleep and Ivan was glad. Sleep was a good thing for Andy now, a good thing, he thought, even though he couldn't help but think of Kate. Strange how their lovemaking seemed such a small part of what was happening now. What would she do now that Andy was gone? A small fear of losing her welled up inside him.

"We're doing the right thing for you now, hear me, Andy?"

Andy's eyes opened slightly, and he looked over at Ivan. "I'm a failure, Ivan." He turned his face to the window and began to cry.

Ivan wanted to tell Andy that his loving Kate was a big mistake and he was sorry and somehow they would recover from all this.

Ivan pushed his fingers through his hair.

He remembered how much he had dreaded Will coming home after being in the hospital so long. Ivan could still feel the revulsion when he first looked at his father coming through the door, his face ghostly with blue and red and black lines of stitched flesh.

He remembered the fishermen coming to welcome Will home—"Good man, Will!" "Glad to be home, not." "You look good, you." And how he and Lena worried that Will would end up down on the rocks with them again.

But he left the fishermen and came back to the house.

And then, they sat around the table, and Lena dished out the hot scallops and vegetables on her best porcelain plates, the sound of the metal servers clinking, low sunlight falling across the tablecloth.

"Welcome home, Will," she said.

— 68 —

KATE ALWAYS THOUGHT OF PETEY SLEEPING NOW, as she memorized the small hairs of his eyebrows and lashes, the full ripeness of his lips. Though she waited every day for him to wake up, she'd grown calm with his being at rest, she liked to call it. She'd watch the screen revealing his heartbeat and she'd study the needle in his arm that fed him and the breathing tube in his mouth, and she imagined him growing a bit each day as he always had, and she'd massage the muscles of his legs and arms and tell herself that she had all the patience in the world for him to wake up.

She could still see the heat in his cheeks when he ran over the yellow fields. She could still see him holding his model British Spitfire fighter plane and mimicking engine sounds as he flew it through the air.

One afternoon, she went to the small United Church on the edge of Slate Harbour. No one was there and she walked into the silence of this sacred place and knelt in the wooden pew. Looking up at the cross in the vestibule, she thought of the first time she went to church with Margaret. A warm peace flowed through her body as she thought of the angels in Margaret's painting; the way they flew in triads out of columns of light. Now she was relieved to be in front of an altar again with angels behind it and prayed to those angels to wake Petey up.

Her father had brought her that painting on his last trip. She needed to find it, and unwrap it.

 app

There were days when she didn't feel patient. In fact, some days when she was purely agitated. That's when she tried to remember the good times. Like that one time walking with Petey along the shore. The tide was at its lowest ebb, and they were headed to look for gold in the cave and the rocks smelled sweet.

A shape loosened up in their gaze, six feet up from the sea's edge. Not hard like stone, this shape had a ridge of fur. Blown seagrass whipped around it. They walked closer; the shape did not move. Gulls loomed around them, and the smell of washed-up oyster shells.

"It's a baby seal," Kate said.

"Is he dead?" asked Petey.

The baby seal was still, its fur gray-streaked, head tucked under. Though gusts of wind blew hard, no life responded.

"Maybe it's hurt," Kate said, worried.

They arched over the seal, wondering what to do. Petey reached for a piece of driftwood. "Maybe we should return him to the sea," he said.

"Perhaps."

Petey began to push the wood beneath the seal's small body.

Suddenly its head rose up. Startled, Petey stepped back. They both could see the seal's brown and murky eyes, and that it was startled too.

"It's alive!" Petey whispered.

Within seconds, a dark shape rose from the sea. Turning, they saw a large seal staring right at them. The mother seal. There was no sound except the breaking of the water.

Quickly, as if it had been summoned, the baby seal awkwardly wriggled towards the ocean.

"The seal was sleeping while the mother fished," Kate guessed.

And just before the little seal dove back in the water, it turned and gave a quick look back at Petey, before disappearing into the sea.

Did Kate dream this, now in the hospital room? She believed she could find a way to wake Petey up. So she went over and stood beside him lying in his bed. Nudging his arm, she waited for his eyes to open. They did not. She nudged him again, and called out, *Petey*. But he didn't wake up.

ฅฅ

Back home from the hospital, Kate looked out over the cove in Slate Harbour. The *Lena* was tied at the end of the wharf, her hull so still on the windless water. A figure moved on board, and Kate guessed it was Will.

The sun blazed from the sky as she approached the wharf. Will did not hear her coming; he was bent over, scrubbing the deck. Water sounds rocked along the hull.

"Will," Kate called out.

Will looked up, his thick brows under his cap. He got to his feet, holding the large yellow sponge in his hand. Surprised, he tipped back his cap. Gulls cried.

Kate spoke. "I had to come down here."

"Yep." Will's gray eyes squinted over the water.

"What do you think?" Kate's voice was low.

Will took in a deep breath, folded his arms tight against his chest. "Kate, I wasn't out there, now."

"Where was Petey thrown?"

"Where?"

"I need to know."

Kate lowered herself onto the deck of the Cape Islander, the smell of gas and salt overwhelming her. Will put the sponge down on the railing of the boat. He reached over, lifted the canvas off the engine box, and drew it back. Underneath, the cold black metal of the engine sat in the shadow of the canvas, gas fumes rising in the air. Kate's eyes traveled over the angles and smooth curves of the engine and the dull layer of grease that coated them.

"There's nothing sharp," she said.

Will nodded. "He hit the edge of the box."

Kate leaned back against the railing of the boat, her breath gone.

Will flipped the canvas back over the engine.

"It's never safe out on that water." Will sat on the railing, crossed his legs. Then he looked directly at Kate, his eyes penetrating. "The way I figure it, Andy got out on a shoal off the point. A roller came across it, lifted the boat, and knocked Petey onto the engine."

Kate looked out past the point over the surface of the ocean.

"Most shoals are marked," Will went on. "But not all of them. See, in shoal water, the waves from under the boat get different. They're short, tight heaves, you. When the wind blows up, and there's a ground sea on, a roller can come in, just like that, you, and swamp your boat."

Kate sat, heavy on the railing, thinking of the notes she'd taken at the library. "Andy blames himself," she said finally, "for not putting the cover of the engine box back on."

Will turned and spat into the water. "I know," he said, tipping back his cap. "Shoal water's a dangerous place to be, see. It's like being caught between two places. You're not out on the deep water, and you're not inshore, on land, see. You're in the place in-between, and that's dangerous. Petey hit his head on a sharp point, and that sharp point was there with or without the cover. God knows, I'm not trying to make excuses for Andy... Forgive me, Kate, if I sound that way."

Kate and Will sat facing each other for a long time. The afternoon sun deepened its heat on their backs and Kate, exhausted and no longer able to think, leaned over the railing to look down into the water. A brilliant green wave swept in the sun's low tide and she smelled the rockweed along the shoreline. There was a lapping motion, and for one moment she was not on the railing, she was somewhere else where there was no longer the unbearable weight of sorrow. Perhaps she was like those seals swimming far beyond this day.

Bending close to the water's surface, she heard a voice and looked up. In the wharf's shadow, she saw Ivan, who reached out his hand toward her. "Don't fall in, now," he said softly.

69

WHEN KATE JUMPED UP ONTO THE WHARF. Ivan didn't let go of her hand.

"Andy's now in the detox center in Halifax," Ivan said finally, his voice quiet as his eyes looked into hers.

Kate leaned into him then, nodding. "Yes, thank you, Ivan." The words caught in her throat.

They leaned closer, and Ivan brushed away the hair that blew across her face, his fingertips lightly on her skin.

Blindly he led Kate to Lena's front door, and then stopped and turned toward her. He let Kate see the war in his eyes. "Andy will do fine in detox," he made himself say. "It's good that he's there. I'll drive you to Halifax to see him anytime, Kate..."

Kate clung to Ivan's hand. She stepped closer. "Ivan, I—"

"He'll want to see you," Ivan interrupted, drawing away his hand. He could hear Craig through Lena's door. "I'll come see you later."

Ivan turned and waved as he walked away.

— 70 —

HOURS LATER, Kate walked out to the end of Skerry Point. She had just kissed Craig and put him into bed. When he had fallen into a deep sleep, she knew she had to go outside. She longed for some fresh air.

Now Kate walked through the windswept grass fired by the setting sun and looked out to the northeast over the Atlantic. She imagined that Ivan might find her here. She lay down in the field. The air was darkening into purple light while the line of the horizon began to fade between the water and sky, and she listened to the rhythmic heave of the Atlantic breaking at the foot of the cliff.

Staring at the rocks, she saw seals emerge from the watery lift of the sea, their forms absorbing the last of the evening's light. She watched them raise their heads as they sniffed the wind and she counted five or six, huddled close together. A large one moved its flipper down the rocky ledge. A wave came up, and the seal rolled into it.

Ivan said her name. "Kate."

She heard the sound but she couldn't respond.

"Kate." A hand touched her gently on the shoulder.

In the dim light, they could barely see each other's eyes. His smell was warm and strong as he lay down beside her.

"Ivan. I was watching the seals," Kate said. She pushed her hand along the muscles of his back that were beginning to feel more familiar to her.

"I love you, Kate, all this time," he whispered, his breath steamy against her face. He unbuttoned her blouse and slipped his hand over her breast and held it there. Together they sank and lay still for a few moments, until Ivan pressed harder and Kate helped Ivan pull down her jeans all the way off from her feet, and then he lowered his own as though peeling back the skin from his body. Lying in their nakedness, Kate tried to lift herself from the itchy grass so that Ivan could come inside her, but Ivan moved farther up, he could not come inside her, as if Andy and the accident were too real in his mind, and he held himself raw on top of her, shuddering. They rolled—heated—feeling their love for whatever it could be on this night, one on top of the other, until Ivan burst into the soft well of Kate's belly.

Panting, they lay there, holding each other tightly. Kate felt a shiver run through Ivan; she felt his comfort. The warm fluid spread in a trickle down her side, and Ivan lifted himself off her, and leaned on one elbow, looking down at Kate.

"I do know our love isn't wrong, Ivan," she said, drawing her hand down.

Flattening her palm, she pressed his semen into her skin and then drew it up like a fine oil over her breast, where she rubbed it in a small circle around her nipple. Then she moved her hand down onto her thighs and, drawing in her breath, smelled the evening air mixed with Ivan.

"It smells like the sea, Ivan," she said in a whisper. "It smells like life..."

Ivan kissed her forehead, her cheeks, and her eyes as she stroked herself with the thick, milky fluid. And as Ivan caressed her while she spread his semen into a perfect film over her body, they dozed in each other's arms while the night air closed in around them.

= 71 =

THE NEXT MORNING, Kate stood in the window. She had
barely slept, yet her whole body felt light. The sun lifted
over the Atlantic and brightened the stones of the harbor,
and she let the rays pour over her. Her eyes followed two Cape
Islanders going out through the mist of the channel onto the
ocean floor and she wondered if Ivan was watching them like
she was, or hearing them like she was, and the knock of their
gasoline engines slightly shook the walls of the old house.

Kate looked out toward the point where she had lain with
Ivan, and the summer grass—lit with dew—sparkled in a
storm of crystals. The exaggeration of light had a calming effect
on Kate, for it reflected her mood that did not ask whether it
had been right or wrong to be with Ivan. It was a part of these
last days when reality and unreality crossed back and forth
from each other, and the only thing true was the crossing.

She turned from the window and went up the stairs to
Craig's room. She turned the brass knob. The door opened into
his room where a drawn canvas shade held back the blazing light
of early morning. It clicked against the window with a rattling
sound, and in the dimness of the opposite corner, Kate saw
Craig's head sunken in the pillows, his small body contoured
under the thin plaid blanket spread on his bed. Joy filled her

almost dizzily as she stepped closer, and she leaned over his bed. His breath—with its slow meter—had a musical sound.

She looked around the room, and the sight of Petey's model planes in Craig's room flooded her eyes—planes Andy helped to build—and for the first time she felt overwhelmed by Andy's loss and not by her own. It was Andy who had been there through Petey's terrible accident.

Should she have known months ago to take Andy to detox? She had known vaguely that detox was where the fishermen got put when they were too drunk to work. But she had never thought about it for Andy.

A crash came from downstairs. Startled, she went down and into the kitchen. Verlene was on the floor, picking up pieces of lasagne.

This would be her weakest moment, facing her friend. It was too late to change what happened; and even if she'd had that chance, she would not want to change it. For a moment, she wanted to be asleep upstairs. She couldn't stand looking into Verlene's eyes with the guilt inside her. Was what happened with Ivan already half-ruined? Was it going to be reduced to sleeping with your best friend's husband? There was Verlene on her floor, cleaning up the dish she'd made. Her blond curls were bouncing around her face as she navigated picking up the mess.

She looked up. "Oh, Kate, I'm so clumsy." She shoveled some of the lasagne back into the metal pan. "I think you can still eat some of this, your floor isn't that dirty…"

Verlene stopped then and looked at Kate, who stood unmoving by the kitchen hallway. Kate opened her mouth, but no words could come out.

"Are you okay?" Verlene asked, looking confused.

"Oh, I... I was just upstairs looking at Craig while he was sleeping, wishing Petey would wake up."

"Kate, just know I'm here to help you in any way I can." Verlene turned away, continuing her cleaning. As Kate watched Verlene wipe the floor and straighten some salvaged lasagna back in the pan, she knew she could not save her from being hurt.

She walked over and put her hand on Verlene's shoulder. "I'm sorry it's such a hard time right now, Verlene. I barely know myself anymore..." At least this is true, she thought.

Verlene looked at Kate. She put the remaining lasagna on the stove and took a deep breath.

"Okay," she said, straightening her hair. "I shouldn't have brought this so early. I probably woke you up. In any case, I have to be off to work now."

Verlene turned and went back out the kitchen door, and Kate watched her walk against the wind coming hard over the point.

ᚱᚲ

With some urgency, Kate opened the door to the attic. Here were stored boxes—books, clothes, dishware, childhood things her father had brought her—and Kate moved the boxes, smelling cardboard mixed with the old woody air. After a short time, she found a box with "fragile" marked on it. Eagerly she peeled back the masking tape, opened the four flaps at the top. Bunched newspaper surrounded a rectangular piece wrapped in a layer of tissue paper. Kate carefully uncovered it, and Margaret's painting lay in her hands. Kate had forgotten how the painting shimmered in its mirrored frame, even in the dim attic light. She searched the familiar images—Margaret in a white uniform, with soft gray hair, holding a young girl's hands Kate knew to be herself.

Tears burned in her eyes. She gazed at the painting as if she were seeking her innocence again, the child standing there in a green meadow beneath a cobalt sky. Small childlike beings flew over their heads, their faces with serene expressions, their small wings sprouted from their backs. She remembered how this painting had leaned on the altar beside her crayon drawings, and she wondered why she had kept it wrapped and put away. She remembered how she had danced with the angel and how that had comforted her. Now she wanted to bring that comfort to Craig.

Hurriedly, Kate took the painting from the attic, ran down to the cellar to get a hammer and nails from Andy's workbench. Then she ran back upstairs to Craig's bedroom—it was now seven o' clock—and Craig was just rolling over in his bed, rubbing his eyes.

"Hi, Mommy," he said.

"Hi, Craig," Kate said, distracted, searching the walls of his room. Her eyes landed on a spot just over the head of Craig's bed. But she would have to move the dog poster.

"What's that, Mommy?"

Kate walked over and sat down on Craig's bed. "I have something to show you," she said, holding out the picture for Craig to see. The glass of the frame reflected parts of their faces as they looked at the watercolor.

"A special person painted this. Can I put this over your bed? It might mean we'd have to move your dog poster."

Craig looked behind him, then turned around again. He considered the picture. "Why are the babies flying?"

"Because they are angels, and angels can fly. Angels can help you when you are sad. They helped me when I was sad."

"Really?"

They both sat for a moment, regarding the watercolor.

Then Craig looked at Kate. "Okay," he said.

"Okay?"

"You can put it over my bed."

Kate felt almost giddy. She stood up, took the dog poster down, and hung Margaret's painting over Craig's bed. It beamed from the flat space of the wall.

"Where do you want me to hang the dog poster?" Kate asked, and Craig pointed, "Oh, over there," even though he was still staring at the angels.

ATER, AFTER LENA took Craig for the afternoon, Kate didn't go to the hospital. She needed to be outside, so she headed for Skerry Point. She was agitated, with very little sleep. Walking to the cliff edge, she knew the path that dropped to the sea. She stepped her way down.

What if she went to the cave? What if she challenged herself now? The air roared around her and the waves heaved in slow, rhythmic rolls.

The tide was low, and Kate grappled along the slippery rocks to the mouth of the cave. She remembered her fear when Andy first brought her here, the same fear she had now, watching the waves beat inside a place she couldn't see.

Balancing her body, she climbed just above the hissing water, sea drops pricking her skin, a chill numbing her fingers that gripped the rock. Deeper inside the chamber, steamy water blanketed her face, the inner rock grew dark around her.

Sucked into the stone, she pushed herself on. Her mind loosened up, and she knew the danger she felt was more in her mind than in the cave. She was so tired of blame; for Andy, for herself, for the horrible pain, for the alcohol, the wave, the engine cover; she had to push herself on now. She was angry— why hadn't she insisted on seeing Dr. Russell, telling him about

Andy's drinking? How could two intelligent men sit in therapy and not get to the bottom of Andy's addiction?

The water sloshed back and forth, covering her ankles. She saw the pyrite thread like gold through the black rock and she imagined Andy and Ivan hunting for it. She could understand how they had become friends here, small boys out of time from the world. It made her shiver, the thought of betrayal. She was inside her own chaos now.

A shape traversed the field of light outside the cave's opening. Kate looked, her hands braced on the rock. A seal appeared on the water outside, its head arched, its black eyes centered on her. It swam closer, and Kate saw its sweet expression: eyes full of skylight.

She knew it was time to leave.

Stronger waves came in, shook her off balance. Within seconds, the sea surged around Kate's thighs while she held onto the gravelly ledges and let herself slither, half-crawling through the water, pulling herself with her hands through the rock. More surf came in and, beginning to swim now, she stared at the cave's opening with vigilance, her face now in the roar of water that was not too cold. She managed to slip out from the cave mouth, clawing the stone that bit her skin, and just before another wave struck, she pulled herself up and high onto a boulder. The tide was coming in swiftly.

She lay back on the shore, her whole body drenched, a cut from the rock bruising her arm. Her nose burned from inhaling water, and she peered down the shoreline.

It seemed that whenever a seal appeared in a time of danger, it gave back life to those who saw it, and to those who believed in it. Then slipped back beneath the water.

73

THREE DAYS LATER, Kate sat beside Petey in the hospital room. She'd drifted off to sleep to the sound of Petey's breathing, and woke up with a start, feeling someone watching her.

She looked up.

Petey's eyes were open, and he was looking in her direction.

Tears of disbelief sprang into her eyes as she got up and walked over to him. Superstitious about her movements, she worried that if she made too much noise, Petey would close his eyes again.

She leaned over and looked at him.

Petey blinked, lids hovering over his eyes, puzzled by the brightness around him. All this seemed to gather in thick light beneath his eyelashes, and he was hesitant to look at her, as if he wasn't sure where he was. Kate knew she was watching someone returning from an underworld, a place far too deep for her to imagine, after these long two weeks. She looked into his eyes, his pupils dilated black, with huge iridescent circles around them. Their crystal gray radiance overwhelmed her, as if she were looking right into the heart of the rogue wave. She grew faint and clung to the bed rail.

Petey looked as if he might recognize her.

Kate put her hands around his face and kissed him. He tried to smile.

"Petey's eyes are open!" she cried out to the nurses.

Turbulence, the nurses and doctor came running.

They circled around Petey. Some moments passed while they watched Petey blink. Then the doctor leaned in.

Do you know your name?

Petey.

Do you know where you live?

A nod of the head.

Do you know how old you are?

A nod of the head.

Do you know where your mother is?

And Petey looked at Kate.

≡74≡

WHEN IVAN WAVED, Kate stopped the car, the dry dust of late summer circling them. He'd not seen her since Petey woke, only congratulated her by phone. She rolled the window down.

"Where are you off to?" he asked softly.

Kate's lips were unsteady. "There's a lot to do," she said. "I'm talking to the doctor today about how soon we can bring Petey home. And then, I need to be in touch with Andy. I called and told him Petey woke from his coma. And my father and Lizzie are coming the day after tomorrow. They want to help."

Ivan nodded, hearing the strong tone in her voice different from before. He reached through the window, put his hand against Kate's cheek. She turned her head so that her lips rested in his palm, and their warmth mixed with his skin and the memory of their lovemaking.

"Have a good trip," Ivan said in a low voice.

She looked back up. "Thank you, Ivan."

"Can I see you later tonight?"

"Yes."

Relief lifted his spirits. *Yes,* she had said, and this calmed him. What a beautiful word, he thought, *Yes.*

ﬡﬡ

At five that same evening, Ivan sat at the kitchen table, waiting for Verlene to come home. At a distance, he saw Karl on the *Lena* tied to the wharf. They had made plans to go fishing.

The door opened and Verlene walked in with a bag of groceries. Ivan pushed his mug away and sat back from the table.

"Ivan," Verlene said. "I thought you'd be at work."

"I took the day off." Ivan drew in his breath.

She turned and faced him. "Ivan, what's happened?"

"I don't like working at the plant. I need some time to think it over."

"But, Ivan, you're a supervisor, it's a good job..."

Ivan stood up and walked over to Verlene. He looked down into her face, her eyes, and her blond curls. He saw how they had both lived here much longer than their own lives—a life longer than Lena's and Will's and Karl's—and that they shared this together. They exchanged this knowledge in the way they looked at each other now without speaking.

"I'm in love with Kate," Ivan said.

"I know," Verlene said, tears filling her eyes.

"I don't want to hurt you, Verlene," he said, but Verlene turned away. She put her hands on the counter, held her head down.

"It won't work, Ivan." Her voice was angry. "You're from two *different* worlds." Defiantly, she began putting the groceries away.

Ivan stood in silence, watching Verlene, listening to the thumping sounds of cereal boxes and juice, vegetables and toilet paper. In the pit of his stomach, he wondered if Verlene was right. Then he said, "I'm going out with Karl on the *Lena* this evening. We're going to jig for some cod."

The tears now were cascading down her face, her mascara in dark stream over her cheeks. She wiped her face with the edge of her blouse, and the only thing Ivan could take refuge in was not lying to Verlene. A profound sorrow overwhelmed him.

He walked to the door, calling back, "Good-bye, Verlene," but she did not respond.

∾

Outside he quickened his pace to the wharf. Gulls lifted from the pilings. Karl was ready, starting up the engine. Ivan released the line from the cleats.

"Feels good to take a day off, you! And take the *Lena* out!" Karl called back, as he pointed the bow of the boat out of the harbor.

"Yep!" Ivan called, coiling the line.

"That's pretty wonderful Petey woke up, not."

"You bet!"

"Lena guesses Kate might move with the boys back to the States."

Ivan's heart stopped then, the sea air whipping around him while he coiled the lines. *Yes,* he heard her voice say. *Yes,* he could see her tonight.

"Really," he said to Karl.

Karl looked him. "It might be the best thing, you. I'm sure her father would look after them, you know, until she got settled and all."

Ivan couldn't bring himself to say anything.

"You can't blame her for not wanting to be with Andy."

Ivan grew light-headed. And what *were* his dreams?

"I'm quitting my job, Karl," he said. The sea smelled sweet and sang to him.

"You've got a good job, now, Ivan."

"Yeah, everyone tells me that."

"Don't go romanticizing fishing," Karl said, raising his voice over the knock of the engine. "Go work for the Coast Guard if you want to be on the sea." Karl looked straight ahead of him, out across the broad reach of the Atlantic, and the ocean swell rocked the *Lena* as they moved out from the harbor.

Ivan turned, watching the shoreline grow smaller. Maybe all that mattered was that he had told Kate how much he loved her, and anything after that wasn't important.

I T WASN'T EASY FOR KATE TO TELL IVAN she was going to move back to the States. Even more, she knew she needed to see Andy before she left. Lizzie and her father had come to help her pack and be with Petey and Craig, so she drove to Halifax on a Sunday afternoon.

The fog combed over her as she got out of the car. Kate knew she was on the opposite side of the dream that had first led her to Nova Scotia. She walked to the front door of the big understated building that sat beside the harbor. Her body was numb as she went inside, the white walls and gray rugs with the faint smell of dried flowers floating around her. She walked up to the front desk and a pale-eyed receptionist greeted her.

"I'm here to see Andy Farrell," she said, her chest thumping so hard she became light-headed.

Within minutes, Andy walked down the hall and came up to her tentatively, his gray eyes more vibrant than she remembered, and gave her a polite hug. Kate had never experienced this before; how someone you once loved could feel so distant. They sat down in the modest chairs in the vestibule and Andy looked at her with a calmness Kate wished she could possess. His black hair was combed back from his forehead and he looked unusually rested.

"Thanks for coming," he said.

"Yes." She fidgeted. "I wanted to see you and assure you that Petey is going to be okay. He's beginning to speak more coherently and his motor skills are good."

"That's good to hear," he said, putting his head down, looking between his knees in his customary way. "I think of Petey, and Craig too, all the time."

"Andy," she said, "I know my words were harsh. Yes, I wish you hadn't taken Petey out, but I know you didn't cause the accident."

He looked away.

She went on nervously. "There's so much I wish to say to you now. I'm so glad you're getting help in this place."

She looked around, seeing some people walk down the hallway, a few scattered nurses in uniform. She remembered her days at the Harbour House.

"Yes, I'm learning, and it might take a long time," Andy finally said. "I'm lucky to be here, to get ahold of things, you know what I mean."

"Yes. We should have known this sooner."

"It was my mistake. I thought I could do it on my own."

"Andy," she said. "I fell in love with Ivan. I betrayed you. I'm sorry." Kate began to cry, she couldn't help herself, and the room turned askew with the truth she spoke out loud to him.

"I know," he said, still clenching his hands.

"I know it interfered with what was happening to us."

"We were a mess, Kate."

"I'm going back to New York," Kate said. "My father will help out financially for a while, and I've found a special school for Petey."

He took a deep breath. "That sounds good," he finally said. "And you?"

"I don't know. I will be here for a while. I might fix up that space over the bookstore, where I can live. I can't imagine going back to the house."

"Yes, I understand."

Then Andy stood up, taking Kate by surprise that he wanted to say good-bye so quickly. She stood up too and could feel Andy trying to keep his composure. "Have a safe trip," he whispered. "Thanks for coming… Tell the boys I love them."

And he turned abruptly, and Kate could see him breaking down somewhere deep inside his chest as he walked with long strides down the hall.

═ 76 ═

HEY LEFT IN THE EARLY MORNING, just when the sun rose from the east. Long streams of gold flowed over the ocean while Will, Lena, and Ivan waved good-bye. Kate's father drove the small U-Haul trailer, and Kate and the boys were in Lizzie's cream-colored Volvo station wagon. Even in the six years Kate lived here, there wasn't too much to take; other than clothes, sentimental things she'd collected, and some furniture and toys for the boys. All the rest belonged to the Tannard house.

Ivan watched them slip up through the village and disappear over the rocks. By now, he was staying at Will and Lena's, who didn't ask questions, but understood what was happening. They didn't flinch when Ivan told them, "I've applied to the Coast Guard. I quit my job at the plant."

And now, he'd be on his way. The Coast Guard had called him. He figured it would take him a couple of hours to drive to Point Edward. He wanted to get a good night's sleep for his interview in the morning.

Just after dark he walked out once more to the Tannard house. Those same steps he took years ago, when he'd run out there for a smoke, crawl through the broken window, and sit on the crate barrel, listening to the Atlantic's eternal rumble.

313

They'd left the house unlocked since Will would look after it until Andy returned. But Ivan knew Andy didn't want to come back here.

He turned the knob and stepped inside. Smells of fresh wax, newspaper, and cardboard lingered. Plastic toys now gone. They'd left the house so clean, and the furniture in the living room was placed neatly around the big window facing the sea.

He grabbed a chair and put it in the middle of the room where he used to smoke, for old time's sake. It felt strange to be the trespasser now, since it was Andy who'd been the trespasser those years ago.

He peered through the windows, the view still the same out toward the reef in the Atlantic. He looked around, a pit forming in his stomach, knowing what he was going to do. He remembered the day he'd learned that the old house had sold, his great sorrow. He remembered digging potatoes for Lena when Will was in the hospital, and throwing himself into the dirt and sobbing. He remembered wanting the house to die like a respectful old man, and how he dug a grave for it with his bare hands.

He got up and went to the kitchen. He found some matches beside the woodstove and went back into the middle of the room. He stood for a while, his reality upside down now with Kate leaving and Andy being in detox. This house should have died a long time ago and none of these things would have happened. He knew Basil Tannard had tried to warn them. All along it should have been Basil's house after he returned from the sea. Basil's ghost must be tired now, and lonely. It was time for everyone to leave.

Ivan went to the fireplace and found some newspaper and kindling. He returned to the living room and knelt beside the small table with an old lamp at the end of the sofa. The old lamp would have faulty wiring going into the socket in the wall—he knew this as a fireman. He crumpled the newspaper right under the table, made a tent of kindling around it. Then he brought four pieces of larger wood from the woodbin, leaned them around the table stand. He struck the match and lit the paper. He knew now he was in a dream, watching himself from afar.

The flame caught, ate up the paper, and leaned into the kindling, crackling. Ivan stood up and walked to the door. When he turned around, he saw the fire beginning to burn strongly into the larger pieces of wood, catching the table and the chair in its blaze. Everything seemed to be in slow motion as Ivan stood there watching. The rug began to smolder and light up too. Then the sofa beside the chair, and the small table at the other end of the sofa. Heat and cracking sounds exploded in the air.

That's when Ivan thought it was safe to leave. He knew the fire wouldn't take very long to catch other things. The lamps, the curtains, the old wood chairs resting under the window sills.

He went out the door and walked up the path. He turned to look back and saw fire filling up the living room through the windows. He could hear the window glass shattering, then the first flame reach out and stroke the western side of the house.

Pretty soon everyone would see it.

He ran. Once more, he was running from fire. But this time it was a good thing. This time he didn't see Will, he saw only the ghosts of the past that would finally disappear. He got into his car and drove through the village, knowing he'd have enough time to get to Point Edward. He would stay in a motel and get a good night's sleep for his interview in the morning.

77

THREE MONTHS LATER, Kate got up from her bed and walked down the hall of her New York City rental apartment. She walked down to the door next to her own and leaned in to it, listening. Her boys slept behind that door but she didn't try to turn the knob. She knew she must learn to believe they were safe inside their room.

Outside the hall window, the early morning began to grow its light through the broad east coast sky. She was relieved she could not see the sea.

Kate put her head against the door. The old paint smelled oddly fresh. She didn't cry and was struck by the healing nature of time. She thought about Lena and how she owed her a letter. Today, after the boys leave for school, she'd write her.

Lena frequently appeared in Kate's dreams, the good ones that didn't wake her. They came during the day with Lena sitting quietly in a sunlit room of her memory. Lena who had welcomed Kate right from the beginning to Slate Harbour.

Dearest Lena,

Thank you for your letter! I so appreciate the clothes you sent for Petey and Craig. You know the things they love to wear so well! Petey particularly loved the brown down jacket. It fits him perfectly and will keep him very warm through the winter. The T-shirts are wonderful and will be well worn.

Today was a good day. I took Petey to school (he is in first grade) and helped in the classroom. I like Petey's special education teacher who is young and very kind. Petey calls her Marmar, even though her name is Marcia. Really that is quite close, don't you think? He's getting much better at pronouncing letters, and I have confidence his speech will improve over time. Please find the enclosed pictures!

Craig is enjoying preschool very much and believes he is a big boy going there at the same time Petey goes to school.

Being back in New York City is an adjustment, but the school system is good and I'm getting to know the parents in my boys' classes. The city has very good special education programs. The kids are nice to Petey and have problems like he does. But really, Lena, if someone were to meet Petey for the first time and not know how he'd been before, you might just think he was almost a normal boy.

Andy and I are working out custody for the boys. He might leave Nova Scotia eventually and come here to be closer to them. He has not relapsed as far as I can tell, but I do still feel nervous. That's nice of you to report that Farrell's Books continues to do well in Greenport. I'm glad Andy is living in the small apartment above the store— it's good for him to be back at work.

As for the Tannard house, I still don't know what to say... I'm glad they've determined faulty wiring was the cause of the fire. Maybe it's for the best the old house is gone... Maybe now Basil can be at peace.

Ivan will be coming tonight, and I will be excited to see him. I'm curious to see how he will like the city! Thank you for your advice about Verlene, and I agree with you that she's a very strong person. I'm glad to hear she is dating.

I miss you, Lena. Give my love to everyone.

Much love to you,

Kate

Kate put down her pen and prepared to seal the letter. Later tonight, she'd wait for Ivan to arrive. The late-night traffic shouldn't be too bad. She marveled that he was now attending the Canadian Coast Guard College in Point Edward, Nova Scotia, and that she was now in New York City. He was driving his truck to visit her during his time off. This was who they were now. Still, when she closed her eyes, the sun blazed over the ocean while the wind made shapes through the grass. Shoulders of fog were just coming up over the point and she was watching Ivan come up to her garden on the tractor. He was waving at her.

᠄᠄

Later, in bed beside him, Kate pressed her naked body against his, and told him, "I'm proud of you, Ivan."

He rolled and kissed her. They embraced and made love in the smell of clean sheets. Though they smelled fresh, she missed hanging the wash out on the line the way she did in Nova Scotia. The large sheets filling up like sails going downwind. And now while they touched each other, she smelled Ivan's salty skin and she saw the Atlantic.

In the morning, she made breakfast. The boys were happy to see Ivan and roughhoused with him, and Ivan was careful with Petey. After the boys had gone to school, they sat together in the kitchen.

"How is Verlene?" Kate asked, tentatively.

"She's filed for divorce. It's been hard on her and she doesn't want to talk to me now. But I've heard her hair-cutting business is doing well. Lena told me she's dating Bernie Mosher, who works for the Greenport Foundry right next door to her shop."

"I'm glad to hear that," she said, running her hands through her own short hair.

"Will you come see me in Nova Scotia?" Ivan asked her. "We can stay in a motel near the college."

"Really, I'm not sure. It's so hard to leave the boys now with this big change."

Ivan looked at her then. "Is it Andy?"

"No. We've talked, and we both know our marriage is over. It's just that I worry about money and need to get a job. I have an interview at Barnes & Noble coming up. My father's been kind, but I need to pull my own weight."

But Kate knew that wasn't what she was really worried about as she sat in the kitchen with Ivan. It wasn't just about money. She worried more about Ivan beside her and wondered where he'd be stationed after he graduated. She worried that the man she loved looked out of place visiting her in her New York City apartment. His shoes seemed large on her oak kitchen floor, his khaki pants and plaid shirts, a bit rugged. So she looked at Ivan's face, the face she loved, and his hands. And the further truth was, Kate saw herself loving Ivan because he was there in Nova Scotia when she didn't know what she wanted and was deeply confused. She still couldn't believe the deep, dark hole she fell into with Andy. And she remembered Ivan's strength now, and she still saw that strength in him as he sat beside her, looking at her, so open and clear.

"I love you, Ivan," she said suddenly, feeling the guilt in this.

He looked at her. "I love you too," he said, sounding sad, as though he knew everything she was feeling. He said, "I'll need to go visit Andy at the bookstore sometime."

Later, when they stood beside his truck and he kissed her good-bye, she heard that same sadness in his voice. It was early morning on the Upper West Side, and the traffic didn't look too bad. Kate knew Ivan had enjoyed himself in the city, being with the boys, and going to the Museum of Natural History.

"Pretty soon I should know where I'll be stationed," he said. "Maybe we'll work something out, and you can come visit me there. Maybe I'll be someplace exciting, like British Columbia!"

"That sounds like fun, Ivan. I'd love to travel out west to such a beautiful place."

He held her close for a few moments. He leaned in and brought his lips close to her ear. "You will always mean more to me than I can ever say, Kate. You take good care now. We helped each other, you. To find the right path."

"Yes, Ivan." Now the tears were burning her eyes.

He climbed into the truck, closed the door, and rolled down the window. He stretched out his arm to hold her hand one last time, and his gray eyes were watery. "Hey, you, you haven't even seen me in my uniform yet! I'll send you a picture."

They both laughed then, and Kate, tears still streaming, watched him drive away.

A light rain had begun to fall.

She thought of Skerry Point reaching its rocky arm out into the North Atlantic, and the Tannard house standing dark and changing in the middle of the long yellow field Ivan mowed every year. She saw the slope where she worked such long hours in her garden, planting scarlet runners and beets and hanging the wash while her children lay sleeping. The spruce were on the west horizon, their tips all singed yellow from the angled sun, and the smell of salt water and air poured like an invisible river over the glacial scrubbed land.

She knew she was on her own now.

And then a brightening called her.
The ocean appeared on her horizon
where a symmetry of waves cast up a rogue.
But this time she wasn't frightened,
this time within the hollow of its cresting
a dark seal swam swiftly toward her
through the pale blue turmoil of foam,
and took her from one world to another
leaving no mark upon the shore

CREDITS

T. S. Eliot, "The Love Song of J. Alfred Prufrock"

"There are Jewels," a poem written by my mother, Anne
   Grosvenor Robinson

'The Mermaid's Song,' Traditional, (Lewis, Western Isles,
   Scotland)

Willard Bascom, *Waves and Beaches* (Anchor Books,
   Doubleday & Company, Inc., 1964)

ACKNOWLEDGMENTS

Writing this book over so many years has brought many writers and dear friends into my life and I wish to express my heartfelt gratitude to all of them:

Peter Barss, whose book *Images of Lunenburg County* (McClelland and Stewart, 1978) was my guide. Filled with photographs and recorded interviews with many inshore fishermen, this book lay on my desk through all the years I wrote *Shoal Water* and inspired me to give voice to the land and seascape of Nova Scotia and several of the main characters.

L. B. Jensen, whose book *Fishermen of Nova Scotia* (Petheric Press, Halifax, Nova Scotia, 1980) helped give me the correct details for the fishermen's work.

Alie Wiegersma Smaalders, Marcia Simpson, John Sangster, Georgie Muska, and Marcia Barthelow, who were in my first writers group and witnessed the beginnings of *Shoal Water* and tirelessly offered their support. Though some are no longer with us, I continually feel their presence.

My teacher and mentor, Brenda Peterson, with whom I have studied for many years, alongside Clare Hodgson Meeker, I thank them both for helping me shape the story and learn more about the craft of writing.

My agent, Anne Depue, who believed in the story enough to keep asking me the right questions to encourage me to write better drafts.

My copy editor, Kate Griggs, who appeared miraculously in time to meet my manuscript deadline.

To Peter Mountford, a writing teacher at Hugo House, who taught me the necessity of making each word count.

To my present writing group, Nancy Ewert, Dianne Dyer, and Marcia Barthelow, who are still on the creative writing journey with me.

Other fellow writers I have sat around a table with include Iris Graville, Lorna Reese, Migael Scherer, Mary Murphy Bayley, Laurie Parker, Helen Sanders, and Sandra Chait.

A special gratitude to Karen Fisher who read drafts of *Shoal Water* over the years and was my last brilliant reader and editor.

I thank Leslie M. Browning, editor, publisher, and founder of Homebound Publications, who selected *Shoal Water* for the Landmark Prize for Fiction and offered me a publishing contract. She has become my invaluable editor and source of inspiration.

To my parents, Dwight Edwards Robinson and Anne Grosvenor Robinson, both of whom were writers and imbued in me a love of poetry, fairy tales, and literature.

To my family, Becca Robinson, Mark McDonald, Daisy, and Will; Jenny Robinson-Hartley, Jason Hartley, Oran, and Narwhal, all of whom never gave up asking me when my novel would be published.

To my Lopez community of friends, who encouraged me through all the years.

And finally to my beloved husband, Stanley, who wrote the song "Shoal Water" with me, and never stopped believing that someday *Shoal Water* would come into the world. I dedicate this book to him.

HOMEBOUND
PUBLICATIONS

We are an award-winning independent publisher founded in 2011 striving to ensure that the mainstream is not the only stream. More than a company, we are a community of writers and readers exploring the larger questions we face as a global village. It is our intention to preserve contemplative storytelling. We publish full-length introspective works of creative non-fiction, literary fiction, and poetry. *Fly with us into our 10ᵗʰ year.*

WWW.HOMEBOUNDPUBLICATIONS.COM

ABOUT THE AUTHOR

Kip Robinson Greenthal, a graduate of Sarah Lawrence College, worked eighteen years as a librarian in schools and public libraries. In 1993, she founded and directed the award-winning Seattle Arts & Lectures' Writers in the Schools program. She was selected for the Jack Straw Writers Program and awarded a Hedgebrook residency. Her short story, "Tattoo Emporium," was published in *Secret Histories: Stories of Courage, Risk, and Revelation*, and another short story, "Stealing," was selected by Elizabeth Austen to air on KUOW's *On the Beat*. Kip's first novel, *Shoal Water*, won the 2020 Landmark Prize for Fiction sponsored by Homebound Publications, to be published in Autumn 2021. Kip lives with her husband on Lopez Island, Washington.